The Ancient Stones Speak

A Journey To The World's Most Mysterious Megalithic Sites

We all agree that your theory is mad. The problem that divides us is this: is it sufficiently crazy to be right?

Niels Bohr

The Ancient

A Journey To Mysterious

Stones Speak

The World's Most Megalithic Sites

David D. Zink

A Jonathan-James Book

A Dutton Paperback
E.P. Dutton New York

First American edition published 1979 by E.P. Dutton,
a Division of Elsevier-Dutton Publishing Co. Inc.,
New York

A Jonathan-James Book

For information contact: E.P. Dutton, 2 Park Avenue,
New York, N.Y. 10016

Library of Congress Catalog Card Number: 79-51188

Design by: Howard Albert
Edited by: Conrad Wieczorek

ISBN: 0-525-47587-7
Printed in the United States of America.
10 9 8 7 6 5 4 3 2 1

To my mother,
who stirred my curiosity
about the distant past.

Contents

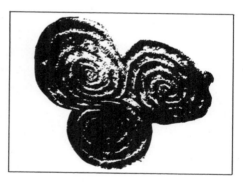

STONE GIANTS

Rising from the pure earth,
Where once the stars did gather overhead,
the stones of time weather and wait,
remembering what the wise men said.

See through the fields the figures dance
'round standing stone on sacred hill.
The solemn white-robed figures wait —
re-animate the cell, the will;

Know purpose and a promise,
(star patterns on the ground),
repeat the cosmic rhythm,
reflect the cosmic sound.

Men plow these fields while monuments
silent *shout* of ancient days!
Curious we look and blandly wait
for truth to pierce our downward gaze.

Joan Zink

Acknowledgements

My travels and research for the present work have been made both more enjoyable and productive through the kindnesses of many people in over a dozen countries. To those not mentioned by name, my warm personal thanks.

In particular I want to express my gratitude to the following: C.W. Conn, Jr. who underwrote several important research trips; Karen Getsla who shared her psychic impressions in Bolivia; Carlos Ponce Sanginés who gave me perspective in certain problems of Bolivian archaeology; Francisco A. Flores Andino who shared his experiences in the Mosquitia of Honduras; Jim Woodman who shared his knowledge and photographs of Easter Island as well as his hospitality during the Ciudad Blanca project; Professor Harold Edgerton whose generosity and expertise in electronics made the 1978 Bimini expedition a success; Barbara Boden, Jon Singer, J.R. Jochmans and Cindy Jones for helpful research suggestions; Braniff Airlines for the use of the San Agustin photos; French Government Tourist Office for photos of Carnac; Shirley Charbeneaux who shared a psychic impression of megalithic sites; Sandra Sennett and John Parks for their drawings; Janet Anderson who typed a very exotic manuscript with extraordinary care; Robert E. Stone, for assistance with Mystery Hill; Allan Stormont, my publisher who made possible the writing of this book; and, last but not least, my love and appreciation to my wife, Joan, who has again supported an involved and demanding project.

As I am dealing with the frontiers of knowledge in various areas, I fully expect that certain aspects of this book will be controversial. I assume full responsibility for all views not specifically credited to others.

D.D.Z.

Preface

Ancient stone giants, the monumental legacy of the modern world's long-dead ancestors, speak to us today. And, though they are silent, we can hear them, if we make use of all the resources (old as well as radically new) available to us for tuning them in. These structures of massive stone are found all over the world — often at places of intense seismic activity — in locations which, after thousands of years of occupation by changing cultures with changing beliefs, continue to evoke in those who visit them some instinct for the sacred. The megalithic sites of the world raise unsettling questions with respect to the generally accepted version of human prehistory. They suggest a past marked by a mobility and by an intellectual and technological sophistication that approaches or even equals our own. By demonstrating Early Man's intense sense of harmony with his environment, these sites also indicate valuable lines of thought for the world today which seems to be standing on the brink of self-extinction.

The sites still evoke what we have called a sense of the sacred — what others might describe as a heightened consciousness. It may be a bit too simple to explain the occupation of these sites over thousands of years by a succession of cultures with distinct beliefs as being merely the result of habit or convenience — the repeated use of a developed site and available structures. Could not the continued occupancy suggest a once powerful, but now only vestigial, sensitivity on the part of human beings to the earth-energies given off at the sites themselves?

Many of the sites are situated in a definite pattern on the surface of the planet. They exhibit a surprising level of astronomical, mathematical, and geophysical information. And, in their structures, they reveal common engineering strategies to deal with earthquakes.

The evidence presented by the megalithic sites described in *The Ancient Stones Speak* suggests a worldwide response to catastrophic changes in the earth's crust. But, at the same time, these cultures are spread over a considerable time-span, and they are widely separated geographically. These facts would argue against a single worldwide culture — *unless* the local cultures known today at each site are actually built over various centers of an earlier, single worldwide culture which is now unknown. There is no archaeological evidence presently available to support the idea of such a culture — *unless* the stonework of megalithic structures like the Great Pyramid, Tiahuanaco, and Stonehenge is much older than now generally believed.

The evidence hints at a previously unsuspected awareness in prehistoric times of then-approaching cataclysmic events caused by the planet's geological evolution. Such violence, associated with the ice ages, has been periodic in the earth's history. From 53,000 B.C. to 48,000 B.C. the earth's north magnetic pole shifted from the Greenland Sea to Hudson Bay. Evidence of the violence which swept the surface of the earth at that time was found in Siberia in 1901 when the still-frozen carcass of a mammoth was discovered at Beresovka. The beast died sometime between 45,000 B.C. and 37,000 B.C. while feeding on buttercups and other summer vegetation. Its body was flash-frozen, not to thaw again until 1901. Such a thing could have been brought about only by stupendous and overwhelming geological and metereological events. There are indications that we may be returning to a period of increasing planetary instability with increasing earthquakes and volcanic activity. The strength of the geomagnetic field appears to be diminishing as we move toward the next reversal of the earth's magnetic poles (predicted by J.M. Harwood and S.R.C. Malin for 2030 A.D.). Past field reversals of the planet have correlated with the extinction of various forms of life (possibly a result of increased cosmic radiation), the onset of ice ages, volcanism, and earthquakes. (This last has increased so much in recent years that much effort is now being made to improve earthquake prediction.) People who are short-sighted enough to build major structures on an important active plate boundary like the San Andreas fault-line certainly need more information.

My approach to dealing with the many questions and lines of thought raised by the megalithic sites is to take you to the sites themselves with the best available photography (including my own) to recount their history and prehistory (including conventional archaeology). This material is enriched by the ongoing wore at many sites, my own on-site interpretations and psychic impressions of the activities carried on at these sites when they were actually functioning in prehistoric times. The psychics, or sensitives, who gave me their assistance were Anne (a pseudonym) and Karen Getsla. Anne spent several days on the sites in Peru, the United Kingdom, at Teotihuacan, and at Bimini; Karen Getsla was present on-site at Bimini and at Tiahuanaco. Impressions of the other sites were transmitted in trance states at a distance from the sites. Like all psychics, they found these experiences emotionally exhausting because of their perceptions of so much of what had happened at the various locations.

This journey to the world's megalithic enigmas takes place at a time of considerable excitement in the world of archaeology. In the Old World, improvements in the radiocarbon dating method have shown that some cultures in western Europe built stone monuments earlier than those of the Middle East. This development calls into question the traditional concept of the origin of Western civilization in the Fertile Crescent, a concept basic to Jacob Bronowski's *The Ascent of Man.*

On the other side of the globe, in the New World, the Maya of Central America have been back-dated radically in the last two years. In 1975 a Maya site in Belize was found to be 1,700 years older than any previous site of this culture. It was dated at 2,600 B.C. The following year, the same site yielded the astonishing date of 4,000 B.C. Some hint of the surprises in store for us can be seen in the dating of an archaeological site at Valsequillo in the Valley of Mexico. Until recently, the oldest date there was 20,000 B.C. Not long ago, Dr. Virginia Steen-McIntyre, a geologist with the United States Geological Survey, reported a new date for the evidences of Early Man at this site: 250,000 years! The date was arrived at by two new sophisticated dating procedures, but it will probably be ignored or at least played down as long as possible because of the violence it does to current conceptions of the New World's past.

In addition to these exciting new developments, a remarkable innovation is taking place in archaeological methods. Years of research in a new discipline, *parapsychology,* have added a new dimension to archaeology. The result is a new tool, psychic or intuitive archaeology which has already facilitated fieldwork in the United States and in Canada; as we have just indicated, it's one of the approaches used to gain insight into the sites described in this book. At present, there are a number of psychics who are offering information on the varying functions of sites which are, as yet, unconfirmed by standard archaeological methods. Working with psychics of proven ability, it is possible to construct testable hypotheses, both about ancient sites and the mental development of their builders. The pioneers in this field are surely Dr. J. Norman Emerson of the University of Toronto and the archaeologist Dr. Jeffrey D. Goodman. Working at a site near Flagstaff, Arizona, between 1971 and 1973, Goodman used psychic information to help him locate an area for excavation. His psychic directed him to a spot described by experienced archaeologists as unlikely to yield any artifacts. The outcome was the location of the first known deep excavation in the area. Goodman credited his psychic assistant with: "Correctly locating a site inconsistent with the traditional model. (2) Correctly predicting the key geologic and archaeological contents. (3) Discovering a new Early Man site of major importance."

In the methods of traditional archaeology, aided now by the refinements of radiocarbon dating, and supplemented with the new tool of intuitive archaeology, we have now at our disposal a multidimensional approach for the investigation of the world's megalithic sites and to provide the reader with a total feel for these unique locations on the planet.

We are, I believe, on the eve of a radical revision of our understanding of the evolution of human consciousness. Discoveries are now being made that hint at unknown chapters in our history. It appears that a number of civilizations, hitherto ignored by students of prehistory, probably rose and fell before recorded history. Developments in archaeology, some of which we have already noted, have begun to encourage a more open attitude toward the possibility of such prehistoric civilizations.

The roots of our understanding of prehistory go back only to the eighteenth century. At that time, an Italian named Giambattista Vico conceived of a new approach in historical research: examination of ancient stonework. He believed that, while historians, for various reasons, might lie or distort, the relics of past civilizations could still speak their own truths. In the next century, a new science appeared: archaeology. Launched in the Victorian era, this discipline has made incredible inroads into the unknown past.

Unfortunately, from that time until fairly recently, we have evaluated the achievements of prehistoric societies from the perspective of an inflated notion of the achievements of our own civilization. Caught up in its material manifestations, we have assumed that our lives have improved with the development of a better technology. But there are telltale signs that such is not the case: fouling of our environment, wasting of resources, millions of unfed, uncared-for people, an increase in mental health problems, a dramatic increase in divorce, a greater de-

pendence on drugs, a startling increase in the past few years of alcoholism as a major health problem. All of these social phenomena indicate something deeply wrong within. What exactly is wrong can be explained in many ways. Some, however, see it as a crisis of meaning. Rollo May has described the twentieth century as the "age of anxiety." Viktor Frankl, the eminent psychotherapist, has said that the endemic plague of this century, what most people suffer from is an "existential vacuum." Our material success, and the high technology which made it possible, have brought us an emptiness which is deeply unsettling to many and destructive to others. Many people now speak frankly of the vacuum within their lives — of a lack of meaning or direction. This situation has intensified the search for meaning in western culture which became obvious after World War II. This search for meaning has taken many forms; one of them is a more determined search into ancient human consciousness through its archaeological remains.

Among serious thinkers, an important milestone in the quest for the ancient consciousness came in 1969. Giorgio de Santillana wrote in *Hamlet's Mill* that he had perceived among the ancients a "common language which ignored local beliefs and cults. It concentrated on numbers, motions (astronomical), measures, overall frames, schemas, or the structure of numbers, or geometry." Santillana was saying

that, contrary to others before him who saw in the ancient myths an arbitrary and capricious response by primitive minds to the order of the universe, he saw an intelligent recording and synthesizing.

In *The Ancient Stones Speak* I want to deepen the reader's awareness of the ancients' artistic, scientific, mathematical, and technological development. The ancient stones *do* still speak, and their message is becoming clearer to those who have escaped certain preconceptions about the early achievements of the human race. We find solid clues that, through observational astronomy they not only created more accurate calendars than ours but also predicted lunar eclipses. They were aware of astronomical secrets revealed to us only after the invention of the telescope and were even apparently aware of the basically mathematical nature of the universe. Stones whose size and tonnage are pretty much beyond our present technology were cut and moved, and their buildings seem to have been proof against earthquakes.

To move from the concrete into the realm of the abstract, we can say that, for a small but increasing number of investigators, the ancient stones imply the following state of knowledge among the ancient builders:

1   They had a *geometry* based on a subtle understanding of the physical universe which is, once again, beginning to be comprehended.

2   They had an *astronomical understanding* far beyond that

justified by any presently remaining evidence, one which allowed maximum utilization of solar, lunar, and stellar energies.

3 They possessed a subtle *geophysics* in which the now-known earth's magnetic fields are but the grossest manifestation of a planetary system of energy which, in fact, responds like a living organism to solar, lunar, and stellar energies, and, perhaps, even to the mental energy of entire populations.

4 They employed a *sacred architecture* whose temples were located so as to derive maximum advantage from the energies understood by these unified sciences; temples, that is whose structure enhanced the planet's energy within them for healing and the raising of consciousness; thus, psychology, physiology, geophysics, and architecture were welded together in an empirical spiritual experience.

5 They had an engineering capability that allowed them to capitalize on the benefits to be derived from the use of large stones at power points in a worldwide energy system.

Certain lines of investigation outside traditional archaeological methods have led to the admittedly startling hypothesis embodied in these statements. They include:

1 Research into the ancient esoteric texts and myths of all cultures in the light of today's scientific knowledge.

2 Recovery of ancient astronomical knowledge through more accurate on-site surveys, application of detailed astronomical knowledge, and the application of statistical analysis.

3 Research into the possibility of an ancient common unit of measurement, again, by means of accurate on-site surveys and statistical analysis.

4 Investigation of the personal responses of sensitives to the remaining on-site energy patterns. Positive psychological transformations such as permanently enhanced powers of concentration are reported by sojourners at such locations.

5 The use of conventional detectors such as the magnetometer to investigate claims of telluric energy points advanced by psychics.

6 Development of unconventional energy detectors so that repeatable experiments can be conducted with the more subtle energies of the planet. This technology is under continuing investigation by researchers such as Pat Flanagan and Marcel Vogel.

7 The ongoing investigation within the earth sciences concerned with the various physical phenomena which seem to correlate with the planet's grid system such as plate boundaries, geomagnetism, and meteorology.

8 Attempts to discover the various geophysical and astrophysical mechanisms affecting the planet's climate and, possibly, its geology. Included are changes in the earth's orbital geometry, variations in sunspot activity, and changes in the earth's magnetic fields. From time to time these periodic changes may have wiped clean the historical slate through cataclysmic earth changes including the ice ages, worldwide earthquakes, and volcanic activity.

9 Clairvoyant accounts of past earth changes.

We are now ready to set out for some of the megalithic sites of the world. We shall go first to the Old World — to England, Ireland, and Scotland; to Malta and Egypt. We shall then journey to the New World to explore sites in the United States, Bolivia, Peru, Mexico, and Colombia. Our photographic and archaeological atlas will be rounded out with a discussion of some of the megalithic sites to be found in the Pacific. We want to hear what the ancient stones have to say to us. They do still speak. In the past we have not heard or we have preferred not to listen. Today we have exciting new ways of communicating with the earliest members of the human family. We have scarcely begun the conversation with the past; but, already, there is emerging the story of people as intelligent and as sophisticated as we are and who lived in a harmony with nature that we can only envy. This book aims to intensify the dialog. To listen more closely to the ancient stones. They can stir up in us a healthy sense of wonder at our past, a sense of perspective on our present, and a sense of hope for our future.

Triple spiral design, New Grange

1 Does Science Have a Prehistory?

Stereotypes are stubborn and dangerous. They are difficult to dispose of, and they distort our perceptions of reality, both past and present. One of our most strongly-rooted stereotypes is that of our prehistoric predecessors as rather brutish, scientifically unsophisticated cave-dwellers. At the present time, however, new techniques of investigation and many new discoveries — especially in three areas directly related to the scientific knowledge of our ancestors on this planet — are stretching the time sense of prehistorians. There are positive signs that we are approaching the time of an entirely new conception of the course of human evolution.

The first of these three areas of investigation raises the question of human mobility in prehistoric times: did various cultures develop essentially in isolation or did many worldwide migrations lead to cross-fertilization? In other words, did human culture diffuse from some ancient center or did it develop in many separate locations, evolving through independent invention? The second field of inquiry is to determine just how much astronomical knowledge prehistoric societies possessed and the uses to which this knowledge was put. The third topic has to do with important new discoveries in geophysics and oceanography. These have spawned a set of relatively new and intriguing questions. How aware were ancient peoples of the geophysical characteristics of this planet? Did they actually sense its magnetic properties? Did they have the ability to predict earthquakes? Did they realize that certain locations on the planet were more conducive to human development than others?

The first topic is a matter of debate within anthropology. The second area is under investigation by astronomers and archaeologists working together. The third has been brought into focus by a new Russian theory — the planetary grid system.

Most of the remainder of this chapter will sketch out the more important — and, as yet, more or less controversial — findings of current investigations into these three areas.

From the outset, the reader must realize that, even though scientists cannot as yet agree on the implications of this new research, its results have significantly upgraded our earlier impressions of prehistoric man's consciousness. More than that, these findings have presented a direct challenge to concepts like Jacob Bronowski's neat picture of the linear evolution of our present civilization over the past 10,000 years, variations of which are still being taught in the universities.

The Ancient Navigators

For a long time it was widely believed by scholars that the technological innovations of early man originated in one location on the planet and were then spread from there to other centers on the globe. This unique source was usually identified with that part of the Middle East known as the Fertile Crescent. This belief, known as *cultural diffusion,* was used to explain the cultures of the Old World as well as certain worldwide cultural phenomena such as megalithic structures like the dolmen. Over the past century, however, a number of archaeologists and prehistorians have held an opposing view: that the discoveries that men expressed through their technology originated independently in a number of locations. This idea is called *independent invention*. In practice neither of these extreme views is ordinarily held today.

Cultural diffusion has held the field for many years, but recently, as a result of the revolution in archaeological dating caused by improvements in radiocarbon dating, the tide has begun to turn (See Appendix: The Next Archaeological Revolution?) Some archaeologists, Colin Renfrew in the United Kingdom for one, have become somewhat aggressive "independent inventionists". In

2

Before Civilization he wrote, "Clearly, the effects of culture contact must continue to play a major role in our thinking. But even if the pendulum swings again towards explanations of this kind (cultural diffusion), no valid meaning or explanatory power can again be assigned to the term 'diffusion'." This sweeping statement is followed by one even more incredible: "Movements and migrations of peoples are no longer acceptable as explanations for the changes seen in the archaeological record." This amazing comment flies in the face of worldwide evidence for many migrations which could not have failed to leave some mark on culture and its artifacts. One case in point is the evidence at the megalithic site of Mystery Hill in New Hampshire for a Celtiberian migration, one which appears to have introduced megalithic building practices.

We might better speak of *cultural evolution,* a larger concept which embraces both cultural diffusion and independent invention. Perhaps, to be more descriptive, the term cultural evolution should denote change through time (evolution and devolution). Quite obviously, cultural change has taken place both by the exchange of information and by local innovation (independent invention).

Current investigations in the West into the processes of human creativity suggest yet another possible

insight into the causes of cultural change. No one will dispute that a particular cultural setting is indeed the matrix out of which new discoveries emerge; but these new discoveries do not always develop in ways that can be fully accounted for by the ideas of the culture. Sometimes there occurs a quantum leap forward which cannot be seen as a logical development from existing knowledge.

Albert Einstein's equation, $E=mc^2$, is a dramatic example of such a leap. Einstein had mastered the physics of his day and had sensed its limits. Then, either in a dream or a vision, the new idea came to him. Only afterward was the new idea elaborated mathematically and, later, tested in the first atomic bomb. In the literature on creativity there have been many occasions on which the initial clue has come from dreams or waking visions or even from chance words or phrases. There are enough of these cases to suggest the possible reality of Plato's world of ideas or, to put it in modern terms, the Collective Unconscious of Carl Jung. Jung, limiting himself to phenomenological psychology, spoke of the Collective Unconscious as something deep within everyone's psyche. It may, in fact, be an actual energy-field functioning as a reservoir of ideas. If these notions are valid, then "independent invention" would actually be the consequence of sensitive individuals' tapping a

universal realm of ideas through their own deeper selves. A position not to be rejected out-of-hand. Once contemporary materialistic biases give way in the face of more and more compelling evidence coming from parapsychology, then the original notions of the psychic unity of mankind found in nineteenth century anthropology take on much greater weight.

The evidence collected in the preparation of this book goes against the emerging emphasis on independent invention as it's now understood. Certainly, independent invention is the simplest way of explaining the megalithic structures found throughout the world. That is to say that: (i) they are all the product of local, indigenous cultures which adapted local materials to local social or religious needs (such as burial); (ii) there are no common elements to be found among these cultures, and (iii) it was simply the local availability of large stones which led the ancients to work with them. Because of the cultural diversity found in pottery and other artifacts at these sites, this belief is far easier to support than the much more subtle concept of a *worldwide employment of megalithic constructions,* a view which, at present, can only be called speculative. Yet it's this very idea which is the underlying premise of this book. It is based on many hints of a science, a technology, and a belief system held in common, even though the expression or the understanding of these things might not be exactly the same in different parts of the world.

My own research has led me to believe that there are good reasons for speaking about a *mother-culture* (such as Atlantis) from which, however remotely descended, certain worldwide cultural traits could have derived. It could be that only dim echoes of such mother-cultures have survived for thousands of years in religious oral traditions. One possible mother-culture, Atlantis, was likely located in the Atlantic; another (perhaps the original mother-culture), Lemuria, may have been in the Pacific. More than likely, both cultures included many individuals who were sensitive to the earth's energies; it also seems that the Lemurian culture may have possessed a more evolved technology for enhancing or intensifying these energies.

In the case of both cultures, the end came through cataclysmic earth changes triggered by various geophysical and astrophysical phenomena associated with the Ice Ages. Even in the conventional paleontological record, this was a time of rapid human evolution. The causes of this rapid evolution are, at present, unknown, though the paleontologist, Loren Eiseley, has suggested a possible explanation.

In conventional archaeology, megalithic culture is usually limited to Western Europe. Is there any basis for speculation about a possible diffusion of megalithic culture from the Old World to the New? Yes, evidence is beginning to accumulate for migrations across the Atlantic even much earlier than the usual date assigned to European megalithic culture, about 5,000 to 2,000 B.C.

In 1963, E.F. Greenman, an anthropologist at the University of Michigan, proposed an idea that drew a mixed reaction from his colleagues. The professional response ranged from a rabid, emotional suggestion that he himself set out across the Atlantic in a kayak (go drown himself!) to a cautious acceptance of some of his ideas. Writing in *Current Anthropology* (February 1963), in a long, carefully reasoned essay with hundreds of illustrations, Greenman suggested that Upper Paleolithic cultures such as the Solutrean and Magdalenian (situated around the Bay of Biscay in what is today southern France and northern Spain) had influenced New World cultures as early as 10,000 years ago. He also claimed to see some Mousterian cultural traits in the New World. At that time, of course, there was no serious criticism being leveled against the prevailing idea that humans had come to the New World from Asia 20,000 years earlier — across the Bering Strait.

Since the publication of Greenman's article, his thesis has become more difficult for conventional anthropologists to accept. This is because of the fact that the dates of cultures in the Old World have been pushed back. The Mousterian culture is the product of Neanderthal Man, formerly dated from about 60,000 to 39,000 years ago. Recently, Neanderthal Man was backdated to 120,000 B.P. (Before Present) in Germany; then in 1977, in Greece, datings at another site put this man-type back to 700,000 years! Mousterian sites closest to the Bay of Biscay have been carbon dated from about 46,000 B.C. to about 32,000 B.C. Sites of the Solutrean and Magdalenian cultures have been dated from about 19,000 to 18,000 B.C. and from about 15,000 to 13,000 B.C. respectively.

Greenman sees evidence of diffusion across the Atlantic from the Bay of Biscay to various New World locations including Newfoundland, the St. Lawrence area, the Great Lakes, and the Southwestern United States. He believes that the ice fields, extending much farther south during the Ice Ages, would have facilitated small-boat crossings of the Atlantic.

To understand the negative reactions of Greenman's critics, the reader must realize that even by 1971, one of the world's authorities in prehistory, Grahame Clark, gave a range of carbon-14 dates for Early Man in the New World which only

4

ranged from about 10,000 to about 6,000 B.C. However, since that time, dates in the New World have been put back radically. While Clark's dates allowed the continued acceptance of the Bering Strait theory of Asiatic origins for Early Man in the New World, the new dates showed its limitations. A carbon-14 date of about 36,000 B.C. was found for a site at Lewisville, Texas. Then, at San Diego, California, a date of about 50,000 B.C. for man was derived by a new dating method. In Peru, at Ayacucho, and at Valsequillo, Mexico, dates of 20,000 B.C. were assigned to early human sites. A carved bone pendant found at Holly Oak in northern Delaware was reevaluated and assigned a date no later than 38,000 B.C., perhaps as early as 98,000 B.C. In light of these facts, early human presence in the New World could not be limited to a Bering Strait crossing a mere 20,000 years ago. As Greenman was writing, Okladnikov, a Soviet specialist in Siberian archaeology, said, "It is important that we do not see a connection with America. To us it is a mystery how people have come to America."

These new dates add plausibility not only to Greenman's thesis but also to other claims for more recent transoceanic diffusion. The most spectacular theorizing (along with actual experiments) among anthropologists has come from the Norwegian explorer, Thor Heyerdahl. In

1947 he sailed a balsa raft, *Kon Tiki,* from Callao, the port of Lima, Peru, to the Tuamotus in the South Pacific. He wanted to show the possibility of a South American influence by sea in the peopling of Polynesia. Twenty-two years later he began the first of two voyages in reed boats *(Ra* and *Ra II)* from Safi on the west coast of Africa to Barbados in the West Indies. The first voyage was a failure because his reed boat became waterlogged; but the second was successful. Heyerdahl was trying on these voyages to show a possible sea connection between the ancient Egyptian culture and Mesoamerica.

Ra's design was taken from an Egyptian bas-relief. Since the rediscovery, in 1840, of the Maya culture in the Yucatan of Mexico, strong parallels have been noted between the Mexican culture and Egypt. They include: step pyramids, columns, obelisks, stelae (upright slabs of stone with inscriptions or sculpturing), the use of hieroglyphics as ornamentation, bas-reliefs, and an absence of the true arch. Both cultures used the corbeled arch as did ancient Mycenaean Greece.[1] Finally, both worshipped the sun. Heyerdah's successful voyage in 1970 adds weight to some unified explanation of these cultural parallels.[2]

However, as with Greenman, so also with Heyerdahl; his theories as well have not been accepted by very

many anthropologists. The reception given to even more conservative ideas than theirs shows the current attitude toward the notion of cultural diffusion. Betty J. Meggers of the Smithsonian Institution, and an Ecuadorian specialist, found Jomon-style pottery (from Kyushu, Japan, c. 3,000 B.C.) at Valdivia in Ecuador. This find led her to theorize that an ancient sea-migration had taken place from Japan to South America. Later, discovering at least seven interesting parallels between the Olmec culture in Mexico (c. 1,200 B.C. to 600 B.C.) and the Shang culture of China (c. 1,750 B.C. to 1,100 B.C.), she suggested that a later migration may have taken place between China and Mexico. While Greenman had received openly hostile criticism, and Heyerdahl was written off as an adventurer, Meggers was patronized in the professional journals as someone who had simply not done her homework. Such is the price of pioneering in science.

Indeed, the burden of proof is upon those who achieve new insights, and their critics play an essential role in the advance of science. Nevertheless, the critics should always be aware of the way their own assumptions can blind them to new evidence. In all of these controversies it has become evident to me that, having prejudged early man as incapable of such voyages, we have, in all likelihood, overlooked many prehistoric migrations by sea. This is a feeling shared by Charles H. Hapgood and Cyrus H. Gordon as well.

Hapgood, a cartographer and historian, was asked to examine the 1513 Piri Re'is chart. A copy of this chart, which came from the library of the sixteenth-century Turkish admiral for whom it is named, is in the Library of Congress. Professor Hapgood and his students concluded that the chart was based on a polar projection, and, for a number of reasons, they felt that it was a composite of much more ancient sources. In *Maps of the Ancient Sea Kings* (1979), Hapgood theorizes that the source charts, supposedly Bronze Age, required knowledge of spherical trigonometry for their construction. If he is right, the Piri Re'is chart constitutes circumstantial evidence of a prehistoric civilization with a science not equaled in historical times until recent centuries.

Working from Hapgood's theory and evidence of his own, Cyrus Gordon, a linguist now at New York University, theorized that an advanced civilization of sea lords ranged over and controlled the world's oceans, carrying on trade and exploration all through the Bronze Age (from c. 3,000 B.C. to 1,200 B.C.). In addition to reliance on Hapgood's work, Gordon based his book, *Before Columbus: Links Between the Old World and Ancient America* (1971), on a connection he saw between pre-Columbian cultures and the Mediterranean. He points to a parallel between the image of man-serpents on the Athenian Acropolis in Greece and the Plumed Serpent of the Aztecs, Quetzalcoatl, called Kulkulkan by the Maya and Viracocha by the Inca. As might be expected, this observation has drawn fire from those opposed to the idea of trans-Atlantic diffusion. Maintaining that Quetzalcoatl is a native tradition, they contend that accounts of Quetzalcoatl's arrival from the east by sea are misunderstandings of primary sources.

In any case, there are also cultural puzzles like the Bat Creek (Tennessee) stone, which seem to support Gordon's view. This artifact was found by Smithsonian archaeologists in 1885, and, from its inscriptions, it was labeled the work of the Cherokee Indians. Much later, an amateur archaeologist versed in Cherokee challenged this conclusion and showed a photograph of the inscriptions to Gordon. He identified them as the work of Hebrews living in Palestine during the Bronze Age.

So far, in looking at the possibilities for the diffusion of megalithic culture across the Atlantic to the New World, we have pointed out evidence that Early Man inhabited the New World thousands of years earlier than we had imagined. In addition, there is evidence that some trans-Atlantic migrations may have taken place earlier than 10,000 years ago, and that the probability of such migrations increases about 5,000 years ago. At present, the earliest dates for megalithic culture in Western Europe are a bit earlier than this last date. Based on the earliest known dates of European megalithic sites, the culture ranges between 4,800 B.C. and 1,500 B.C. The oldest site is found in Brittany, followed by sites in Ireland, Portugal, Spain and, lastly, England.

In the New World, there are two, as yet controversial sites which exhibit megalithic characteristics and which may be old enough to have a relationship with the European culture. One of these is underwater off Bimini Island in the Bahamas where, because of rising sea levels, the latest plausible date of occupation would have been about 6,000 B.C. (See "Bimini"). The other site is Mystery Hill, about thirty miles north of Boston, just outside of North Salem, New Hampshire. Long thought to have been constructed by an eccentric nineteenth-century farmer, the Mystery Hill site, which contains megaliths weighing over six tons, includes standing stones which mark the summer and winter solstices. Its construction is quite reminiscent of the Neolithic village of Skara Brae in the Orkney Islands of Scotland.

In 1975 the case for the authentici-

6

ty of Mystery Hill became much stronger. Based on a C-14 date, the earliest occupancy of the site may be as early as 2000 B.C. Furthermore, Dr. Barry Fell, professor of invertebrate zoology at Harvard University and president of the Epigraphic Society (a group which examines and translates the inscriptions on ancient stones), has translated, from a single stone at Mystery Hill, inscriptions to the Celtic sun-god Bel and to Baal, the chief deity of the Phoenicians. This evidence strongly suggests the ancient presence of these two cultures in America at least as far back as 800 B.C. At the present writing, the group exploring the site, the New England Antiquities Research Association, is also at work in Vermont on another site which is abundant in Celtic artifacts and inscriptions.

Should the Mystery Hill claims stand up, the prehistory of the New World suddenly becomes much more complicated. The evidence for a prehistoric trans-Atlantic connection brings to mind other claims and theories that are offensive to those committed to conventional views of prehistory. These claims and theories have one thing in common: all of them picture prehistoric people as far more mobile and much more scientifically sophisticated than heretofore suspected.

The Ancient Astronomers

Until recently, the megalithic sites of prehistory have raised more questions than they have answered. For this reason we are fortunate that a new discipline, *archaeoastronomy*, has begun to shed new light on these archaeological enigmas and to reveal the surprisingly sophisticated consciousness behind their construction. With great precision, archaeoastronomy combines the archaeologist's methods of site survey with the methods of the astronomer to analyze stone alignments for astronomical significance.

At first, when only a few astronomical alignments had been found in the prehistoric sites, such evidence could be dismissed as simply the result of chance. Today, the number of these alignments as well as their appearance in many cultures over the planet's surface clearly indicate purpose.

Despite this, in a recent attempt to preserve modern beliefs about the limited mental capacity of prehistoric humans, it was conceded that the alignments were, doubtless, the product of actual astronomical observations, but it was suggested that they probably served only superstitious purposes. This implies that ancient astronomy had no logical basis. The evidence offered in the present work shows the con-

trary. For example, actual cataclysmic earth changes having been experienced, it is probable that astronomical knowledge was used to warn of further changes. Astronomy was certainly used to set calendars and, thereby, planting and harvesting seasons.

At the present time, the work of archaeoastronomy is beginning to bear fruit. In Ohio, for example, Indian mounds have been shown to align to the lunar extremes that have a cycle of 18.61 years. Such alignments require deliberate, sustained observation. The idea, once thought unfounded, that the Maya were close to recognition of the fact that Venus orbits the sun, has begun to be reconsidered. After over a decade of controversy, it is now recognized that Stonehenge is aligned to the summer solstice sunrise, though more sophisticated functions, such as lunar eclipse prediction are still being debated. Even in conventional circles, the ancients' interest in astronomy is being pushed farther back in time. In *The Once and Future Star,* George Michanowsky, a specialist in Mesopotamian astronomy, says that Sumerian cuneiform tablets record the observation of a very brilliant supernova 6,000 to 10,000 years ago and that this marked the birth of Mesopotamian astronomy.

Pioneering work in archaeoastronomy began in the nineteenth century. Various investigators sought to learn whether or not the Great Pyramid at Giza held any astronomical secrets. Almost at once the same approach was begun at Stonehenge, sometimes by the same people. For years, however, the low estimation of the prehistoric mind blinded most scientists to the real nature and function of much ancient architecture. From the time of Sir Norman Lockyer's *Dawn of Astronomy* in 1894 until the Stonehenge controversy of the 1960's, archaeoastronomy was the rejected stepchild of both the physical and social sciences. Lockyer was the first to put forth solid evidence of the astronomical orientation of Egyptian temples such as that of Amon-Ra at Karnak and that of Isis at Denderah — the former being oriented toward the midwinter sunrise and the latter toward the rising of Sirius.

The Stonehenge controversy of the 1960's precipitated rapid advances in archaeoastronomy. It began with two provocative articles in the British periodical *Nature* by Professor Gerald S. Hawkins of the Smithsonian Astrophysical Observatory. The articles were entitled: "Stonehenge Decoded" (1963) and "Stonehenge: A Neolithic Computer" (1964). At the time, Professor Alexander Thom of Oxford University had been at work for more than twenty years on more than fifty megalithic sites in the United Kingdom; but his scholarly articles were ahead of their time. It took Hawkins' claims that Stonehenge presented "unwritten evidence for astronomical knowledge of a high order in a prehistoric culture" to ignite the controversy. This view was an outrage to many prehistorians.

In his book, *A Little History of Astro-archaeology,* John Michell tried to explain the passionate opposition to archaeoastronomy — and its implications. Its basis is the antagonism between two widely differing world views: "The modern view, informed by the theory of evolutionary progress, is of civilization as a recent and unique phenomenon. Against this is the older orthodoxy of Plato and the pagan philosophers, that civilization proceeds in cycles, from primitive settlement, through the development of agriculture and technology, to empire, decadence, and oblivion — a pattern of events constantly repeated." The modern view is the basis for contemporary faith in our political, academic, and scientific opinions, and, consequently, it will be vigorously defended.

Our understanding of the human march toward civilization is based on written history — beginning about five thousand years ago. The archaeological record allows us to extend the roots of civilization back another five thousand years in the Fertile Crescent, but this is actually prehistory. By limiting focus to this narrow segment of 2.75 million years of human existence on this planet, the historian can describe a steady, logical climb to our present highly technological civilization. Such a view is very satisfying to the modern ego. However, other reconstructions of prehistory may be possible. There are even grounds for arguing that geometry, perhaps even mathematics, may have preceded language. If that is true, then written records diminish in importance. Put another way, the absence of written records may not tell us what we had assumed about the level of a given culture. Perhaps we have been wrong to use not only our present technology but even the more basic elements of our culture — such as written language — as standards for evaluating previous cultures. Listen to astronomer Fred Hoyle, who sided with Hawkins in *From Stonehenge to Modern Cosmology* (1972): "It will probably be hard for the historian to accept the idea of geometrical arrangements of stones and holes providing evidence much stronger than a document, but I believe this to be true."

Hawkins himself, with the imaginative use of modern science, had successfully attacked the problem of Stonehenge. Working from a photogrammetric survey, he established the possible sighting lines, then fed the astronomical data into the computer. He thereby discovered that Stonehenge provided sighting arrangements, not only for the sun at the times of the equinoxes, but also for the extremes of the moon. He made the further startling discovery that the site could be used as a computer to predict eclipses of the moon. Naturally, this represented a severe challenge to the crude conceptions of megalithic culture based simply on the unearthing of rather simple artifacts.

Alexander Thom published two books, *Megalithic Sites in Britain* (1967) and *Megalithic Lunar Observatories* (1971). He has been working for over thirty years on a theory that the builders of stone circles and standing stones in prehistoric Britain and Brittany had practical field surveying techniques as well as a knowledge of geometry and observational astronomy, particularly of solar and lunar phenomena. With what we presently know about available early Bronze-Age technology (c. 2,500 to 1,800 B.C.), the slow change in declination (movement north or south of the celestial circle — equivalent to the earth's equator) of the sun as it approached the solstice (the winter or summer extreme in declination) could only be detected accurately with long sight lines to the horizon such as the Maya used. Surprising accuracy is possible with this system. At one Scottish site, the sighting arrangement is between several standing stones and mountain peaks eighteen miles distant. As the sun approaches its extreme at the solstice, the final

two-tenths of a degree of arc move the observer a lateral distance of six feet. This sighting arrangement is capable of an incredible angular accuracy of six minutes of arc, despite the Bronze-Age technology. Thom has amassed clear evidence that ancient Britons used this system 4,000 years ago. His work shows that a substantial proportion of British and Breton standing-stone sites serve an astronomical purpose. Apparently the usual site was planned to observe one phenomenon such as the winter solstice sunrise. A wider range of astronomical phenomena was found at Stonehenge.

Thom also credits megalithic culture with a geometry that anticipated the "sacred" triangles of Pythagoras. In his careful surveys of megalithic sites, he determined the common unit of measurement used during their construction, the megalithic yard equal to 2.72 feet (.829 m).[3] Finally, despite Hawkins' scientific reasons for denying the validity of distant hills as possible foresights, Thom has demonstrated the ancient use of such sights.[4]

By 1974, the new discipline of archaeoastronomy had authority. The astronomer, John A. Eddy writing in *Science,* could say, "The solstitial alignments of Stonehenge and other European megalithic monuments, of Egyptian pyramids and temples, and of Mayan temples are by now generally recognized."

Eddy himself, working at the American "Stonehenge," the Medicine Wheel, located in the Big Horn Mountains of northern Wyoming, had moved off to the investigation of more sophisticated phenomena, the *heliacal risings of stars.* Eddy's investigations led him to claim that, in Wyoming, the summer solstitial observation was also accompanied by the heliacal rising of Aldebaran, the bright star in Taurus. A heliacal rising, important to the ancients for calendrical purposes, occurs when a star rises momentarily before sunrise and is then extinguished by the light of the predawn sky. For example, the ancient Egyptians used the heliacal rising of Sirius to help time the summer solstice which signaled the annual rise of the Nile. The flooding of the fields by the Nile was necessary for productive agriculture; but the people required warning to leave their fields for the hills.

In Mesoamerican archaeology, archaeoastronomers have realized that the meridian passages of the star-cluster, the Pleiades, as well as two other constellations, were important to the Maya. Deep wells and towers would make such observations possible.

In addition to meridian passages of the Pleiades, Mesoamerican archaeologists also suspect the importance of rising and setting directions for this constellation. The azimuth (direction expressed in degrees clockwise from true north) of one of the streets at Teotihuacán, north of Mexico City, happens to coincide with that of the setting of the Pleiades at the time of its use.

Thus it is beginning to be clear that observations of solar and lunar risings and settings, the meridian transits of stars, the heliacal risings of stars, and even predictions of eclipses were probably made by ancient astronomers. Furthermore, many of these phenomena were demonstrably a part of megalithic astronomy.[5] The obvious reasons for such observations include calendrical information for agriculture and navigation seasons and the conservation of the power of the priests of the culture, this latter through the ability to predict eclipses. Yet more subtle elements of megalithic culture will likely be uncovered.[6]

Rediscovering an Ancient Geophysics?

In 1975, writing for *New Age Journal* in an article entitled "Planetary Grid," Chris Bird reported an exciting new Russian theory. According to this theory, significant natural and cultural phenomena on the earth's surface could be located at strategic points of a geometric grid system composed of pentagons and equilateral triangles. The Russian theorists who devised the grid system noted that a number of civilizations were initiated at intersections of the system. Until the present work, however, no one has pointed out the surprising number of megalithic structures located at or near these intersections.

The Russian grid system appears to coordinate a number of seemingly unrelated geophysical, biological, and cultural phenomena on this planet. Visualizing the earth in terms of the system, we see it as two interpenetrating spherical solids. One of these (like a stone cut by a jeweller) has twelve pentagonal surfaces (a dodecahedron). The other has twenty faces, each of which is an equilateral triangle (an icosahedron). The geometry of this system must have been, at least in part an element of the ancient Pythagorean teachings. Plato said that the "earth viewed from above resembles a ball sewn from twelve pieces of skin" (the dodecahedron). The dodecahedron highlights the edges of the continental plates which geologists have recently recognized in a dynamic new view of the earth called plate tectonics. These plate boundaries are the site of much volcanic and earthquake activity as well as of magnetic anomalies. One such plate boundary, the mid-Atlantic ridge, is one of the planet's hottest areas for earthquake and volcanic activity.

Intersections of the two solids, as well as of their boundaries, pinpoint specific areas of minimum and maximum barometric pressure, the locales where hurricanes, prevailing winds, and ocean currents are spawned, and where oil and mineral deposits and the birthplaces of a number of ancient cultures are found. Is magnetic energy at these points the cause of all this?

In addition to exhibiting a surprisingly high order of astronomical and mathematical knowledge, many of the megalithic sites described in the present work seem to have been located at or near intersections of the grid system. This suggests that ancient man may have responded to the planet's energies, deliberately locating his megalithic structures to capitalize on them. While design, materials, and apparent sacred use vary from locale to locale, this common principle for siting many of the remaining megalithic structures is significant.

In the Russian theory, the grid system is the result of the geological evolution of the planet. Believed to have been at one time a crystal, the earth is thought to exhibit some magnetic and electrical properties at its former crystalline boundaries. More subtle forms of energy may also be involved. The boundaries are now concealed by subsequent rounding of the planet. It might be worth pointing out here that certain crystals can make a connection

10

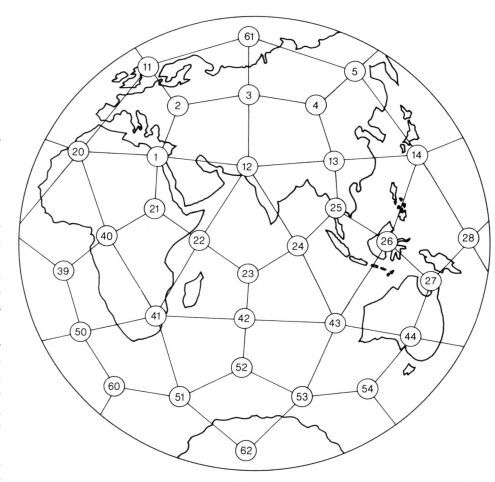

between mechanical and electrical energy — the so-called piezo-electric effect: A sharp blow to a quartz crystal under pressure can cause thousands of volts of electricity to be discharged from it. Perhaps the boundaries of the moving plates of the earth's surface as conceived in plate tectonics also generate electrical effects (in addition to their known magnetic effects). Sensitives report seeing some sort of energy field around crystals and also say that the energy field varies with the presence or absence of music. These phenomena hint at the possibility that the planet is not the dead matter of Newtonian physics but is instead somewhere in the process of a transformation of energy to matter. This would not conflict with current physics, and, if this is actually the case, then the planet's geological evolution has some very subtle aspects yet to be discovered.

My theory is that ancient man sensed the energies at the intersections of the planetary grid system, found them to be beneficial in healing and raising consciousness, and learned how to enhance these energies through architecture. Furthermore, he developed his astronomy in order to predict the seasonal ebb and flow of these energies and also to warn him of instability in the earth's motions.

Two earlier ways of describing the earth as an energy system may give us clues as to subdivisions of the grid

system. One is the English *"ley line" system;* the other is the Chinese concept of *dragon currents:* positive ("Yang", the male principle) and negative ("Yin", the female principle). The positive dragon current is thought to follow the high terrain (hills and mountains), the negative current the low (valleys and underground passages). As Peter Tompkins put it, the dragon energy is "curative, invigorating, and consciousness-expanding."

The English ley line system was first posited by Alfred Watkins in 1925 (*The Old Straight Track*). Watkins perceived that many antiquities such as standing stones, stone circles, and cathedrals are situated on straight lines which run across the English countryside. In some cases, these ley lines appear to coincide with long astronomical sighting-lines which radiate from megalithic monuments such as Stonehenge. This coincidence hints

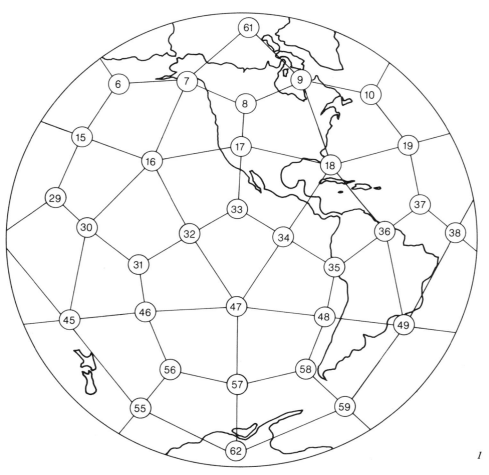

1 The Planetary Grid System
Some significant features of the major intersections: (1) Giza, The Great Pyramid; (3) Tyumen oil field, USSR; (4) Lake Baikal, USSR, many unique plants and animals; (9) Hudson Bay, present location of north magnetic pole; (11) northern British Isles, Maes Howe, Ring of Brodgar, Callanish; (12) Mohenjo Daro culture; (14) southern Japan, great seismic activity; (16) nearby lies Hawaii, scene of high volcanic and earthquake activity; (18) Bimini; (20) Algerian megalithic ruins; (21) Zimbabwe, Africa; (25) Bangkok, Ankor Wat; (26) Sarawak, Borneo, megalithic structures; (28) Ponapé, Caroline Islands; (35) Lima, Peru, boundary of Nazca plate, Stones of Ica; (40) Gabon, west Africa, natural atomic reactor in operation about 1.7 million years ago; (47) Easter Island. The cultures associated with these megalithic sites are separated widely in time. The only logical conclusion is that they represent a continuing response to the energy of these intersections.

1

at a connection between astronomical phenomena and earth energies. Authorities like John Michell claim that, in the ley system, the ancient monuments represent "hot spots" of magnetic energy first located by clairvoyants and dowsers and then commemorated with a stone structure.

What produces these local hot spots? Apparently they have some relation to the behavior of the earth's magnetic field. We know that underground streams, particularly where they cross, have magnetic effects. Running water is a conductor of electricity, and in motion it generates a local magnetic field. Major geological faults have magnetic anomalies present. Ore deposits may also induce local magnetic anomalies.

How could such subtle earth-effects have been noticed by the ancients who then built monuments over them? Today, we have scientific instruments that record such phenomena. Without this technology, however, sensitive human beings have long been capable of sensing such anomalies with their bodies.

In *Earth Magic*, Francis Hitching describes a very interesting sequence in which a clairvoyant said that he saw spirals of energy around a particular English standing stone. He also said that, depending on the moon, the spiral periodically changed direction and strength. On one particular occasion, he marked with chalk the lines where he said the spiral intersected with the surface of the stone. A magnetometer, which records subtle changes in the intensity of the earth's magnetic fields, was then brought to the stone. The first surprise was that the magnetic field around the stone was *double* that of the usual intensity in England. Next, after running the magnetometer up the stone, the local magnetic field was seen to vary in strength just where the sensitive had chalked his bands to indicate intersections with the spiral!

If ancient man actually possessed such sensitivity to his environment, our own science certainly has much to do if we are to understand the more subtle aspects of our planetary home — and to benefit from this knowledge. The following pages, in guiding you around megalithic sites in the Old World, the New World, and the Pacific, will marshall the evidence for this ancient awareness.

The megalithic sites included in this atlas were selected according to a quite definite set of criteria: 1. The relation of the site to the planetary grid system. 2. Evidence at the site of astronomical and mathematical knowledge and the use of standard units of measure. 3. Evidence of structural configurations, mineral content of stones and orientation which apparently enhance terrestrial and astronomical energies capable of healing and raising conscious-

ness. 4. Site of an enigmatic culture whose consciousness, in my opinion, may have been greatly underestimated. 5. Evidence at the site which suggests a worldwide engineering instinct for constructing massive stoneworks as nearly as possible proof against earthquakes and other natural cataclysms. Finally, 6. The geographical location of the site to illustrate the worldwide distribution of the type of knowledge suggested by the other criteria.

A Psychic Impression of Megalithic Sites

. . . I suddenly saw a circle of large stones, phallic-shaped and in standing positions, with the energy field around them such that those who were involved in a ritual could leave their bodies and enter the stones, passing on, then, to higher realms, or states of consciousness as a result of passing through the higher energy field of the stones. Conversely, I saw entities arriving from higher states of consciousness entering the stones and appearing, then, in either etheric or flesh form (it didn't seem to matter which). The entities seeking to leave were obviously of a lower state with great desire to accomplish this mission . . .

My thoughts were then turned to the Pyramids — and I saw those who had prepared themselves by living in the high energy field of the pyramid, ridding themselves of "self", highly disciplined, lying down in the King's Chamber at certain times in a ritual (very delicate and almost zero in emotions) to receive a higher state of consciousness through the channel in the chamber designed to accept the beaming down of the 'higher state'. The body had to have lived in this high energy field for a long time and had to have been disciplined in a manner which would allow the 'higher state' to reside in it for periods of time, not readily discernable.

Notes

1 The present work adds two more rather specific cultural traits found both in the New World and the Old. Compare the masonry corner details in the Egyptian and Peruvian sections (Karnak and Machu Pichu). The interlocking pattern is most distinctive and would be an effective technique for stabilizing buildings against earthquakes and similar violence affecting the earth's surface. Observe also the possible Hindu influence at Tiahuanaco in Bolivia (another writer has already noted a different Hindu influence at Teotihuacán).

2 The latest successful sea experiment in Hyerdahl's tradition, again, one intended to demonstrate the real possibility of prehistoric trans-Atlantic voyaging, was that of Timothy Severin. He was trying to show that the legendary seven-year voyage of the Irish St. Brendan to the New World sometime before 700 A.D. could have been real. In a leather curragh such as Brendan was supposed to have used, Severin sailed from Brandon Creek, Ireland, in May, 1976, wintered in Iceland, and then landed in Newfoundland the following June.

3 In the present work, measurements at archaeological sites and descriptions of the ancient units of measure in relation to the planet's dimensions are given with varying degrees of accuracy because of the present state of knowledge. For perspective on this matter, consider the fact that, even in the twentieth century, a unit of measure as basic as the meter varies slightly in various parts of the world.

4 Clearly, not all prehistorians accept the intellectual capacity implied for megalithic man in Thom's work. However, in 1975, after years of opposition, the prehistorian R.J.C. Atkinson made this concession: "It is hardly surprising that many prehistorians either ignore the implications of Thom's work, because they do not understand them, or resist them because it is more confortable to do so. I myself have come to the conclusion that to reject Thom's thesis because it does not conform to the model of prehistory on which I was brought up involves also the acceptance of improbabilities of an even higher order. I am prepared, in other words, to believe that my model of European prehistory is wrong rather than that the results presented by Thom are due to nothing but chance."

5 The terms megalithic science and megalithic astronomy should not lead the reader to assume that all megalithic sites have demonstrable astronomical functions. This is simply not the case.

6 So far, serious field work in archaeoastronomy seems to be restricted to the areas of western Europe, Mesoamerica, and Egypt. Surprisingly, even Malta in the Mediterranean has had little astronomical analysis. When you reach the Pacific, the astronomical information, except for Easter Island, is almost exclusively ethnological in nature. Precise on-site surveys for possible astronomical significance in site orientations are rare. The discipline of archaeoastronomy is, however, quite new and has a relatively small group of workers.

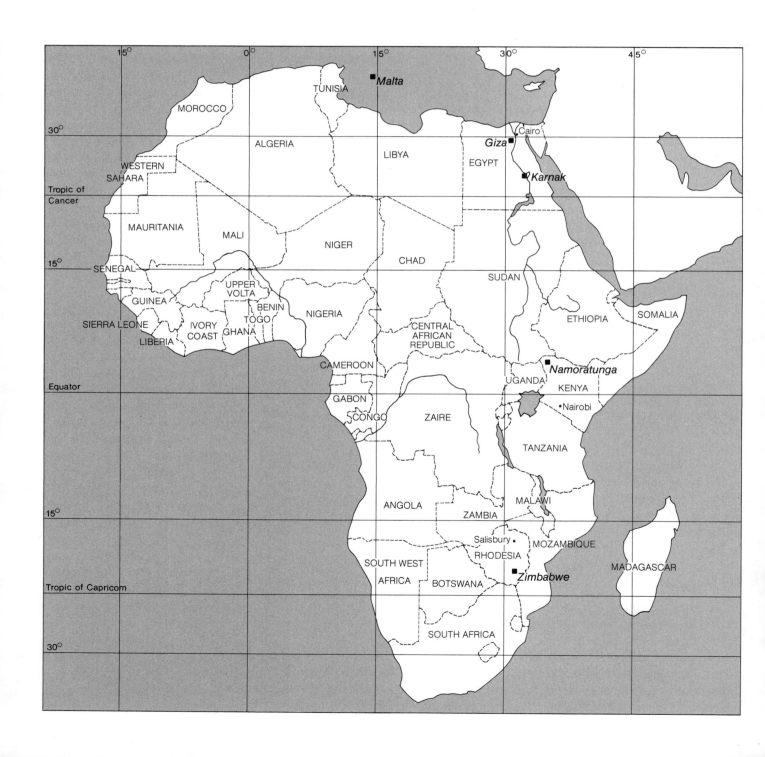

2

The Old World

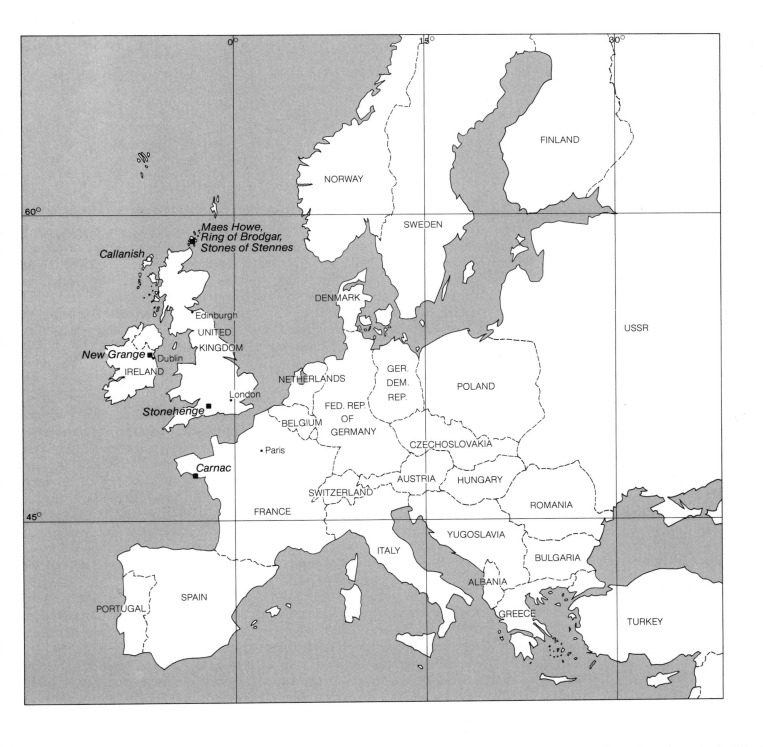

Maes Howe,
Ring of Brodgar,
Stones of Stennes

Callanish

NORWAY

SWEDEN

FINLAND

DENMARK

Edinburgh

UNITED

KINGDOM

New Grange ■ Dublin

IRELAND

NETHERLANDS

GER.
DEM.
REP.

POLAND

USSR

London

London

Stonehenge

BELGIUM

FED. REP.
OF
GERMANY

CZECHOSLOVAKIA

• Paris

Carnac

AUSTRIA

HUNGARY

SWITZERLAND

ROMANIA

FRANCE

YUGOSLAVIA

BULGARIA

ITALY

PORTUGAL

SPAIN

ALBANIA

GREECE

TURKEY

0°

15°

30°

60°

45°

As strictly defined in European archaeology, the only sites which exhibit megalithic culture are those to be found in western Europe and the United Kingdom. The oldest of these are located in Brittany, although some nearly as old are found in Ireland. Probably the best known site in this area is Stonehenge, a stone circle having demonstrable astronomical functions. It is one of about 900 such sites in the United Kingdom. Two other stone circles with astronomical orientations are Callanish (with a Pleiades orientation) in Scotland's Outer Hebrides and the Ring of Brodgar in the Scottish Orkneys. Two magnificent passage graves can also be seen in this part of the world, one at New Grange, north of Dublin, and the other at Maes Howe in the Orkneys.

Megalithic structures, including standing stones, circles, and dolmens are found on the island of Corsica, and to the southwest on Malta there are a number of spectacular megalithic temples dedicated to the mother goddess about 3000 B.C.; older, therefore, than the Great Pyramid at Giza, according to the conventional dating.

In Africa a megalithic observatory for stars (including the Pleiades) is found in Kenya at Namoratunga; its date is about 300 B.C. South of this, in Rhodesia, is the famous Zimbabwe ("venerated houses") occupied by the Shona people from the fifteenth to the nineteenth centuries A.D. Its oval masonry towers are the backdrop for monoliths within the main enclosure. Their meaning is uncertain.

The Iberian peninsula is rich in megalithic structures. Representative sites, such as the famous passage grave site of Los Millares, which

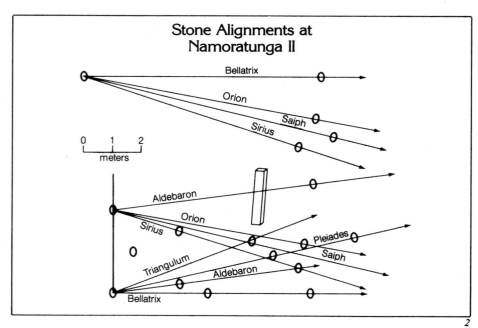

dates from about 3300 B.C., can be visited in the south of Spain. Another megalithic site on the peninsula is a megalithic tomb at Orca dos Castenaires in Portugal dating from about 3800 B.C.

To the north in Germany, Holland, and Scandinavia megalithic sites are abundant. In Scandinavia they range from about 3500 B.C. to 1500 B.C. and, as elsewhere in megalithic Europe, consist of passage graves and dolmens.

Among the oldest megalithic structures of Europe, however, are those in Brittany. The megalithic passage grave at Kercado dates from about 4800 B.C.; megalithic tombs with corbeled vaults are found at Île Carn dating from about 4200 to 4000 B.C. Brittany also boasts the famous stone alignments such as Carnac which has eleven rows of standing stones running parallel for 1,097 meters (c. 1,200 yds), an alignment apparently intended as an enormous graph to predict lunar positions. Nearby is the enormous standing stone, the Grand Menhir

Brisé, now broken and lying horizontal. According to Professor Thom, when its nearly 350-ton bulk stood over sixty feet high, this stone served as the foresight for lunar backsights up to ten miles around. It thus constituted a complex lunar observatory.

At the eastern end of the Mediterranean lies northern Galilee. A number of dolmens and other megalithic structures were found here including a group of twenty-one dolmens near the village of Beit Jahun. Built of roughly dressed limestone, the majority are oriented with their entrances to the northeast. Some are long with eight to nine vertical slabs as at San Agustin in Colombia. North, in Lebanon, is found the famous temple of Baalbek which incorporates the largest stones used in construction by man. Three of the platform stones average 63 feet by 13 feet by 10 feet and are estimated at over 750 tons. Still in the quarry is one 70 feet by 14 feet by 13 feet believed to weigh over 1,000 tons.

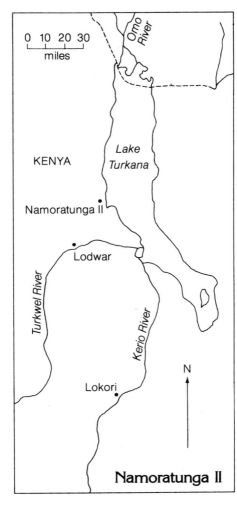

Namoratunga II

3

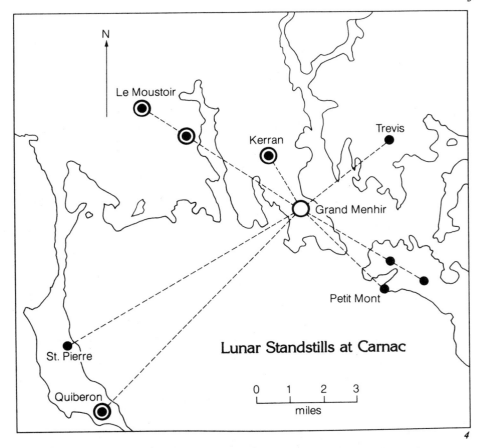

Lunar Standstills at Carnac

4

Still further north, near the Black Sea, Russian archaeologists are investigating megalithic sites with dolmens similar to those of northern Europe.

Finally, to the south, on the Nile River, lies the most enigmatic of the world's megalithic structures. Even if the Great Pyramid at Giza is not as old as many of the other structures, the level of geographical, mathematical and engineering knowledge it exhibits should give us pause about all that has been thus far lost to prehistory.

2   Stone Alignments at Namoratunga II. The alignments at Namoratunga indicate the strong worldwide interest among the ancients in the Pleiades.

3   Aerial view of one of the major standing stone alignments at Carnac in Brittany.

4   Lunar Standstills at Carnac.
In the center, the Grand Menhir Brise: This enormous standing stone, when vertical, stood about sixty feet tall. Possibly as old as 4000 B.C., it was the foresight for the district. Five actual backsights have been located up to 10 miles away.

18

5   *Callanish in a snow shower. View is to
south with circle in the center and west-
oriented stone row on right.*

Callanish
The Isle of Lewis, Outer Hebrides

5

I flew from Inverness, Scotland to the Outer Hebrides. There was not time for the sea passage, which would have been dramatic. The British Airways turbo-prop flight to Stornoway on the Isle of Lewis took me to "The farthest Hebrides" of William Wordsworth's romantic poem "The Solitary Reaper." Stornoway, with a population of over 5,000, has a snug harbor which shelters its herring-trawler fleet. It is also the center for tweed manufacture in the outer islands. The flight passed over the North Minch which opens northward to the Atlantic. Below, the seas were wild and wooly, grey green with long streaks of spindrift. Openings in the clouds also revealed huge breakers pounding the rugged rocks off the Scottish coast.

I went to Stornoway to visit the famous megalithic site of Callanish. It was November, and the North Atlantic had already worked up one of its aggressive winter moods. The taxi-driver who brought me in from the airport thanked me for bringing the sun which they had not seen for three weeks. During that time winds exceeding hurricane velocity had lashed the Outer Hebrides. Nature's moods dominate the low heather moors undulating into peat bogs where cuttings for fuel still continue.

In Stornoway I checked into the County Hotel whose proprietor, Bill Low, an Aberdeen man, extended me the most gracious hospitality of my travels.

Fortified for the weather with a marvelous bar lunch, I went by taxi twelve miles west to Callanish. There, between snow showers, I found more magic lighting like that previously experienced at the Ring of Brodgar in the Orkneys. After one snow shower, the sun appeared briefly to silhouette the standing stones starkly under lowering clouds, suggesting, as Evan Hadingham puts it, "a strange, unnatural forest against the sky." Even in the bitter cold, the place had a special mystique of its own.

Later, back in town, I found a bookseller with some rather sophisticated titles. I expressed surprise at the presence of two Oxford Univer-

sity Press books by Professor Alexander Thom on megalithic astronomy. The bookseller's reply was that his Dutch and German visitors had a keen interest in the subject and often requested the standard works.

The standing stones of Callanish constitute one of the most dramatic megalithic monuments in Britain, ranking in appeal to visitors with Stonehenge and the Ring of Brodgar.

This impressive site is on a ridge overlooking East Loch Roag and the surrounding hills. The ground plan of the stones takes the form of a skewed Celtic cross extending over 400 feet north and south and about 140 feet east and west. On the high ground in the vicinity are found four

8

6 *Looking south along the avenue of stones leading to stone circle.*

7 *The circle of standing stones.*

8 *View to the west through circle and along west-oriented row of standing stones.*

9

Construction Material:
Lewisean gneiss, a very hard metamorphic rock. Central standing stone estimated at five to six tons is 15.5 feet tall (4.72 meters).

Approximate geographic coordinates:
58° 12′ 12″ North Latitude
 6° 45′ 25″ West Longitude

Historical Background

Between the construction of this site (c. 2000 B.C.) and its nineteenth-century excavation, peat was deposited to a depth of about five feet because of the onset of a cooler and damper climate. Thus the earliest known account, Martin Martin's 1695 *Description of the Western Islands of Scotland* would naturally contain an inaccurate representation of the site. Martin said that local traditions linked the site with the Druids. One of these traditions, still current in the twentieth century, calls for all fires on the Island of Lewis to be extinguished on May first (Beltane). The priest then starts a new fire and distributes it to the people within the stone circle of Callanish. This suggests a possible link with the worship of the sun-god Bel (Baal).

First measurements were taken by John McCulloch in 1819; but these

other stone circles which seem to make up a complex of interrelated sites. The best estimate of the construction date is late Neolithic, perhaps about 2000 B.C. At that time the climate was warmer and drier, the situation prior to the accumulation of the present peat bogs.

The origin of the name "Callan-

ish" is not settled. It seems to be a word with a possible geographical meaning.

Within the circle of stones, actually an ellipse about 40 feet across, stands a huge single stone which may be a phallic symbol.

Significant astronomical functions have been seen in this site since 1909.

are useful only to establish the general location of stones which have since been moved in restoration. In 1857, the five-foot deposit of peat was cleared away by the proprietor of Lewis, Sir James Matheson. At that time, the chambered grave with skeletal remains was found; unfortunately, modern dating methods were not then available to apply to these remains. In the opinion of some modern authorities, this burial was intrusive — or, the work of a later culture.

The first detailed site plan based on modern surveying methods was done by Rear Admiral Boyle T. Somerville. Interested in Sir Norman Lockyer's pioneering work in archaeoastronomy, Somerville introduced the idea that megalithic culture used standing stones for lunar observations. He also claimed a Pleiades-rising orientation in 1750 B.C. for Callanish. To my knowledge this is the only such orientation in the British Isles.

Theories, then, about Callanish are varied; they link the site with Druid worship, astronomical observations, and fertility cults (phallus worship). One of the more exotic ideas is that the stones focused energy flowing along ley lines (see "Planetary Grid System").

The relatively intact state of

9   *Callanish, burial cairn visible within circle.*

10   *Callanish: Stone Alignments*

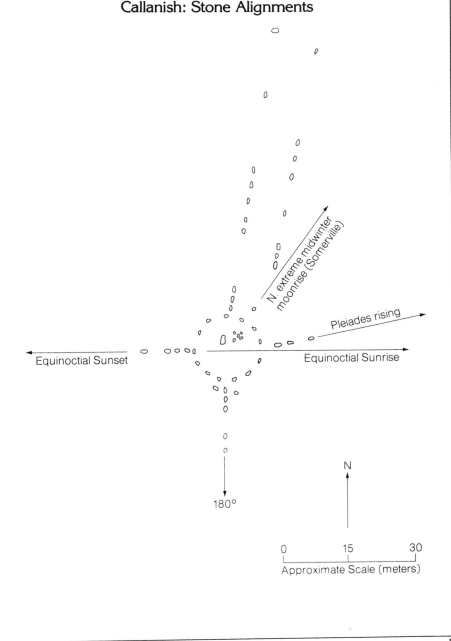

Callanish: Stone Alignments

Equinoctial Sunset

Equinoctial Sunrise

N. extreme midwinter moonrise (Somerville)

Pleiades rising

180°

N

0   15   30
Approximate Scale (meters)

Callanish has allowed investigators to put forward more solidly based astronomical theories. The first claim that the site had an astronomical function was that of one of the pioneers, Sir Norman Lockyer. Using the available maps of the site, he claimed that two alignments of stones had once been established for stellar phenomena: the rising of the Pleiades in 1330 B.C. and Capella in 1720 B.C. Soon after, the first modern survey of Callanish was done by Rear Admiral Boyle T. Somerville who subsequently published a paper in 1912 claiming alignments to the rise of the Pleiades in 1750 B.C. and Capella in 1800 B.C. His major contribution was the assertion that one of the alignments defined the northern extreme of the midwinter moonrise, thus introducing the idea that megalithic monuments were not confined to solar alignments but included also the more complicated lunar observations over the 18.61 year cycle.

A young engineer was impressed by this paper but did not act upon it until 1934. Then, the serendipity that sometimes advances science operated. As Evan Hadingham tells the story, Alexander Thom was forced to seek shelter from an Atlantic storm in Loch Roag. Anchoring his sailboat, he went ashore for a meal. That night, observing the pole star over the central megalith and northward up the "avenue" of standing stones, he was irrevocably pulled back into the problem of astronomical alignments in megalithic sites. Eventually, his

extremely accurate surveys would provide the basis for identification of the megalithic yard, 2.72 feet (.829 meters). In 1967 Thom published his *Megalithic Sites in Britain.* His work includes the notion that the skewed construction of the east-west arms could only be explained by the astronomical purposes of the site. He describes the "circle" as an ellipse based on a Pythagorean triangle with sides of 3-4-5. Instead of a Pleiades-rising orientation for the eastern arm, Thom claims it as pointing to the rising of Altair in 1800 B.C. Finally, there is the expressed need for a more accurate survey of Callanish.

In 1965, Gerald Hawkins had published a paper entitled "Callanish, a Scottish Stonehenge," later included in his *Stonehenge Decoded.* Seeing more possible alignments by means of a compuer analysis of existing site plans, he called Callanish a primitive computer and saw, even, that it might be used for eclipse prediction.

In 1974, the Geography Department of the University of Glasgow produced a new, more accurate survey which, while not yet correlated with astronomical alignments, challenges certain features of Somerville's survey — the basis for both Hawkins' and Thom's astronomical concepts. The principal problem seems to lie with the southerly extreme of the moon, apparently obscured by a nearby hill.

Despite the superior condition of the site in relation to others, the issue here is still one of precision. Sighting

arrangements which are only one hundred feet apart produce limited precision. Were the alignments first established by other means, then memorialized by the standing stones?

A Psychic's Impressions of Callanish

Questions asked: (1) date of construction, (2) cultural origins, and (3) possible connections with the Druids?

The answers: "4400 B.C. The Druids occasionally used this spot as a haven, a place of intercepting space, order, light, energy. As their organization changed and grew, frequent out-of-the-way retreats were fortified with stone and embedded with powerful frequencies [By the Druids]. Only the evolved could tarry here. The energies created vortices of strength which disoriented many. So the superstitions began, that it was haunted by forces, demons, witches. These Druidical meetings took place at summer solstice and fall equinox."

Question: Were there any other people involved with this place?

Answer: "Dwarfs. Picts, small people, very barbaric. They frequented this place from time to time on migrations. Nomadic tribal societies [with] sheep. Dark haired, pinched brown skin, I.Q. ranged 50 to 100. Tribal dances held here. [Is this the culture which was the source of the small, intrusive cairn?] This is a spiritual center because of Pleiades rising and fall equinoctial alignment of sunrise and sunsets."

Maes Howe
Orkney Islands

11

11 Aerial view of mound over passage

Construction Material:
Red sandstone

Geographical Coordinates:
58° 59′ 56″ North Latitude
3° 11′ 20″ West Longitude

Visiting several megalithic sites in the northern British Isles during November, my wife Joan and I missed our train connection in Edinburgh, had a chilly night in the Palmerston Hotel, then set off by British Air the next morning for Kirkwall in the Orkneys. Thirty-five minutes flying in the rain took us to Aberdeen, an important center of North Sea oil production; another forty minutes over the North Sea in a Viscount turboprop put us into the Kirkwall airport in the Orkneys. Snow was evident in the Highlands of Scotland and it was bright, cold, and windy. We checked into the Kirkwall Hotel which had excellent meals and set off 15 kilometers west of Kirkwall to visit Maes Howe, described by the archaeologist Aubrey Burl as "surely one of the most

12

awe-inspiring monuments in Europe." It is the most spectacular of twelve similar passage graves in the Orkneys. Three quarters of a mile to the west lies the dramatic circle-henge of Stenness, and beyond Stenness, the magic Ring of Brodgar.

The latest corrected radiocarbon date for Maes Howe (1974) is 3100± 100 B.C. Contributing to the regularity and finish of the structure is the fact that the local flagstones of **Old Red Sandstone** readily split into rectangular forms. The main chamber measures about 4.57 meters (15 feet) on a side, and about 1.83 meters (6 feet) up. The walls of this square main chamber are corbeled inward to a 3.05 meter (10 feet) square at the 3.96 meter (13 feet) height. A passage, about 1.37 meters (4.5 feet) high, leaves this chamber and runs 15.85 meters (52 feet) in a southwesterly direction. The overall layout is, like New Grange, cruciform with alcoves on three sides and the passage entrance on the fourth. The entire structure is covered by an earthen mound 10.97 meters (36 feet) high and 30.48 meters (150 feet) in diameter.

The main chamber of Maes Howe was broken into during a twelfth-century Viking raid. Runic graffiti, recording the theft of the grave's

13

treasure, were left behind. When entered in the nineteenth century, the tomb revealed only the bones of a horse and a fragment of a human skull.

Archaeoastronomy at Maes Howe

The passage into the main chamber points approximately southwest over an outlying stone. It was evidently intended for a midwinter-solstice sunset, but, at present, it points to a sunset somewhat earlier in December.

12 Slab-lined entrance passage; may once have been oriented to winter solstice sunset.

13 What remains of original corbeled roof; lighter area above is reconstruction.

14 Maes Howe, corner detail in main chamber of passage grave.

The Ring of Brodgar
The Stones of Stenness

16

The Ring of Brodgar is 18 km from the town of Kirkwall, past Maes Howe and the Stones of Stenness. The Ring of Brodgar and Stenness represent the two most northerly circle-henges of the British Isles. About 1.6 km (1 mile) apart, the two sites are separated by the narrow isthmus between the lochs of Stenness and Harray.

The Stones of Stenness were originally a ring, twelve in number; about 1300 tons of sandstone were quarried from the surrounding ditch. Today only four very dramatic, thin, unshaped flagstones about five meters (c. 16.4 feet) high remain. Aubrey Burl dates this site as third millenium B.C. or late Neolithic.

The Ring of Brodgar is one of the largest stone circles of the British

15 *Ring of Brodgar silhouetted by afternoon sun.*

16 *Ring of Brodgar, aerial view.*

Isles. Like the inner circles at New Grange and Avebury, its diameter is about 125 megalithic yards (103.6 m). The stones were set six degrees apart, beginning with geographical north. Astronomically, its date has been estimated at about 1560 B.C. by Dr. Alexander Thom. The Scottish archaeologist, Dr. Euan MacKie, noting that many stones of the circle were snapped off at the ground, wonders if this was the result of some natural catastrophe.

The Ring is surrounded by a ditch cut into solid bedrock three meters (9.8 feet) deep to a width of nine meters (29.5 feet). This may have been the source of the original sixty standing stones. Only thirty-six now remain; some are but stumps.

Various mounds and standing stones are to be found about the Ring. In the 1850's one mound was excavated to reveal a steatite urn with cremated bones. When exposed to the air, it disintegrated.

Archaeoastronomy at Brodgar

According to Alexander Thom and A.S. Thom, the Ring of Brodgar was an important observatory for observing lunar declinations, both the major and minor standstills during the lunar cycle. No solar orientations were discovered in several years of investigation (1971-74).

17

18

19

Construction Material:
Sandstone

Geographical Coordinates:
59° North Latitude
3° 13′ 22″ West Longitude

17   Ring of Brodgar, looking south.

*18   Three of the standing stones of
Stennes near the Ring of Brodgar. The
tallest stands over four meters.*

19   Eastern part of Ring, looking south.

Psychic Reading: Ring of Brodgar

Horizon extends (to?) Arctic Circle. The Arctic nights changed dramatically over the course of 20,000 years. Further annoyances were the strange fluctuations of the seasons at the times of meteorite showers and, until the beginning of the last Ice Ages, man remained in ignorance as to the fluctuations. I guess some news of alarm would spread through the continent as these ice masses changed .... I think the people retreated in the face of those — picked up and just left when the movements were slow. So it was a celestial observation place — concerned with the Arctic north, navigation, seasonal fluctuations, rotation of constellations (precession) and some azimuth points. Knowledge imparted to past generations of such observations enabled men to more carefully regulate their living conditions. There were times of great upheavals in the earth and the panic may not be known by the modern mind. No similar crises have disturbed man on such a worldwide scale, the global destruction connected with the Ice Ages. Waves whipped to fury in the seas at such times; it must have been a big swing around or something. Earthquakes. The earth was like a roaring, bellowing creature. The tar pits (at La Brea?) yes, are from the days of such intense pressures ... In the future the evidence will show that the Ice Ages succeeded in finishing off large remnants of civilization. That known? (No) Many unhappy souls have had to go through these experiences on this earth. These souls have been rejuvenated through time, so the memories are very dim. The price of paying too much attention to these things will be an inner disturbance to people.

32

New Grange
Irish Republic

Located about thirty-five road miles north of Dublin and about five miles east of Slane off the road to Drogheda, New Grange is situated on a hill partly surrounded by a bend of the River Boyne in County Meath. This spectacular passage grave ringed with a standing-stone circle vies with Maes Howe in the Orkneys for the title of most impressive megalithic tomb in Europe. More rough-hewn, New Grange yet possesses its own awe-inspiring architectural and engineering elements.

Low clouds and mist crowded the hill surmounted by the massive mound of New Grange on the rainy day I first visited the locale. About the mound stood the twelve stones which remained from an estimated thirty-five. The tallest was about eight feet (2.4 meters) above ground. From Thom's work I knew that this circle, about 340 feet in diameter (103.6 meters), had probably been constructed to a diameter of 125 megalithic yards, thus giving evidence of its being related to the other megalithic stone circles. Likely too, in its original configuration, it had an astronomical function now lost to us. Standing stones around chambered tombs are rare in the British Isles except for the Clava cairns near Inverness, Scotland.

Within the circle the immense flat-topped mound rose to a height of about 36 feet (11 meters). It is one of the most impressive of the 300

20

New Grange (after O'Kelly)

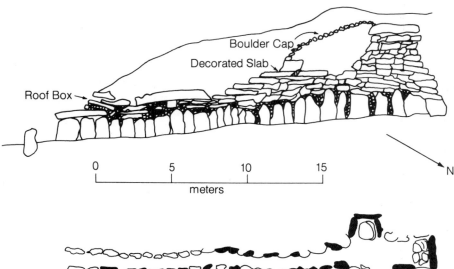

Neolithic passage graves now known in Ireland and located, for the most part, in the northern half of the country. All in all, about 1200 megalithic tombs of all types exist in Ireland; they are thought to have been communal burial places in use for many centuries. They are usually located on hilltops and are built of dry-stone construction, usually of stones which are megalithic in size.

The New Grange mound is surrounded with decorated curbstones, which had the function of a retaining wall but which also carried the symbolic message of its builders expressed as an art form. Within the mound massive linteled stones line each side of a dramatic passage which penetrates about sixty-two feet (18.9 meters) to a central chamber from which open three smaller chambers. The ground plan is cruciform, and the passage opens to the southeast to admit the midwinter sunrise. The main chamber has a dramatic corbeled beehive roof which rises to about twenty feet (six meters). The forty-three orthostats which line the sides of the main passage average about five feet in height. These orthostats are grit (an impure form of sandstone). The seventeen lintels or capstones contain some huge stones; the first and third from the entrance weigh six to eight tons.

21

22

Construction date: c. 3300 B.C.

Construction Materials: Earth, white quartz pebbles, river-worn boulders of grey granite, syenite (an igneous rock with the minerals feldspar and hornblende). Source of latter stone: Pomeroy about sixty miles distant.

Culture: Unknown, possibly the legendary Túatha Dé Danann. Earlier claimed relationship with Kings of Tara but, chronologically, are out about three thousand years.

Geographical Coordinates:
53° 41′ North Latitude
6° 28′ West Longitude

20 *Passage grave and standing stones, Clava, near Inverness, Scotland. Site contains a winter solstice sunrise orientation.*

21 *Linteled entrance to passage grave runs in northwesterly direction.*

22 *Corbeled roof structure above main chamber.*

Historical Background

Edward Lhwyd, a road-builder, is credited with the discovery of New Grange in 1699. In the nineteenth century, it was surmised that the Danes had built it (Norsemen had apparently raided it in the ninth century A.D.). Recent radiocarbon dates have, however, put its construction date between 3300 and 3000 B.C., and current archaeology can tell us little of the unknown Neolithic culture which built New Grange. The most basic observation has been that the builders somehow linked sun worship and death. One recent writer bases the name "New Grange" on "an Uamh Greine" which means the cave of the sun ("grian" sun). For reasons given at the end of this section, I associate the fascinating spirals of New Grange with the positive lifegiving forces of nature and the unfolding of creation itself.

Aside from these bare facts there are some very interesting questions relating to New Grange and its unknown builders. The actual basis for Irish prehistory is limited to archaeology and to the sagas of the Old Irish. These latter had a long oral tradition and were written down only in the middle ages. Perhaps the earliest known site for man in Ireland is at Kilgreany cave in County Waterford, in the Irish Republic. One skeleton here has an uncorrected C-14 date of about 2630 B.C.; another, because of preservative materials, has an estimated date (by fluorine and nitrogen replacement tests) earlier than 9000 B.C. The earliest generally accepted date for early man in Ireland is, however, about 6800 B.C., the date assigned to Mesolithic (Middle Stone Age) hunters and fishermen in Ireland. After them, a Neolithic (New Stone Age) people who were farmers, using polished stone axes, appeared about 3700 B.C. This latter group was probably responsible for the construction of New Grange. In such a historical vacuum it is not surprising to find speculation on such matters as the Druids.

Conventional prehistory has it that no Druids were in the British Isles before about 300 B.C. This belief may be the result of assuming that Druidism was originally brought from the continent in Celtic invasions; but even if this were the case, Goidelic-speaking Celts arrived in Ireland from Spain probably only as early as 600 B.C.

Some, however, believe the Druids to have been in Ireland long before the Celts, who assimilated them after invading their territory. In *Magical and Mystical Sites,* Elizabeth Pepper and John Wilcock say, "Seing New Grange in relation to the stone monuments of the French Coast and British Isles allows one to anticipate a time in the future when Ireland will be recognized as the center of a lost civilization: a supreme culture as yet unnamed whose elite class, the Druids, held sway for several thousand years." These writers associate the Druids with the Túatha Dé Danann, "people of the goddess Danu," linked in one legend with New Grange. But, if the Túatha Dé Danann were contemporary with New Grange (dated to about 3300 B.C.) they were at least seven hundred years later than the earliest French megalithic sites. On the other hand, one Irish megalithic site, Ballynagilly, County Tyrone, dates to about 4500 B.C.

The Túatha Dé Danann existed as a tribe when the Celts arrived and were "an indigenous mystical culture which deeply influenced the nomadic warriors." Greek and Roman writers noted the civilizing influence of the Druid priests on the Iron-Age Celtic invaders. Egerton Sykes, the foremost student of Atlantis today, has claimed that the Túatha Dé Danann had their origins in the lost Atlantis. And, finally, some speculate that they were the originals of the "little people" in Ireland, a small, dark group which intermarried with the tall blond Celts.

The Spirals of New Grange

Probably the most remarkable example of megalithic art in Europe is the Entrance Stone at New

23

25

24

23　*Entrance stone: decorated with spiral motif, a design of great significance to many cultures of the world, it is 3.2 m long (about 10'6").*

24　*Spiral in west alcove off main chamber.*

25　*Unique triple spiral design in northern alcove off main chamber.*

Archaeoastronomy at New Grange

Beginning in 1962, concurrent with a restoration project, the archaeologist, M.J. O'Kelly, excavated various parts of the mound at New Grange and the nearby standing stones. Perhaps his most interesting discovery was the so-called "roof box", a vertical displacement of about 20 cm between adjacent lintels on stones roofing the entrance passage. On December 21, 1969, Professor O'Kelly waited within the burial chamber within the pre-dawn hours. He wanted to see if his hunch (that the midwinter sunrise would enter the passage) was correct. For about seventeen minutes, around 10:00 A.M., a narrow shaft of sunlight entered the main chamber, ever illuminating its triple spiral. Four satellite tombs in the vicinity of New Grange are also oriented in the same direction. One of these ruined tombs has a stone basis decorated with a rayed circle, like a sun symbol. This evidence has led some to see a connection between sun worship and death. However, after the midwinter solstice sunrise, the days are making way for spring and new life.

Grange. Its spirals are similar to those found on Malta and in Brittany, and there has been considerable speculation as to the symbolism of this very important motif at New Grange. Throughout the ages considerable meaning has accrued to this symbol.

One very plausible explanation for the local meaning (at least at one level) is that the spiral symbolized a natural force of which the builders were aware. In *The Pattern Of The Past,* Guy Underwood, a dowser with extensive experience around the megalithic sites of the British Isles says that "a round barrow [like New Grange's mound] is always located on one or more powerful blind springs. This marks its mystic centre . . . . Blind springs [upwellings of water without an outlet] will be found in the centre of the flat top." Another English dowser, Scott Elliott, believes that such springs usually are sited over geological faults. As we pointed out earlier, faults also often exhibit magnetic anomalies. In his dowsing Underwood traced out right- and left-handed spirals associated with these blind springs. He found that they usually had seven turns.

Some of the spirals at New Grange have seven turns; but this is not usual; they do, however, turn both clockwise and counterclockwise. It is, therefore, not unreasonable to conjecture that the spiral motif at New Grange is more than mere decoration, in fact, that it indicates the builders' awareness of the natural force or energy focussed on the site.[1]

26 *Stonehenge, from the main site to the heel stone, silhouetted in center aperture.*

27 *From the heel stone toward the main site.*

Stonehenge

27

From ground level, Stonehenge is the most impressive of the European megalithic sites. For centuries it has filled visitors with the compulsion to try to explain its origins and functions, but the more that is learned about it, the more enigmatic the unaccountable science of its master-builder becomes. Only recently, have its carefully laid out sighting patterns for solar and lunar risings and settings been recognized for what they are.

The first phase of Stonehenge's construction began about 2800 B.C. This date, corrected from C-14 dates by tree-ring dating, pushes Stonehenge's origins back to the early part of the Old Kingdom in Egypt and to the remarkable science of the era that ushered in the Great Pyramid. The last phase of Stonehenge was likely completed by 1400 B.C. Although its construction was thus contemporary with the ancient Egyptian culture, its master builder, presumably, had no contact with the older culture or its science. In addition to the knowledge of astronomy evident at Stonehenge, its builder had a surprising aesthetic awareness. The sarsen linteled circle by which the visitor is first impressed as he sees the site from the road (or walks up to it) gives evidence of an architectural device common in the columns of classical Greek temples. To correct the effects of perspective, the sarsen stones, which taper in as they rise, are also curved convexly. How did this level of cultural awareness find its way to the Salisbury Plain?

Today's visitor to Stonehenge may at first be disappointed; such a response is commonly reported. Particularly during the summer months, the huge crowds distract

Sarsen Circle

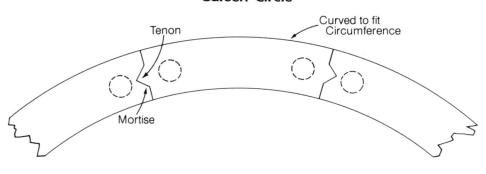

Tenon

Curved to fit
Circumference

Mortise

Mortise in Lintel

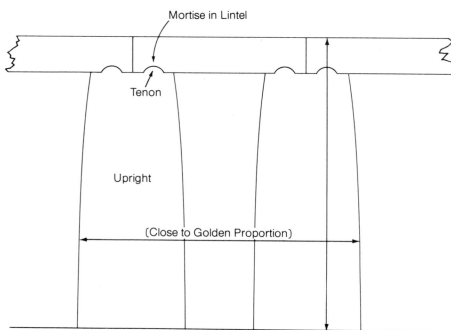

Tenon

Upright

(Close to Golden Proportion)

28 Trilithon detail: exposed by weathering; the mortise and tenon joint is visible at top of right-hand vertical stone.

28

one and dampen any personal response to these ancient stones. From a distance, the massive structure is dwarfed by the chalk downs of Salisbury which surround it. Yet standing among the ancient stones one cannot fail to be impressed by their massive strength. On closer inspection more subtle features are seen, such as the mortise and tenon joints which could represent a kind of earthquake proofing.

Archaeological History

The earliest reference to Stonehenge may have been by a Greek writer, Diodorus Siculus, a contemporary of Julius Caesar. About 8 B.C. Diodorus described a "spherical temple" to the sun-god Apollo in Hyperborea (probably Britain). According to C.A. Newham, a major contributor to the astronomical analysis of Stonehenge, "spherical" was sometimes used by ancient writers to denote "astronomical."

The name "Stonehenge" first appeared in the work of Henry of Huntingdon and was said by him to have meant "hanging stones." A few years later, in 1136 A.D., Geoffrey of Monmouth called the stones the Giants' Dance. In his *History of the Kings of Britain* he included the legend that Arthur's magician, Merlin, had stolen the stones from the Irish and brought them to England.

The eighteenth-century writer William Stukeley claimed a connection between the Druids and Stonehenge. At present this is taken to be purely conjectural, particularly because the Druids are not usually dated as far back as the present date for Stonehenge I.

Daggers carved on one of the sarsen stones originally suggested diffusion from Bronze-Age Greece. However, this influence became impossible with the new dates resulting from the adjustment of radiocarbon dates (see Appendix A). The end result is that the cultural origins of Stonehenge have been restricted to Western European megalithic culture (4000-1500 B.C.).

In 1901, Professor W. Gowland found a trace of copper on the base of a sarsen stone (a part of Stonehenge III); this had suggested a Bronze-Age connection with the last phase of construction. However, extensive modern archaeology was not undertaken on the site until the 1950's; this was the work of Stuart Piggott and R.J.C. Atkinson which can be followed in Atkinson's *Stonehenge* (1956). At first hostile toward astronomical claims for Stonehenge, Atkinson, by 1975 had come to acceptance of Alexander Thom's work in this area.

The prehistory of Britain relevant to this site begins about 4300 B.C.

when Neolithic farmers from Europe joined the indigenous nomadic population. These farmers are called the Windmill Hill People; they built causeways and camps such as the one near Avebury. Later Neolithic people arrived from Europe, merged with the Windmill Hill people and constructed Woodhenge, Silbury Hill, and Stonehenge I (c. 2800 B.C.); thereby inaugurating megalithic building in Britain. The engineering capability of these people (Silbury Hill required a volume of earth equal to the second pyramid at Giza) and their astronomical knowledge (many of the known alignments are found in the earliest stage of Stonehenge) is unsettling to those uninformed about ancient man.

About 2500 B.C. these people were also joined by the Beaker People[2] from Europe; these were responsible for the second stage of Stonehenge and possibly Avebury. Additional Beaker People eventually arrived and a more homogenous Bronze-Age culture, the Wessex people, who actively engaged in trade, then emerged. This culture was probably responsible for the construction of the three stages of Stonehenge III, beginning about 2075 B.C.

The Chronology of Stonehenge

Stonehenge I (dated to c. 2800

B.C. with a calibrated radiocarbon date):

This phase consists of a circular henge monument 350 feet (107 meters) in diameter with a circular bank and ditch surrounding an inner circle of fifty-six Aubrey holes (first noticed by John Aubrey, a seventeenth-century antiquarian who saw a circle of depressions), the four "stations" (based on two mounds and two stones on the Aubrey circle), the Heel Stone and other features. The Heel Stone weighs thirty-five tons and lies about 256 feet northeast of the center. The Aubrey circle was measured by Alexander Thom at about 284 feet (c. 86.6 meters) in diameter.

Stonehenge II (dated to c. 2130 B.C. with a calibrated radiocarbon date):

This phase added the Avenue, two parallel ditches and banks about forty-seven feet apart and about 2.5 miles long (4 km), running from Stonehenge to the skyline and thence to the river Avon by the easiest grade. Also added were two bluestone circles, possibly linteled, and including a blue-green spotted dolerite (an igneous rock), rhyolite, volcanic ash and sandstone. These weigh up to five tons, and they were transported, apparently, over 200 miles from the Prescelly Mountains in southwest Wales, possibly from an earlier monument. The immense labor involved here suggests that these stones had a special quality for

29

30

29 *Sarsen circle: at either end, behind, are
lintels of trilithons.*

30 *Several lintels of the sarsen circle.*

the builders. In Alexander Thom's survey of Stonehenge, these bluestone circles (or what remains of them) did not fit neatly into megalithic geometry, and this suggests a possible intervention by a culture with rather different values.

Stonehenge III (usually divided by archaeologists into three subphases, this phase has been dated by a calibrated radiocarbon date to c. 2075 B.C.):

The third phase of Stonehenge saw the demolition of the two bluestone circles to clear the way for the famous sarsen[3] linteled circle and the massive trilithon horseshoe. Described by Jacquetta Hawkes as "unique in Europe" at least the pattern of a circle and horseshoe — oriented to the winter solstice sunrise (corrected for the Rumanian latitude) — can be seen duplicated in a prehistoric site, Sarmizegetusa, Rumania. The monumental stonework of this phase represents an innovation in megalithic standing-stone circles. The sarsen circle, originally included thirty uprights weighing about twenty-five tons, all connected with lintels mortised and tenoned together and each weighing about seven tons. The sarsen stones are sandstone brought from Marlborough Downs about twenty miles north. The huge trilithons stand as much as twenty-four feet above the ground; the largest is estimated at about fifty tons.

31

Geographical Coordinates:
51° 10′ 42″ North Latitude
1° 49′ 29″ West Longitude

31   Trilithon detail.

32   *Great trilithon: largest stones are estimated to weigh over fifty tons.*

32

Archaeoastronomy at Stonehenge

The story of the astronomical investigation of Stonehenge begins in the year 1740. At that time, William Stukeley claimed (in *Stonehenge, A Temple Restored to the British Druids*) that the central axis was oriented to the summer solstice sunrise. It was not until our own times that the truth of this would be known. By 1771 Dr. John Smith first claimed that the Heel Stone (slightly east of the central axis) was the foresight for the summer solstice sunrise. In this century Gerald Hawkins repeated this assertion — which, as will be seen later, is invalid.

Serious astronomical investigation of Stonehenge did not actually commence until 1901 when Sir Norman Lockyer surveyed the site for possible alignments. Lockyer agreed with the earlier view of the great Egyptologist, Sir Flinders Petrie, that the Heel Stone marked the summer solstice sunrise. This opinion, and his date for Stonehenge I (c. 1880-1840 B.C.), have since been challenged.

In 1963 Gerald Hawkins, then at the Smithsonian Astrophysical Observatory, began publishing a series of professional papers claiming twenty-four astronomical alignments at Stonehenge. He also asserted that Stonehenge served to predict lunar eclipses. Two years later his *Stonehenge Decoded* and a BBC television special stirred many readers and viewers. Hawkins put the crucial alignment, the summer solstice sunrise, over the Heel Stone. More accurate surveys by C.A.

Newham and then by Thom, later placed this key astronomical event back on the central axis where Stukely originally reported it to have been. (See illustration: "Stonehenge: Major Astronomical Alignments").

Hawkins' most ingenious proposal was that the fifty-six Aubrey holes of Stonehenge I had been used to predict lunar eclipses; this was the first attempt to explain the Aubrey circle. Essentially, what Hawkins did was to assume a fifty-six-year eclipse cycle not previously recognized by astronomers. Shortly afterwards, two critics, R. Colton and R.L. Martin demonstrated from actual recorded eclipses that the cycle is sixty-five years, not fifty-six.

Ultimately, the place of Hawkins in the development of Stonehenge astronomy seems to have been as much a dramatic as a scientific role. His investigations began by utilizing the results of site surveys done by others, surveys apparently not executed to astronomical precision. These surveys were later upgraded by a photogrammetric survey and the data interpreted by a digital computer for possible alignments. The omission of the laborious first step, his own on-site survey, left Hawkins open to much criticism, particularly from archaeologists. Prior and subsequent surveys by Newham and Thom highlighted this problem. On the other hand, Hawkins' dramatic ploy with the expensive computer hardware today linked in the public's mind with "good science" put Stonehenge astronomy on the map, so to speak. Probably few scientists would care to view themselves in this light, but style does matter — even in science.

C.A. Newham, an amateur archaeologist and astronomer, whose name we have already mentioned, first visited Stonehenge in 1957. In 1963, about six months before Hawkins' first paper, he published solar and lunar alignments for Stonehenge I. Newham's work was based on his own careful surveys of the site. He advanced fewer but more defensible alignments, based primarily on the "Station Rectangle" of the Aubrey circle (Station Mounds 92 and 94; Station Stones 91 and 95). He suspected distant foresights and later led Alexander Thom to one of them, "Peter's Mound," which is named after him. One of Newham's contributions was the initial recognition of the equinox sunrise alignment, 94 to "G."

In 1972, Velikovsky, criticizing Hawkins' analysis of Stonehenge, calls our attention to an issue which has by no means been resolved. On the one hand, he observes, Hawkins asked us to believe that those who built Stonehenge could design and build an astronomical computer. On the other hand, inquiring into their motives, Hawkins explained their actions by attributing to them a perfectly groundless fear that the sun's movements might become irregular. Whether or not Velikovsky's scenario of past threats to this planet by orbital changes of Venus and Mars is valid, his point is well taken. The immense effort expended in the contruction of Stonehenge and the astronomical understanding displayed therein is inconsistent with a neurotic concern with the sun's actions. It is one of the contentions of the present work that such fears were not groundless, that for reasons not clearly understood today, violence on the earth's surface has repeatedly endangered the survival of our species.

The great theoretical astronomer, Sir Fred Hoyle, beginning from an analysis of Hawkins' work, considered the whole astronomical problem at Stonehenge and subsequently devised his own eclipse prediction system based on the fifty-six Aubrey holes. E.C. Krupp in his *In Search of Ancient Astronomies*, has given a professional astronomer's evaluation of the two systems. In essence, he seems to feel that Hoyle's explanation *On Stonehenge* (1977) would be more valid for a people presumed to possess an observational as opposed to a theoretical astronomy. But even of Hoyle's system Krupp remarks, "If the Stonehengers actually did use the Aubrey circle in this way, they had an ability for abstract thought that exceeds previous assessments."

Aside from the lunar eclipse predictor questions, Hoyle's analysis represents the most solid support for the idea of Stonehenge as an astronomical observatory. However, as should be obvious from descriptions of other sites in the present work, at least one of his statements is fallacious. He said, "Stonehenge *alone* was designed as an astronomical observatory". Hoyle confirmed a number of Hawkins alignments; but rejecting, (by implication) Hawkins' Stonehenge III alignments, he called this phase a degenerate, ritualistic stage of construction, a stage following the observatory phase. In addition to the claim that Stonehenge was the only observatory of its era, Hoyle also claims that it was the first of such megalithic structures. As Eger-

ton Sykes suggested in a review of Hoyle's book, Carnac in Brittany may have been the prototype. Archaeologically, it is earlier, and, as Thom has shown, it, too, is a complicated astronomical computer (See "Carnac, Brittany").

The investigator with the most solid body of field work upon which to assess megalithic astronomy, Stonehenge included, is surely Dr. Alexander Thom whose name has already come up frequently. In the past fifty years, he and his associates have surveyed over 300 megalithic sites in Western Europe. With his son Dr. A.S. Thom he has discovered an unsuspected precision and design complexity in the standing-stone circles of Europe. He has shown them to be based on circles, egg-shapes and ellipses constructed on a standard unit of measure, the *megalithic yard* (MY): 2.72 feet (.829 meters) and the *megalithic rod* (MR): 2.5 MY or 6.803 feet. His work at Stonehenge, as well as at several of the complex sites of Carnac in Brittany is surely his triumph.

Dr. Thom's 1973 survey of Stonehenge revealed that the circumference of the sarsen circle (the inside diameter) 45 MR (or 112.5 MY) was consistent with the megalithic yard he had earlier established in hundreds of site surveys. Also, four of the five trilithons were consistent with megalithic elliptical geometry. The Aubrey circle, as well, had a basis in megalithic geometry; its circumference was equal to 131 MR. From Thom's work, it appears that megalithic builders preferred even MR's for perimeters and the MY for straight-line measurements (such as radii of circles and ellipses and

triangles). In Thom's survey, only the bluestone circles were inconsistent with his knowledge of megalithic geometry; either our knowledge of the locations of the bluestones is faulty or another culture intervened in the construction. This latter possibility will doubtless cause a mild shudder of horror among those archaeologists who have painstakingly reconstructed what is presently assumed about the cultural sequence of this mysterious site.

With suggestions from Newham, Thom's astronomical analysis added the concept of long sight-lines. He found Stonehenge to be a reversal of the setup at Carnac in Brittany, where a central monolith was used as the lunar foresight for a number of distant backsight stations. On the contrary, Stonehenge has, he thought, the backsight for a number of distant foresights. "Peter's Mound," named, as I have said, in honor of Newham, is on the Stonehenge axis 8,981 feet (c. 2737 meters) northeast of the center of the Aubrey circle on the azimuth of the sun at 2700 B.C. Thom feels that perhaps one or two other foresights may exist.

An excellent survey of the astronomical problem at Stonehenge is to be found in Dr. E.C. Krupp's *In Search of Ancient Astronomies*. He concludes with the statement that: "By this stage we can no longer doubt whether Stonehenge had astronomical significance. Instead, we might marvel that it had so much significance."

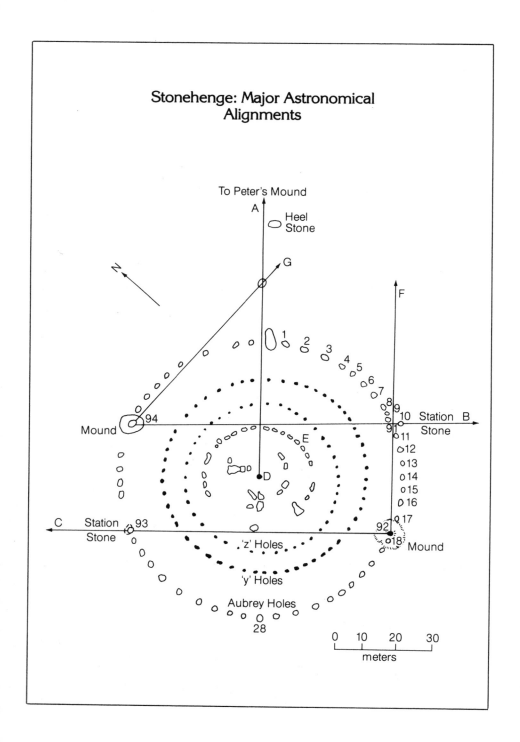

Stonehenge: Major Astronomical Alignments

To Peter's Mound

A

Heel
Stone

G

N

F

1
2
3
4
5
6
7
8 9
10 Station B
9 Stone
94
91 11
Mound 12
13
E 14
15
D 16

C Station 93 92 17
Stone 0 18 Mound

'z' Holes

'y' Holes

Aubrey Holes
28

0 10 20 30
meters

Malta's Temples

33 *Mushroom-shape altars: hint of possible use of hallucinogenics in religious rituals.*

Malta is an archipelago composed of three small islands running about twenty-seven miles northwest to southeast; it lies at the center of the Mediterranean between Sicily and Tunisia. Malta, the largest island, is seventeen miles long and nine wide; Gozo is only nine miles by four and a half; and Comino is but a square mile. The maximum elevation of these barren, dun-yellow limestone islands is 800 feet. The indigenous language, Malti, is Semitic in origin and, though written in Roman characters, shares much with modern Arabic. Its vocabulary includes Sicilian, Italian, Spanish, and English words; Malti and English are the official languages of the islands.

These early periods were followed by the Bronze Ages (2400 B.C.), the Phoenician (850 B.C.), the Punic (600 B.C.), the Roman (218 B.C.) and, finally, early Christian influences (60 A.D.)[5]

The Sites on Malta

The fascinating megalithic temples of Malta are believed to be the oldest free-standing stone structures in the world. They include Hagar Qim, Mnajdra, Hal Tarxien and the Hypogeum, all located on the main island of Malta. The island is composed of various layers of sedimentary rock, primarily limestone of marine origin. Obvious faults have displaced these sedimen-

34

35

36

tary layers and, as recently as 1693, an earthquake destroyed a cathedral at Mdina in the southwest. The survival of these megalithic temples for millenia is, therefore, a tribute to their construction.

Hagar Qim is located on the southern coast of Malta. In the vicinity, spectacular cliffs drop abruptly to the sea from elevations

34 As at Hagar Qim, Mnajdra displays some earthquake-resistant masonry joints.

35 Carved doorway within the temple of Hagar Qim.

36 Hagar Qim, main façade. A phallic stone stands above the wall on right.

of over 400 feet. From Hagar Qim, looking seaward, the tiny rock called Filfla is dimly visible in the afternoon haze. The wonderfully intense, yet soft, light of the Mediterranean sun in winter put a special magic over the site at the time of my visit. Assigned to the Gjantija phase, its corrected radiocarbon date is about 3500 B.C. The impressive façade, which faces in an easterly direction, is badly weathered on its seaward side. This is due to the use of a soft limestone (globigerina); some coralline limestone, which is harder, was also used in the temple's construction. What may be the largest single

stone in the Maltese temples is found in the northern wall of this temple complex. It is over twenty-two feet long, and what is visible may weigh nearly seventy tons.

Maltese temples are usually thought to be the place where an earth-mother fertility goddess was worshiped. At Hagar Qim the evidence for this theory is somewhat equivocal: facing west are four feet believed to be the base for two missing mother-goddess statues, and facing northeast is a phallic shrine, introducing the contrasting male principle.

Within the main temple are found

37

38

Hagar Quim Ġgantija- and Tarxien-phase megalithic temples constructed of limestone.
(c. 3500 B.C. to 2400 B.C.)
Geographical coordinates:
14° 26′ 46″ East Longitude
35° 49′ 40″ North Latitude
Mnajdra Ġgantija- and Tarxien-phase megalithic temples constructed of limestone.
(c. 3500 B.C. to 2400 B.C.)
Geographical coordinates:
14° 26′ 31″ East Longitude
35° 49′ 37″ North Latitude
Hal Tarxien Ġgantija- and Tarxien-phase megalithic temples constructed of limestone. (c. 3500 B.C. to 2400 B.C.; Colin Renfew's date: 3100 B.C.)
Geographical coordinates:
14° 30′ 05″ East Longitude
35° 50′ 00″ North Latitude
Hypogeum An underground rock-cut burial site with many intricate chambers on three levels including replicas of above-ground megalithic structures carved from the solid limestone. Discovered in 1902. Żebbuġ (c. 4000 B.C.) to Tarxien phase (c. 2900 B.C.)
Geographical coordinates:
14° 05′ 45″ East Longitude
35° 52′ 05″ North Latitude

37 *Closeup of main façade seaward.*

38 *Closeup of entrance, main façade.*

39 *Phallic stone from outside the temple.*

40 *Interior chambers: phallic stone in background.*

40

two altars supported by what are thought to be mushroom shapes, hinting at the ancient use of hallucinogenics. Here too, was found the altar (now in the museum at Valletta) with carvings of plants growing in tubs on each of its four sides — the so-called Tree of Life motif.

From where did the impetus for these marvelous temples come? Because the second radiocarbon revolution (See Appendix A: The Next Archaeological Revolution?) invalidated the belief that cultural influences from further east in the Mediterranean affected Malta, Colin Renfrew argues that the Maltese megalithic culture was home-grown. He has also advanced the same theory for European megalithic sites. His views have been challenged by a Maltese archaeologist, Dominic Cutajar, who sees a decisive break in the continuity of Maltese prehis-

41

The Cultural Periods
of Malta

Age and Phase:	Beginning Dates:
Maltese Neolithic Age	5000 B.C.
Cave dwellers and later	
villagers in rubble huts	
(A pronounced cultural	
discontinuity)	
Maltese Copper-Age Phases	
Żebbuġ	4000 B.C.
Mġarr	3600 B.C.
Ġgantija	3500 B.C.
Saflieni	3000 B.C.
Tarxien	2900 B.C.

(Another pronounced cultural discontinuity, suggesting a violent end of the Tarxien culture, perhaps due to an earthquake)

toric culture. According to Cutajar, the break comes between the Neolithic Age and the first phase of the Copper Age, the Żebbuġ, which preceded the era of the megalithic temples, the Ġgantija. In other words he sees the Żebbuġ and the Ġgantija phases as the product of an outside culture coming, possibly, from Sicily.

Discovered in 1915, Hal Tarxien, directly adjacent to a modern Catholic church, is one of Malta's better-known megalithic temple complexes. In front of its façade, which faces to the south, is found a cistern apparently fed by a spring. Readers will recall that sacred sites

42

often appear to have been located with reference to ground water. "Used for libations" is the predictable archaeological explanation. The central, and main, temple contains relief carvings of two rows of bulls. The bull motif ranges from Plato's Atlantis to Crete's Minoan culture. Another important motif here is the running spiral. This spiral design may have ultimately derived from the usual spiral or labyrinth. A local archaeologist has, however, seen the running spiral as symbolic of weaving. At the entrance of the complex is the lower portion of an extremely corpulent fertility goddess. When first excavated, the interior of these temples was noted to have been reddened by fire, indicating either deliberate destruction by human agency, or fire started by earthquake activity. Whatever the explanation, conventional archaeological accounts speak of a

violent end for the Tarxien Copper-Age culture here.

The usual accounts of the use of this complex highlight worship of another goddess concerned with fertility and death. (See Psychic Vision).

The Hypogeum, when first excavated in 1904, yielded about 7000 skeletons; evidently its major use was as a cemetery. Occupation of the Hypogeum extends back to the Żebbuġ phase (c. 4000 B.C.). Within these complex artificial caverns, about thirty-five feet below the modern surface, are two replicas of the megalithic trilithons found in the above-ground temples. Also, a large cistern has been cut out of the living rock. The most famous artifact from this site is a terracotta figurine of a lady who seems to be asleep, the so-called "Sleeping Lady."

41 Looking out through trilithon entrance. Note Maltese version of spiral motif.

42 Bull motif removed from Hal Tarxien to museum.

43

44

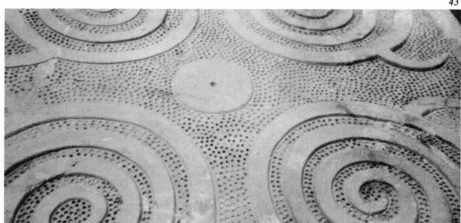

45

43 Altar inside entrance.

44 Lower half of Mother Goddess, entrance of Hal Tarxien.

45 Detail of spiral removed to protection of museum.

46 Interior section of Hypogeum, unique Maltese burial site carved out of living limestone on three levels. Some architectural motifs of above-ground temples, such as the trilithon are repeated here.

47 Trilithon doorway.

*48   Looking out of main entrance of
Mnajdra, up the hill, toward Hagar Qim.*

Archaeoastronomy at Hagar Qim and Mnajdra

Christopher Kininmonth, who wrote one of the major guides to Malta, says that there are no astronomical alignments at Maltese temples. "They are all inward-looking." In preliminary compass-work at Hagar Qim and Mnajdra, I satisfied myself that this was true — at least in one sense. None of the major axes of these two clusters of temples seemed to correspond with any important astronomical orientation at 3500 B.C. — the conventional archaeological date of the two sites. For those interested in technical details, I worked with a mirror sighting compass which could be read to 1° and compared my observations both with site maps and Professor Anthony Aveni's computer-generated astronomical tables.

Despite the belief of the archaeological authorities, Gerald Formosa, in his book *Megalithic Monuments of Malta,* claims to have observed (and photographed) the summer solstice sunset and (the day after) the sunrise. Formosa's site-map, the claimed path of the solar phenomena, his photographs, and the orientations of solar phenomena extrapolated from Aveni's table fell together — for the sunset. The claimed sunrise was not so clear-cut. The calculated angle was 59° 12′; Formosa claimed the sun's path was 68° — which could be the case with a 12° to 15° elevation of the path (for example, slanted over a stone in the wall as on the actual site). This claim, however, must be checked out very carefully by observation. I concluded that Formosa's case was strong enough to justify further on-site work with a theodolite and executed with the modern surveyor's precision.

On a tip from a Maltese archaeologist, I went through several years of the *Malta Sunday Times* in Valletta. There I found an interesting series of articles which ran from May to September in 1976. These were largely critical of Formosa and his "mystical archaeology" and even sarcastic and patronizing when referring to his claim of solar phenomena at Hagar Qim. One reviewer apparently believed that Formosa was unaware of the consequences of astronomical precession. Working back in Professor Aveni's tables (and figures furnished in Professor Gerald Hawkin's writings) I calculated that, given the dimensions of the temple and the changes in the sun's azimuth due to precession (back at 3500 B.C.), light from the sun would have moved 4 cm to the left within the temple, and, thus, its target would have been closer to a significant stone in the temple. None of Formosa's critics gave evidence of having made on-site astronomical observations.

Psychic Reading on Maltese Temples

The Maltese stones of strange construction emphasize rigidity in placement. The angles fit known constellation patterns. There are jumbled areas of construction because of past ice ages, erosion.

The fat-legged being represents a maiden goddess worshiped here whose beauty transcribed into earthly terms symbolized fertile pleasure. The ruins' position was used to foretell ecliptical passages of stars, moon and sun. The crossing at right angles of solar movement interfered with harmony it was felt. Harmony was greatly stressed at this period.

Thirdly, the accumulated knowledge here ranked high and pilgrimages were made here. The three sites (Hagar Qim, Hal Tarxien, Hypogeum) served one purpose — communion with extra-terrestrial beings who were expected from legends. None of the sites was abandoned until 1100 B.C.

At funerary sites these people relished games in conjunction with burial procedures. Such games included drawing lots for the widow or wife. Pagan influences were felt to be dangerous later. There was no known admixture to culture here — mostly Siberian. In search of new fertile lands wandering tribes sought Italy. Little is known now of these migrations, yet Siberian huskies made such an overland connection possible. Fertility sought and established in first wave; later, astronomers developed and added idea of heavenly harmony. Yet a third group migrated here from Spain and undertook to reclaim the land with the use of watersheds.

Hagar Qim the last constructed, most efficient group. Use of materials here created atmosphere of worship and cleansing. Stones mined nearby. Adjusted view south for most beneficial rays. Large amounts of water taken over site (?) for irrigation.

The Great Pyramid of Giza

The Great Pyramid is the most substantial megalithic structure of the world and the monument which most clearly testifies to the level of ancient mathematics and astronomy. Its location and geometry also reveal, at the very least, a high geographic science. Furthermore, this edifice is located at a crucial intersection on the planetary grid system, a fact which demonstrates, on the part of its builders, a subtle awareness of the planet's energy patterns.

The real significance of the structure continues to be debated. Ideas range from the utilitarian notion that the pyramids were the first public works project to the claim that the Great Pyramid represents an indestructible record of the level of astronomy, mathematics and geography 5000 years ago. Tradition or present evidence lend support to the notions that it could have been an observatory (before its completion) an initiation temple, and a geodetic marker. Although the pyramids are often described as tombs, it should be noted that no original burials were found in the principal chambers of any of the large pyramids.

Located ten miles west of Cairo, on a rocky height leveled by men, this wonder of the ancient world began drawing its first tourists from the classical world. Planned and executed with mathematical and, at times, optical precision, this incredible monument contains over six million tons of limestone and granite.

Its original height was 481.4 feet (146.73 m); but the top thirty-one feet are now missing. The difference between its longest and shortest sides (756.08 feet and 755.43 feet) is a mere 7.9 inches, and its sides are no more than 5.5 minutes of arc from the true cardinal directions.

Aside from its more subtle mathematical information, one basic geographic fact has been recognized since the end of the second century B.C. In modern surveys, the sum of all four sides (the perimeter) has been found to be 3023.16 feet (921.46 m). Twice this figure (1842.922 m) is extremely close to the distance occupied on the equator by one minute of latitude (1842.9 m). This means that the builders had a surprisingly good geographic understanding.

William R. Fix, a recent writer trained as a systems analyst, has seen two other basic measurements in the Great Pyramid's dimensions: the planet's polar radius and its circumference (See "The Archaeology of the Great Pyramid").

49   *Great Pyramid of Giza.*

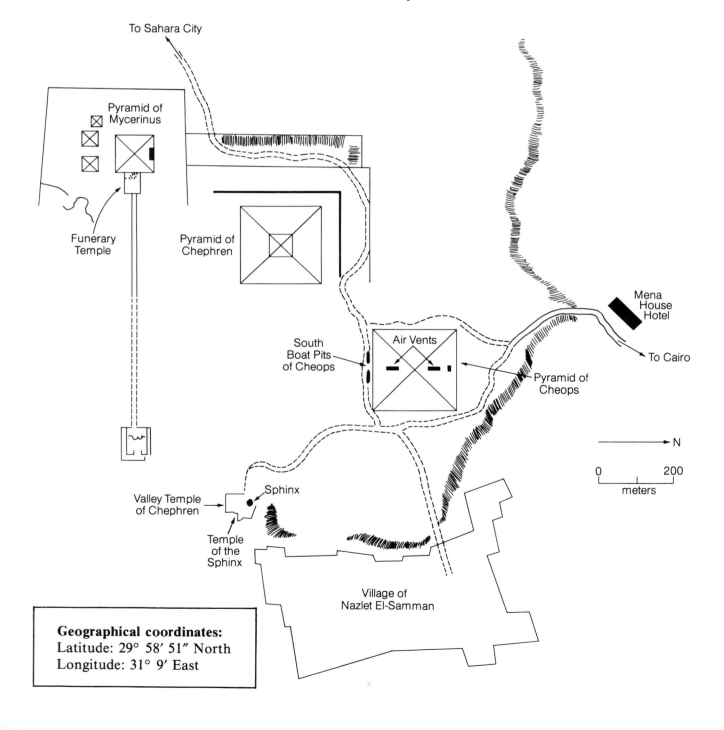

Giza: Necropolis

To Sahara City

Pyramid of Mycerinus

Funerary Temple

Pyramid of Chephren

South Boat Pits of Cheops

Air Vents

Pyramid of Cheops

Mena House Hotel

To Cairo

N

0 200 meters

Valley Temple of Chephren

Sphinx

Temple of the Sphinx

Village of Nazlet El-Samman

Geographical coordinates:
Latitude: 29° 58′ 51″ North
Longitude: 31° 9′ East

The Pyramid Age of Dynastic Egypt

The sparseness of evidence from which the Fourth Dynasty is described, the Great Pyramid is dated, and its construction explained is surprising to a trained scholar. The insubstantial nature of the evidential foundation is all the more puzzling in view of the fact that, from the outside at least, Egyptology appears to be the most solid body of archaeological evidence in existence today. It is true that massive data exists for dynastic Egypt; it is equally true that this data gets thinner and thinner prior to the oldest established calendar date — the reign of the Twelfth-Dynasty pharoah, Sesostris III (1878-1843 B.C.).

Before this date the events of dynastic Egypt become more and more conjectural, so much so that, by the time of the Fourth Dynasty, linking the kings of the dynasty to their respective pyramids seems almost arbitrary. In fact, with present knowledge the term "Pyramid Age" may be more scientific than the present assignment of the now remaining eighty pyramids to the Third through Sixth Dynasties. When the origins are reached (the beginning of the First Dynasty) the first pharoah, traditionally Menes, may really have been Narmer, and the date commonly assigned to his

reign (3100-2890 B.C.) may, perhaps, be as much as a thousand years too recent. The existence of Narmer himself is tied to *one* artifact.

Jean Yoyotte, a contributor to a contemporary French dictionary on Egyptian culture, alluding to existing theories of the origins of Egyptian civilization, put it this way: "The student of Egyptology will thus

> **Old Kingdom Dynasties and Pharoahs**
>
> c. 2686 B.C. - 2613 B.C.
> III Djoser, Huni
> c. 2613 B.C. - 2494 B.C.
> IV Sneferu,
>   Khufu (Greek: *Cheops*),
>   Khafra
>   (Greek: *Chephren*),
>   Menkaura
>   (Greek: *Mycerinus*)
> c. 2494 - 2345 B.C.
> V Sahure, Neuserre, Unas
> c. 2345 - 2181 B.C.
> VI Pepy I - Pepy II

take the numerous 'proto-histories' for what they are worth — as hypothesis, stimulating for research, but all debatable and all debated, always attractive to the theorist, but a little disquieting to the exact scholar, in so far as, by general arguments ... they claim to give shape to an extraordinary and almost inexplicable confusion of human actions about which very little is known."[6]

Of Menes (the Greek version of Meni) Yoyotte says we know of him only through Greek legends. He adds, "We do not know precisely which of the archaic kings mentioned on the monuments is the prototype of the legendary Menes."

The serious student of dynastic Egypt soon gathers two disquieting impressions: (1) that the culture seems to have flowered very quickly without leaving substantial evidence of a long developmental period, and (2) during its existence, the culture seems to have declined as if gradually losing the impetus of an inspired beginning. In *The Idea of Prehistory*, Glynn Daniel speaks of "the obvious facts of Egyptian decay," and in *Beyond Stonehenge*, Gerald Hawkins said, "after thirty dynasties, pharaonic Egypt was a shadow of her former splendor." In fact, repeated visits to the Egyptian collection of the British Museum have led me to the feeling that the decline came long before the end — perhaps midway.

One Egyptologist, Rudolph Anthes, a specialist in Egyptian religion and philosophy, saw it this way: "When all is said and done, Egyptian history suggests that, about 3000 B.C. (First Dynasty), religious and logical matters were in better balance than they were in 1000 B.C. in Egypt, or in the present-day world." Another writer, Andrew Tomas, confirmed my British Museum impressions: "For some reason the workmanship level of jewelry ... was higher in the earlier periods. Rings, necklaces, earrings, diadems, and crowns of the Fifth to Twelfth dynasties are more beautiful than those of the latter dynasties."

Neither these impressions nor the archaeological evidence itself are inconsistent with the idea of a prehistoric contact between the Stone-Age Nile population and an unknown ancient high civilization, all records of which were lost due to earth changes. (See "Psychic Impression of the Great Pyramid"). Such an hypothesis would explain the relatively high level of science and the early presence of engineering skills and writing in Egypt.

Manetho, an Egyptian scholar-priest of the third century B.C. whose writings are only known second hand, is one of the principal sources of the sequence of the thirty-one Egyptian dynasties. He is reported to have said that from the time of Menes to the Persian invasion (525 B.C.), excluding the Fourteenth dynasty, 4750 years had elapsed. For the same period, Herodotus said that about 4950 years had passed. These accounts put the beginning of dynastic Egypt back to between 5475 B.C. and 5275 B.C.

Today, however, the conventional date for the First Dynasty is about 3100 B.C. About four hundred years later the Old Kingdom dynasties

began a period which may also be called the "Pyramid Age."

Djoser, with the leadership of his minister and architect, Imhotep, built the first step pyramid at Saqqara sometime after 2686 B.C. This was also the first cut stone structure, marking a transition from brick to stone. Today, the remains of eighty pyramids are known, basically from the Old Kingdom. They lie between Meidum in the south and Abu Roash in the north. Among the thirty-four major pyramids, only two others approach the Great Pyramid's dimensions. Conventionally dated at 2644 B.C., the Great Pyramid is attributed to Cheops; but this date is not really firm. The great Egyptologist Sir Flinders Petrie gave it a date of about 3800 B.C. The attribution to Cheops is based only on red ochre inscriptions found in the relieving chambers. There is no cartouche or other marking on the sarcophagus which, due to its size, had to have been in place at the time of construction.

Archaeological History of the Great Pyramid — Evidence for an Ancient Science.

In his *Secrets of the Great Pyramid*, (1971), Peter Tompkins recounts the absorbing story of the field surveys of the Great Pyramid which began in the seventeenth century and the theoretical work by those who have attempted to establish the fact that a surprisingly high order of astronomical, mathematical, and geographic knowledge existed among the ancient Egyptians. The specialist will be advised to use caution with the mathematical work: sometimes decimals are rounded off in misleading ways and, in the case of the figure for the megalithic yard, inaccurately. Nonetheless, Tompkins has written a very interesting story from, at times, very technical materials. The archaeologically inclined reader will also want to supplement this introductory reading with a standard work, I.E.S. Edwards' *The Pyramids of Egypt*.

A good point at which to begin this story is with the visit to Giza about 440 B.C. by the Greek historian, Herodotus, who found the Great Pyramid still covered with polished limestone. In his *History* he reported that the Egyptian priests told him the Great Pyramid was designed in such a way that the area of each of its faces was equal to the square of its height. When finally understood in our own times, this meant that the Pyramid's geometry included pi (π) and phi (ϕ). In Egypt, pi or 3.1416 is not usually traced back further than about 1700 B.C. Phi, or 1.618, the Golden Proportion, was described by Plato in his *Timaeus* as the key to the physics of the universe. Only in this century was this proportion recognized as a part of Egyptian Old Kingdom mathematics. To recapitulate, the proportions given to Herodotus describe a structure (The Great Pyramid) whose geometry includes both π and ϕ, a fact not appreciated until very recently.

The account of Herodotus' visit is the most detailed of classical accounts now available. The destruction of the Alexandrian library was doubtless one reason for our understanding of the Great Pyramid being so long delayed. This destruction took place in two stages: first, in 389 A.D. at the hands of a Christian mob under the orders of the Emperor Theodosius, and, second, in 640 A.D., when the Arabs captured Alexandria and used the remaining library materials to heat the city's baths.

About two centuries later, in 820 A.D., drawn by the possibility of hidden treasure, entrance to the Great Pyramid was forced by

Meridian Triangle of Great Pyramid

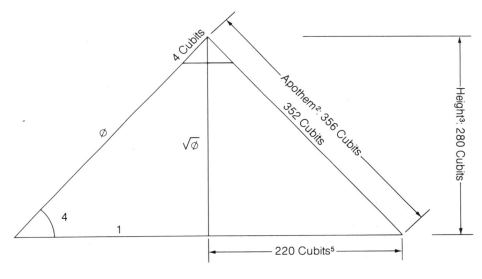

ϕ and π Proportions in Meridian Triangle of the Great Pyramid:

A *pi (π) and phi (ϕ), two geometric proportions, originally thought to have been developed much later, are found in the pyramid's geometry:*
(ϕ) Apothem (356 cubits) – ½ base (220) cubits) = 1.61818 (ϕ)
(π) Height (280 cubits) x 2 π = perimeter (1760 cubits)

B *This geometry also means that the pyramid is a model of the Northern hemisphere, that it is an elegant geometric solution for translating a 90° spherical quadrant (¼ of the Northern hemisphere) onto a flat triangle (the apex corresponds to the North pole, the perimeter to the equator).*

1 *The base is what Stecchini calls the "consensus of responsible interpreters."*
2 *Apothem is in some calculations taken without 4 cubits of pyramidion capping structure.*
3 *With four cubit pyramidion added in calculations, Herodotus' report is valid: square of height approximates area of one face:*
$$280 \times 280 = \frac{440 \times 356}{2}$$
$$78,400 = 78,320$$
4 *Slope angle chosen so that if half of base equals 1, the apothem is ϕ, then the height equals $\sqrt{\phi}$. (The thrust of notes 3 and 4 is that contained within Herodotus' report was the information that the pyramid was proportioned by the Golden Section (ϕ).*
5 *The cubit here is the royal cubit found by Petrie in the King's Chamber: .5241483 meter.*

Abdullah Al Mamun, son of the Caliph of Baghdad. Even at this time the King's chamber was empty.

During the Renaissance, interest in the past led an Italian physician, Girolamo Cardano, to claim that an exact science preceded the Greeks and that clues to this science would be found in Egypt. In 1638 an English mathematician and astronomer, John Greaves, went to Egypt looking for data in the Great Pyramid's measurements which might relate to the planet's dimensions — not then known accurately. Because of rubble at the base, Greaves' measurements were inaccurate. Shortly afterwards, Sir Isaac Newton tried to use Greaves' figures to establish the unit (or units) of measure of the Great Pyramid which he wished to use for correction of the then known circumference of the earth (a figure crucial to his gravitational theory). From then on, until the visit of Napoleon to the pyramid in 1798 with 175 scholars during the French invasion of Egypt, investigation virtually stopped.

After conquering Egypt, Napoleon's force (with Turkish assistance) cleared the rubble at the pyramid's northeast and northwest corners. In so doing, they located the platform underneath and the two shallow depressions (or "sockets") ten by twelve feet at these two corners and measured this side at 230.902 meters. They also determined the apothem (slant height

from bottom center of one side to apex) to be 184.722 meters. One scholar with Napoleon, Edmé-François Jomard, related this length to Greek statements that the Pyramid's apothem was one Greek stadium (or 600 Greek feet). In his research, Jomard then found that the Alexandrian Greek stadium was about 185.5 meters, within a meter of his own measurement. He also learned that the 600-foot stadium was thought to be 1/600 of a geographic degree. Hot on the trail of measurements related to the earth's dimensions, Jomard read that the Greeks reported the perimeter of the Pyramid to equal a half minute of longitude. This and other information led Jomard to claim that the Greeks had gotten their geometry from Egypt where there had existed the astronomical knowledge to measure a geographical degree and thus the knowledge to establish the planet's circumference. Unfortunately, Jomard's measurements were challenged, and his theories were not accepted by his colleagues. Their reverence for ancient Greek science could not allow this elevation of ancient Egyptian science. Perhaps even today this bias, if unconscious, leads many scholars to reject, out of hand, the implications of the Great Pyramid. After all, for educated westerners today, western civilization began in Greece, not Egypt.

The Napoleonic investigations in

50

52

50   Closeup of casing stone shows incredible fit achieved by the ancients with these massive stones.

51   Casing stones rest on the platform stones (right) and then the bedrock.

52   Closeup of one of the sockets.

53   Corner of Great Pyramid.

54   One of the sockets, a depression in bedrock at corner of the pyramid. Sockets provided archaeologists with one of the pyramid's crucial measurements.

53

54

Egypt, including the discovery of the Rosetta Stone, could be said to have inaugurated the oldest of modern archaeological disciplines, Egyptology. Twenty years later, the Rosetta Stone enabled Jean-François Champollion to decipher the hieroglyphics of the ancient Egyptians. This achievement established him as the founder of Egyptology.

Next, John Taylor, English poet, essayist, mathematician, amateur astronomer, and author of *The Great Pyramid: Why Was It Built and Who Built It?* (1864), found that the perimeter of the Great Pyramid divided by twice its height gave a figure close to pi, or 3.144 (pi is actually 3.14159+). Trying to explain the presence of pi, Taylor decided that the perimeter of the pyramid had been designed to represent the circumference of the earth and the height to equal the polar radius. If the earth were a true sphere (which it is not), 2pi would describe the relationship between the polar radius and the circumference: circumference = $2\pi r$. As Taylor put it, the Great Pyramid was built "to make a record of the measure of the earth."

With modern measurements, Taylor's intuition about the pi relationship between the perimeter of the pyramid and its height, as well as the relationship between the planet's polar radius and circumference was confirmed. (See "pi and ϕ proportions in Great Pyramid"). Pi

was not taken to the fourth decimal until the sixth century A.D.

In 1864, convinced that Taylor was on the right track, C. Piazzi Smyth, Astronomer Royal for Scotland went to Egypt to make his own measurements. This was the first survey to modern standards and involved the use of much specially-designed equipment. He agreed with Taylor that the coffin in the King's chamber was a standard of linear and cubic measure. The next visitor would derive the royal cubit from measurements of this artifact. Smyth established the latitude (29° 58' 51") and the actual inclination of the Descending Passage (26° 17'). From this figure, Smyth worked out the astronomical situation (and date) of the pyramid's construction.

After Smyth, the next major survey of the pyramid was that of a man destined to become one of the greatest of Egyptologists. Sir William Flinders Petrie, who began as a professional surveyor, founded the British School of Archaeology in Egypt. In its accuracy, his 1880-1882 survey was not to be superseded until J.H. Cole's 1925 survey. His measurements led him to discard Smyth's cubit of 25.025 inches and settle on the royal cubit of 20.636 inches (.5241483 m). This precise figure, interpreted by Stecchini from Petrie's measurements of the coffin in the King's chamber, still stands. His measurements led him to support Taylor's theory of the pi

relationship between the 440-cubit base and the 280-cubit height. Furthermore, he discovered the "Pythagorean" 3-4-5 and 2-$\sqrt{5}$-3 triangles in the dimensions of the King's chamber. His outer measurements (of the base) were taken, not between the four "sockets" at each corner, but 21.6535 inches higher (on top of the platform). His survey was not to be improved upon until Cole's work which revealed the four sides to be slightly different lengths, the average being about 230.365 meters, a difference of .305 meter (or about twelve inches) from Petrie's figures.

Another British astronomer picked up Smyth's idea of the pyramid as an observatory. This was Richard Anthony Proctor who deduced an astronomical situation for 3400 B.C., a date when he said the pyramid was under construction. At that time, he said, the descending passage pointed to the north (to Alpha Draconis) and the Grand Galley could have been used to observe the meridian passage of Alpha Centauri (in the southern sky).

These astronomical suggestions imply an Egyptian astronomy which is far too sophisticated for most Egyptologists to accept, even today. Near the turn of the century, the real pioneer of archaeoastronomy, Sir Norman Lockyer, in *The Dawn of Astronomy*, (1894), began to suggest that the ancient Egyptians were

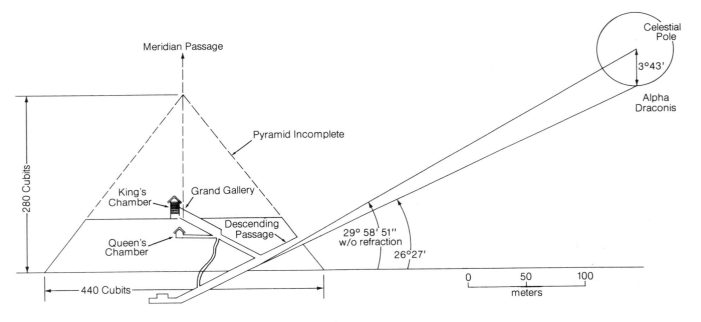

Piazzi Smyth's Astronomical
Assumptions for 2170 B.C.

Meridian Passage

Celestial
Pole

3°43'

Alpha
Draconis

Pyramid Incomplete

280 Cubits

King's
Chamber

Grand Gallery

Descending
Passage

Queen's
Chamber

29° 58' 51"
w/o refraction

26°27'

0   50   100

meters

440 Cubits

aware of precession and periodically reoriented their temples to adjust for its effects. In *Hamlet's Mill*, Giorgio de Santillana and Hertha von Dechend make the point that the entire ancient world possessed a common body of knowledge which transcended local cultures. This information was astronomical, numerical, and geometric. Such knowledge, say Santillana and von Dechend, was the actual basis for worldwide myths. In this work Santillana challenges scholars on their ignorance of astronomy, even a phenomenon so basic as the precession of the equinoxes. For him, the evidence makes it unreasonable to

deny that the Egyptians understood precession.

Because of precession, due to a slow wobble of the earth on its axis over about 26,000 years, at the equinox, the constellations of the zodiac appear to be slipping back 30° (or one constellation) in 2,160 years, or about 50 seconds of arc per year. The constellation in place at the equinox gives the name of an age such as the present Piscean age. While the phenomenon was not explained until Newton's seventeenth-century celestial mechanics, the evidence of ancient zodiacs suggests that observation of the constellations at the equinoxes may

be traced back to at least 4000 B.C.

Precise, observational knowledge of precession depends upon accurate sighting of the meridian passages of the stars *and* an accurate solar calendar to time the equinoxes. At least during its construction, the Grand Gallery of the Great Pyramid could have handled precise meridian passages of stars to the south, such as Alpha Centauri.

Analysis of the now available data on the Great Pyramid has led the foremost authority on ancient weights and measures, Professor Livio Catullo Stecchini, to the view that a high level of astronomy, mathematics and geography existed several thousand years before classical Greece and that Egyptian cultural remains reveal the presence of this knowledge.

The most recent contribution to our understanding of this knowledge is the result of analysis of the pyramid data by William R. Fix in *Pyramid Odyssey* (1978). It will be recalled that one earth measure was found in the perimeter length: one half minute of latitude at the equator. Fix realized that the perimeter was therefore constructed on a scale of 1:43,200. Working out a measurement on this scale equal to equatorial longitude, Fix discovered that such a length (927.66571 meters) was very close to the perimeter measured at the sockets, outside of the corners of the pyramid, or 927.72161. The difference is a mere .0559 of a meter (2.2 inches). The sockets include one (at the southwest corner) which is but an incised line. This fact makes the sockets more logical as reference points than as anchoring locations. The archaeological view of these sockets is consistent with Fix's interpretation. His second contribution to understanding the secrets of the pyramid was realizing that by adding the dimension of the platform upon which the entire structure rests (21.6535 inches or 55 cm) to the height he could get an equivalent to the polar radius: 481.4 feet plus 21.6535 inches = 482.75751 feet; 482.75751 feet = 147.14479 meters;

147.14479 x 43,200 = 6,356, 654.9 meters. The present estimate of the polar radius is 6,356,774 meters.

It is thus clear that, in addition to more subtle mathematical concepts, the significant measures of equatorial latitude, longitude and the polar radius are contained in the Great Pyramid on a scale of 1:43,200.

The Search for the Hall of Records at Giza

The idea that records of the ancient Egyptian mysteries, once understood by the priests, still exist and may someday be found, particularly at Giza, has been put forward many times. In the trance-state, material channeled through the American sensitive, Edgar Cayce, this idea was developed at length. In fact, one reading gave a specific location for the entrance to an underground temple complex where these records are yet supposed to exist.

One historical text which points to the possible existence of such records is a Neo-Platonic treatise, "The Virgin of the World", translated by G.R.S. Mead, a friend of the Irish poet Yeats. Because of the modern bias against the entire Platonic tradition, this text is probably not regarded as seriously as it should be. Based on internal evidence, Robert Temple, author of *The Sirius Mystery* makes a case for its authenticity. "The Virgin of the World" gives a dialog between priests (representing Isis and Horus) which includes the more secret teachings. In essence, Isis and Osiris brought a high culture from elsewhere which, almost overnight, transformed a Stone-Age culture into the Egyptian dynastic civilization.

In the actual dialog between Isis and her son Horus, Hermes is described as a being who came from the stars, taught Isis and Osiris in "God's hidden codes, became the author of the arts, and sciences, and all pursuits which men do practise, and giver of their laws." After his teaching mission was concluded, Hermes, "with charge unto his kinsmen of the Gods to keep sure watch, ... mounted to the stars." Before his departure, Hermes left records bearing the secrets of the cosmos with this pronouncement: "O holy books, who have been made by my immortal hands, by incorruption's mighty spells ... free from decay throughout eternity remain and uncorrupt from time! Become unseeable, unfindable, for every one whose foot shall tread the plains of this land, until old Heaven doth bring forward meet instruments for you, whom the creator shall call souls." In other words, the hidden secrets of Hermes are to remain lost until the right people emerge.

Afterward, the teachings continued through "Tat" (Thoth) which may stand for a priesthood. In sources other than "The Virgin of the World", Hermes' son was Hermes Trismegistus, usually identified with Thoth. The Greeks held this Hermes to be the inventor of writing, geometry, astronomy, medicine, surgery, art and music. Obviously Thoth's talents symbolize the total impact of a high civilization.

In the mainstream of Egyptology, our principal source of information about the Osiris cult derives from the Greek Plutarch's *De Iside et Osirde*. Here, Osiris, the eldest son of the earth-god Geb and the sky-goddess Nut, ruled as a just and benevolent king over the entire earth, instructing mankind in the arts and crafts and thus converting them from savagery to a civilized state. In the Pyramid Age, Isis, also a child of Geb and Nut, was the wife of Osiris who was eventually murdered (and dismembered by his brother Seth). Isis recovered the remains and gave birth to their son Horus. One Egyptologist, I.E.S. Edwards, believes that Osiris was probably the first king before the union of Upper and Lower Egypt under the traditional king (Menes). He then became a local god, was finally identified with a local Nile Delta god, Andjeti, and took his symbols, the shepherd's crook and flail. Isis, the chief Egyptian goddess, was often identified with Sirius, the star most important to the Egyptians.

The Osiris cult was paralleled by a solar cult, the official religion, which is supposed to have originated during the Pyramid Age at a temple near Memphis located a few miles northeast of Cairo at the Biblical On (called "Heliopolis" by the Greeks). By the Fourth Dynasty the solar cult had become dominant. The god Ra (now Re), the sun, was also known at Heliopolis as Atum. The solar cult celebrated life; the Osiris cult, the dead and the underworld. Yet, as Edwards points out, both cults provide a divine example of survival after death and thus support various funerary practices including mummification.

Life after death was not, however, guaranteed. It depended upon following proper rituals and providing material support for the afterlife, hence the importance of the tomb (at one period the pyramid?). This belief flourished for over two thousand years.

"A more advanced conception of a blissful afterlife gained as a reward for virtue may have been entertained by adherents to the Osirian cult from remote antiquity, but the absence of any contemporary evidence of its beliefs and tenets renders any attempt to reconstruct the creed in its primitive form very hazardous," says I.E.S. Edwards.

In *The Sirius Mystery*, Robert Temple highlights the very great antiquity of the names Isis and Osiris: "The meanings of the Egyptian hieroglyphs and names for Isis and Osiris were unknown to the earliest dynastic Egyptians themselves, and the names and signs appear to have a pre-dynastic origin — which means around or before 3200 B.C., in other words 5,000 years ago at least. There has been no living traditional explanation for the meanings of the names and signs for Isis and Osiris since at least 2800 B.C. at the very earliest."

Writing in 1977, the astronomer, Gerald Hawkins, succinctly summarized the obscurity surrounding the origins of Egyptian culture, an obscurity which the discovery of some repository such as The Hall of Records could dispel: "The feeling today is that there was an underlying principle in Egyptian philosophy that has not yet been fully understood. Beyond the inconsistencies in their myths and legends, there seems to have been a basic set of ideas that helped to produce an enduring civilization. At least part of those ideas might have been an appreciation of order and stability in the greater environment, in the cosmos, and in the reliable movement of the heavenly bodies".

The discovery of the Hall of Records will surely constitute the most stunning archaeological find of all times.

Archaeoastronomy in Egypt

In the outline of archaeological history we have seen the discovery of earth-commensurate measurements in the Great Pyramid; this implies an observational astronomy in use by ancient Egyptians from which they derived accurate geographical information. Their astronomical skill also gave them a means of accurately orienting pyramids and other structures. Once the Great Pyramid was completed, however, there appears to be no real basis for saying that it was later used for stellar observations. On the other hand, its precise orientation and great height could have provided a means for timing the solar year — at the equinoxes. However, the Egyptian solar calendar, the so-called "vague year," was 365 days, rather than the 365¼ days necessary to keep the calendar in phase with the actual seasons. Also, unlike the Maya for instance, dynastic Egyptians seemed to have let their civil calendar (a solar one) slide so that only about every 1460 years did the New Year's day of the civil calendar coincide with an important stellar phenomenon, the heliacal rising of the star Sothis (our Sirius) — the so-called Sothic cycle.

The real basis for believing that the priests possibly kept a more realistic solar calendar comes from the evidence of astronomical alignments in the temples. The best example is the Great Temple of Amen-Ra at Karnak in the Thebes district, northeast of the modern town of Luxor. From on-site hieroglyphics and work with local charts, Gerald Hawkins discovered that, before an addition in 1480 B.C., this temple had a clear sight down its central axis to the winter solstice sunrise (between 2000 and 1480 B.C.). Besides the Amen-Ra alignment, Hawkins found another winter solstice sunrise in the time of Ramses II.

Hawkins' work challenged the earlier theory of Sir Norman Lockyer that this temple's alignment had been to the summer solstice sunset. In *The Dawn of Astronomers* Lockyer claimed a total of six solstitial alignments of Egyptian temples. He also found evidence for stellar alignments. In two cases, the temples seemed to have been rebuilt periodically to allow for new stellar alignments due to precession. One was at Luxor (aligned to Vega at four different times); the other at Medinet-Habu, across the Nile from Luxor. The latter includes two temples, the later encroaching upon the earlier and re-oriented by about four degrees. Lockyer said that these two temples were, at different times, oriented to align with the star Phact (Alpha Columbae). Lockyer's stellar alignments are not yet generally accepted. Of course, the level of dynastic Egypt's astronomical knowledge implied in the present work is pretty heady stuff for most conventional Egyptologists.

A Psychic's Impression of the Great Pyramid

The construction of these mighty edifices signified new growth and new understanding for this land. Of course, the original workers were wary and little understanding of the powers or purpose of the pyramids. Alternative cycles of calendars led astronomers to understand the changing earth position (due to precession). The Great Pyramid was a permanent fixture, a fix on the heavens.

The early builders expected earth changes of immense degree. Remember this was after Atlantis. Safety for the remains of the bodies of the high souls who had been leaders was only one purpose. Their restoration of the earth after the great peril *which has not as yet arrived* [Italics mino]. So removing the mummies has been an awesome interference and brought hazard upon the tamperers from the nether worlds. Alas, contemporary man whose wisdom has perished!

The north star orientation was a fixed point for calculation. Floods such as submerged Atlantis were feared so the height of the pyramid was great. We do not understand the modern reluctance to see the numerical knowledge built into the pyramids by astronomer-priests. These priests were mindful of their responsibility to erect many principles into one edifice.

First purpose: calendrical with

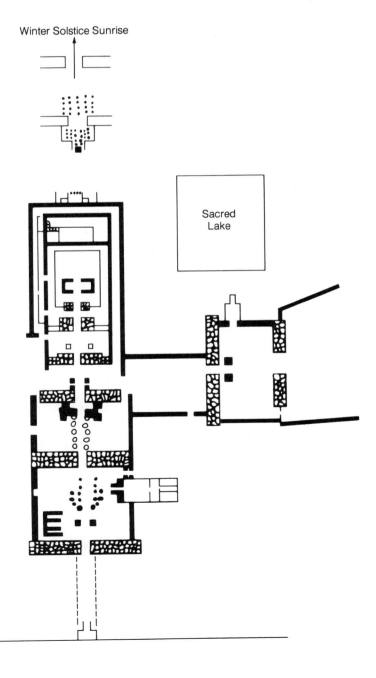

Temple of Amon-Ra, Karnak

Winter Solstice Sunrise

Sacred Lake

material and spiritual counterparts — as above so below.

an energy collector and beacon

a place of burial and a place to amass knowledge and, by the way, great hoards of information are yet to be found (to be) discovered in sealed compartments above stairs in central chamber, Cheops pyramid.

All right now to disseminate these facts. After all, man's innate abilities will stir with the mention of certain sounds, lights, words.

Look to the future for new inspiration and joy.

The initiation of which men speak today took place in many places. The resonances of the stones triggered the out-of-body experience. Modern pyramid inadequate. Other stone dwellings, even standing stones to a lesser degree, have some vibratory effect.

The complete workings, i.e. the mathematical structure, were not built to inaugurate initiations but to record mathematical knowledge. Initiation took place in many temples wherever the subject's body-energy could be raised. Through prayer (churches) chanting, any means to getting it (the body) to a high frequency.

We are through.

Psychic Impressions of the Sphinx

The purpose of the Sphinx was navigational (1) as pertains to flights of souls entering the earth's field, (2) as a target from which energy could be broadcast as pertains to transmissions sent far afield. In several dimensions this energy was useful; in the use of this force-field understand that powerful radiations were used at that period to energize the continent and the area. The animal kingdom was raised through such energy blasts and over Egypt the highest souls in service to the earth could congregate with less friction. Radial lines of energy transmitted to Europe; the power points there aligned with Giza.

Now understand. All centers of radii were chosen from earth's magnetic 'pressure points'. Fields of force were fully recognized by the effect upon the body by the men of old. The field around Giza was of undisputed power. Forceful attractions continued there for centuries and spurred through "mental alignments" to the "idea world" the discoveries and advancements which put Egypt at the pinnacle of power. The decline of that greatness occurred after the sixth century B.C. There lay a vast reservoir of understandings of magnetic force-fields subsequently lost in the world. Atlantean information in Egypt added to the development of this "mystical technology" whose workings propelled the study of gases and ethers, the crystallized atom (particles of matter) and finally the use of the octave of twelve notes. Unlike all other cultures, Egypt strove for purity in consciousness at this period (its greatest period) and pronounced the earth dead of spirit.

The alignments to stars and etheric force-fields was thought indispensable for lifting man out of the mire, the retardation into which he was caught. Every opportunity to reverse this condition was given those who came for initiation, the spiritual elite. In turn, these spirits freed could achieve for their land tremendous accomplishments and understanding. More on the golden disk at a later time.

Notes

1 Incidentally, the Irish passage-grave art is now seen as different from Spanish and French megalithic art, calling into question the earlier assumed links among these megalithic cultures.

2 So-called from their use of elaborate clay beakers.

3 The origin of the word sarsen is not known.

4 Pronunciation of key Maltese place-names (after Kininmonth)

Ġgantija:	Jigantiya
Ghar Dalam:	Ar Dalam
Hagar Qim:	Hajar Eem
Mġarr:	Imjar
Mnajdra:	Imnighdra
Tarxien:	Tarsheen
Żebbuġ:	Zebooj

5 Dates from David H. Trump.

6 *Dictionary of Egyptian Civilization* (French ed. 1959).

55 *The Sphinx, Great Pyramid in background.*

55

72

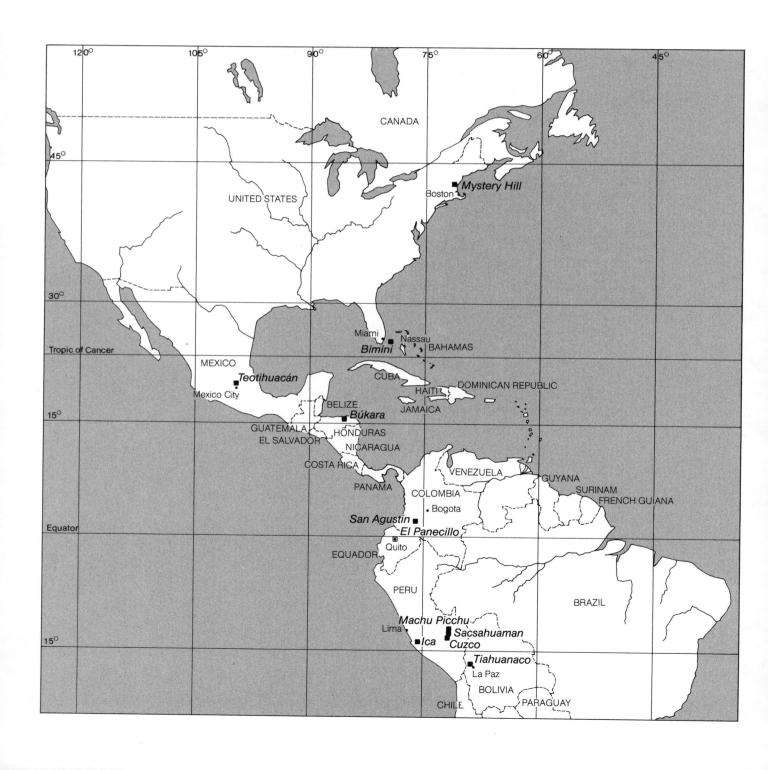

Mystery Hill
Boston

UNITED STATES

CANADA

Miami   Nassau
Bimini   BAHAMAS

CUBA

MEXICO

Teotihuacán

Mexico City

BELIZE
Búkara
GUATEMALA
EL SALVADOR   HONDURAS
NICARAGUA

COSTA RICA

PANAMA

HAITI   DOMINICAN REPUBLIC

JAMAICA

VENEZUELA   GUYANA
                   SURINAM
COLOMBIA   FRENCH GUIANA

Bogota

San Agustin
El Panecillo

Quito

EQUADOR

PERU

BRAZIL

Machu Picchu
Lima   Sacsahuaman
Ica   Cuzco

Tiahuanaco
La Paz

BOLIVIA

CHILE   PARAGUAY

120°   105°   90°   75°   60°   45°

45°

30°

Tropic of Cancer

15°

Equator

15°

3

The New World

The megalithic sites of the New World range geographically from Mystery Hill in New Hampshire to Tiahuanaco, Bolivia. In time they begin with the possible date of last use of the controversial site at Bimini Island in the Bahamas (about 6000 B.C.) and end with the Inca culture in the sixteenth century A.D. Their stone work includes the mammoth stone weighing 440 tons at Sacsahuaman, Peru and stones in excess of 200 tons at Tiahuanaco. As might be expected with the geological instability of the Andes, the most intriguing engineering strategies for stabilizing masonry against earthquakes are to be found in the Peruvian and Bolivian work. Although the Maya were certainly the most knowledgeable in astronomy and mathematics (at least from what is known), the most complex arrangements for observing the heavens appear to be those at Teotihuacán.

This was one of the reasons for including Teotihuacán instead of the Mayan monuments. Inevitably, a work such as this must select, sometimes almost arbitrarily. The principal reason for the omission of the Maya, however, is that very full coverage of this extraordinary culture is available in many excellent, easily available, works. The Maya present clear evidence of an observational astronomy, for example, the Caracol, an astronomical observatory at Chichén Itzá. By this means they maintained a calendar

more accurate than our own. Pyramids were also used for solar and lunar observations. Their study of the motions of Venus allowed them to calculate its orbit within fourteen seconds. They also pioneered the zero and began their calendar with a mysterious date before the Great Pyramid in Egypt was thought to have been built — August 11, 3114 B.C.

Most important of all, their harmony with their environment led to incredible longevity of the culture. One site on the northern coast of Yucatan, Dzibilchaltún, was continuously occupied for at least 2,000 years beginning in 500 B.C. Inclusion of this rich culture would have crowded out lesser-known cultures contributing to a sense of the planetary distribution of megalithic sites.

Not all megalithic sites exhibit astronomical implications. A number of important sites do, however, and thus archaeoastronomy is important in the New World as well as in the Old. Research in New-World astronomy is relatively new, yet in a short period of time it has uncovered surprising sophistication in locations besides Teotihuacán and the sites of the Maya. At Mystery Hill (whose oldest C-14 date is 2000 B.C.) sighting arrangements for lunar and solar observations have been demonstrated. At Medicine Wheel in Wyoming, American Indians built a twenty-

eight spoke wheel of stones eighty feet in diameter. As Dr. John A. Eddy, of the Smithsonian Astrophysical Observatory and the principal researcher here, has shown, in addition to solstice sunrise and sunset phenomena, the site (built about 1760 A.D.) is oriented to the rise of Aldebaran, Rigel and Sirius. Another fact noted by Dr. Eddy is that its twenty-eight spokes parallel the lunar zodiac of the Maya and resemble the twenty-eight stations of the moon in the systems of India and China.

In the southeastern United States the Pueblo Indians even constructed an arrangement by which the summer solstice sun projected a vertical mark on a stone carved with a spiral. It will be recalled that spirals are found at Newgrange in Ireland, which is also a solar-cult location. The Pueblo site is at Fajada Butte in the Chaco Canyon National Monument in northwestern New Mexico.

It appears to be high time to pay much more attention to the astronomical achievements of the lesser-known New-World cultures. Interested readers should see Anthony Aveni's two books, *Archaeoastonomy in Pre-Columbian America* and *Native American Astronomy*.

Two archaeological controversies of the New World, the figures of Acambaro, Mexico and the carved stones of Ica, Peru are treated in Appendix C.

Mystery Hill

North Salem, New Hampshire

It was a rainy October day when I first visited Mystery Hill. An easy drive north of Boston took me to the quiet, wooded hill of the site located just outside North Salem in the southeastern corner of New Hampshire. Once there, I found that, visually, the site lacked the drama of other megalithic sites I had visited. However, the enthusiasm and professional manner of my guide, Dan Leary, carried me over the initial disappointment. Mystery Hill becomes impressive only after the visitor begins to feel its mood and then slowly and carefully absorbs its many features. Both in layout and stonework Mystery Hill's twenty acres has more than a superficial resemblance to the Neolithic site of Skara Brae in the Scottish Orkney Islands. This latter however, has no astronomical orientations of which I am aware.

Among the trees I saw an incredible maze of dry-stone or mortarless walls and standing stones four to five feet in height which have since proven to have astronomical significance. There were also dolmen-like stone slab chambers, one of which has an oracular speaking tube arrangement, and,finally, the mysterious four-and-a-half-ton slab with a guttered edge which has been called the "Sacrificial Table." I already knew that the earliest radiocarbon date (2000 B.C.) made the site contemporary with European megalithic culture and that it shared

56

57

58

59

similarities with megalithic structures in Spain and Portugal.

As I studied surveyor's plans of the site back in the headquarters building, the astronomical complexity of the sighting arrangements compelled my own belief that Mystery Hill is, indeed, an authentic megalithic site. It thus presents a radical challenge to the existing prehistory of North America.

Archaeological History

For decades the conservatism of American archaeology led to a denial of the validity of many pieces

56   Entrance to Oracle Chamber (looking out).

57   Entrance to Oracle Chamber (looking in). Speaking tube located in left wall about eye level.

58   So-called "Watch House".

59   Four-and-a-half-ton "Sacrificial Table." Its guttered edge has given rise to the idea of its use. Over thirty similar tables have been seen at megalithic sites in Portugal; some are associated with burial sites.

of evidence which pointed to Old-World influences in the New. The evidence was ignored, misunderstood or called fraudulent. The Bat Creek Stone found in 1885 by Smithsonian investigators is a good case in point. Identified as Cherokee at the time, it was only recently recognized by Dr. Cyrus H. Gordon (at the time at Brandeis, now at New York University) as a sample of Bronze-Age Hebrew writing. In the absence of dependable written texts, the pursuit of prehistory poses many traps for the unwary, but it also eludes those who try to fit each new find into their own preconceptions. Gordon himself makes this clear in his *Riddles in History* (1974). Here he tackles some of the more interesting archaeological controversies of the past century such as the Paraiba inscription found in Brazil in 1872 which is in Hebrew and Phoenician dating from about 530 B.C.

As we said earlier, various scholars, including Gordon, have posited extensive voyaging to the New World during the Bronze Age. The most recent effort is the work of Dr.

Materials:
Gneisses, schists (metamorphic rocks based on igneous)

Geographical Coordinates:
42° 50′ 35″ North Latitude
71° 12′ 37″ West Longitude

Barry Fell, *America B.C.*, a book which, in effect, turns 2,300 years of American prehistory into history, This stunning book makes it clear that many evidences of trans-Atlantic diffusion before Columbus have been ignored or misunderstood. This was due, in a major way, to over-reliance on the basic concept of an Asiatic migration across the Bering Strait as the sole source of cultural influences in the New World. Dr. Fell presents evidence for deliberate Celtic voyages from Portugal and Spain leading to settlements in New England and Oklahoma no later than 1000 B.C. The earliest date at Mystery Hill, 2000 B.C., argues for earlier accidental voyages. Mystery Hill also possesses Celtic inscriptions in Oggam. Dr. Fell believes, as well, that these original voyages were soon followed by those of Basques, Phoenicians and Libyans from the Old World. They settled in Pennsylvania, West Virginia, Ohio and elsewhere.

Some of these settlements lasted until the fall of Rome.

The most impressive evidence for all of this is the Davenport, Iowa, Stone found in 1874. First seen as a fraud, it has recently been recognized as the American Rosetta Stone — inscribed in Egyptian, Iberian Punic, and Libyan! Dr. Fell presents evidence that Egyptian hieroglyphs were incorporated into the Micmac Indian script.

Given all of this, the claims made for Mystery Hill are not at all surprising. On the other hand, it must be granted that the site's history is sufficient explanation for its cautious reception by archaeologists. Further, the great age of the site, dated at 2000 B.C., challenges conventional views of American prehistory.

From the time of its discovery in historical times, Mystery Hill was subjected to damage which led the prehistorian Geoffrey Ashe to label it "ruins of ruins." It has been estimated that upwards of forty percent of the stones of the original construction were removed during the occupancy of the first known owner. In 1823 a farmer named Jonathan Pattee who settled there used many stones for the foundation of his house. A few years later in the 1860's, the site was used as a quarry for the construction of a nearby dam built in Massachusetts. After a series of owners, the property was bought around 1936 by a retired insurance man, William B. Goodwin. In the intervening years, New England archaeologists had come to believe that the Mystery Hill structures (and others as well) were nothing but colonial "root cellars."

Goodwin believed differently. His view was that the site had been constructed by Irish Culdee monks. However, during the years of his ownership, he compounded the problem for archaeologists by rear-

ranging parts of the site to fit his theory. Nevertheless, whatever damage he may have done, he did bring the ruins to the attention of the world. The immediate response from the archaeologists was that Mystery Hill was simply the work of a "crazy colonial farmer", Jonathan Pattee, but no rational explanation has been offered to account for the prodigious effort Pattee and his eleven daughters would have had to put forth to build structures containing stones weighing up to six tons! And no historical references have been found to document such a project, which would surely have excited comment in a small new England community.

Goodwin died in 1950 at which time the property was leased (and later sold) to Robert E. Stone, an electronics engineer. Stone's leadership and persistence have both preserved the controversial site and encouraged the serious scientific evaluation which has led to understanding its true significance.

In 1967 a series of radiocarbon datings by the Geochron Laboratory of Cambridge, Massachusetts produced one date equivalent to about 2000 B.C. Even the least radical result of these tests rules out the "crazy farmer" theory. A laboratory report by Dr. Harold W. Krueger, dated September 18, 1967 states that one of the buildings identified by archaeologists as Pattee's work was penetrated by tree

roots which dated back to about 1690 A.D., ± 90 years. This means, of course, that the structure was built well before 1823.

Dr. Fell first visited the site on June 14, 1975. Some of the stone-slab chambers reminded him of Goidelic Celtic structures he had seen in Scotland. He was also shown a weathered stone inscribed with what he immediately recognized as a Phoenician dedication, in Iberian Punic script, to the sun-god, Baal. The triangular dedication tablet had been found by James P. Whitall. Subsequently, Robert Stone found an inscription, which Fell recognized as Celtic Oggam, dedicating the temple (at Mystery Hill) and other New England sites, all of which is detailed in his *America B.C.* Fell concluded that the New England megalithic chambers (including Mystery Hill) were built by Celts from Spain and Portugal who had welcomed Phoenician traders on the North American coast. Furthermore, they had allowed the visitors to worship at their shrines and to make dedications in their own language.

On linguistic evidence Professor Fell puts the Celtic occupancy at least as early as 800-600 B.C. and believes that it continued as late as 50 A.D. The functions of the site likely include burial (in passage graves) ceremonial (based on lunar and solar phenomena observed

there) and perhaps living quarters for the priests.

60

61

60 "Tomb of Lost Souls." Like many features of this site, this structure resembles the cist of megalithic cultures in western Europe.

61 Dedication tablet in Mystery Hill museum. Inscribed in Iberian, it is dedicated to Baal of the Caananites (Phoenicians). It was found in a temple observatory used to observe the winter solstice noon transit.

62 *Browne's Hill dolmen, a type of megalithic structure found throughout the world.*

63 *Celtic Beltane stone discovered at Mystery Hill. This stone with Roman numerals signals day 39, Mayday in the Celtic calendar around the time of Christ.*

64 *Largest dolmen in North America, North Salem, New York. Resting on five upright stones, the capstone weighs about ninety tons. Local authorities call it a glacial erratic. Barry Fell considers it Celtiberian in origin. Compare Browne's Hill dolmen, Ireland.*

Psychic Reading on Mystery Hill

At 'Mystery Hill' you will find remnants of an ancient civilization, long before this mound: sheets of papyrus containing information about stolen goods of nearby tribes were buried. Piecing together the evidence will lead you to consider a rash of possibilities: warriors of South American origin traversed this country [Fell sees a South American link with the Iroquois]; their original Semitic neighbors fought long and hard to avail themselves of a secret, the rites of passage which existed in the storehouse of knowledge of the South American tribes. (Rites of passage refers to graves; much information stored in underground tombs: gold disks, devices to attune souls on the way out of the body. These secrets of knowledge were guarded by South American priests. The struggle was over this hardware!) These tribes also tried to contain the fierceness of one who smuggled stolen treasures from their domain. It is hard to deny that some measures among these people seem like behavior of today; but fierce competition existed even then.

At far right of the mound, there is an underground exit. Underground tunnels suggest use of primitive escape and entrances. It is so. Further along, at entrance, traces of battle remain near floor to the left. Kneel, closely examine crystalline structure — Semitic — clasp for holding ajar a large stone door.

Mound built in 1532 BC by warlike inhabitants. From then until 1200 BC it was used primarily for storage of stolen and hoarded goods. Later reconstructed: became a temple for worship of Venus.

Q. How often frequented?

A. Occasionally by many, but major use came later in 10th century AD [BC?] Arriving Spaniards [Iberian Celts?] forced inhabitants of a community underground. 30–40,000 Spanish invaded.

Now let me repeat; watch openings. Parapet on right — forecast seasonal changes. Look to left of entrance for signs of former occupations. Underground caves, caverns. You will be instructed.

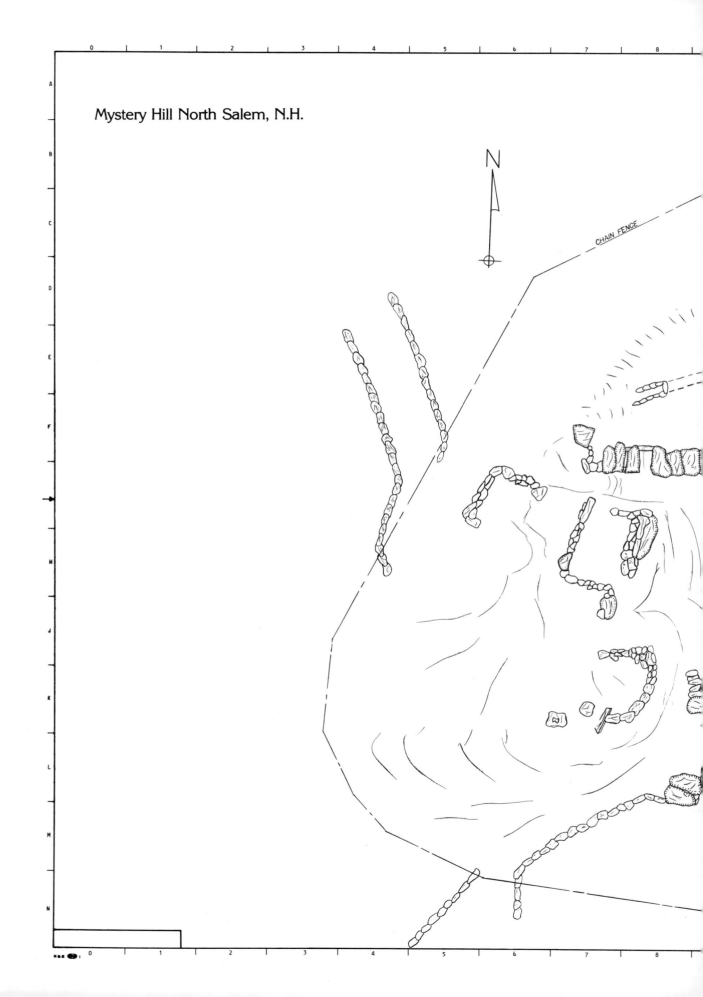

Mystery Hill North Salem, N.H.

N

CHAIN FENCE

79

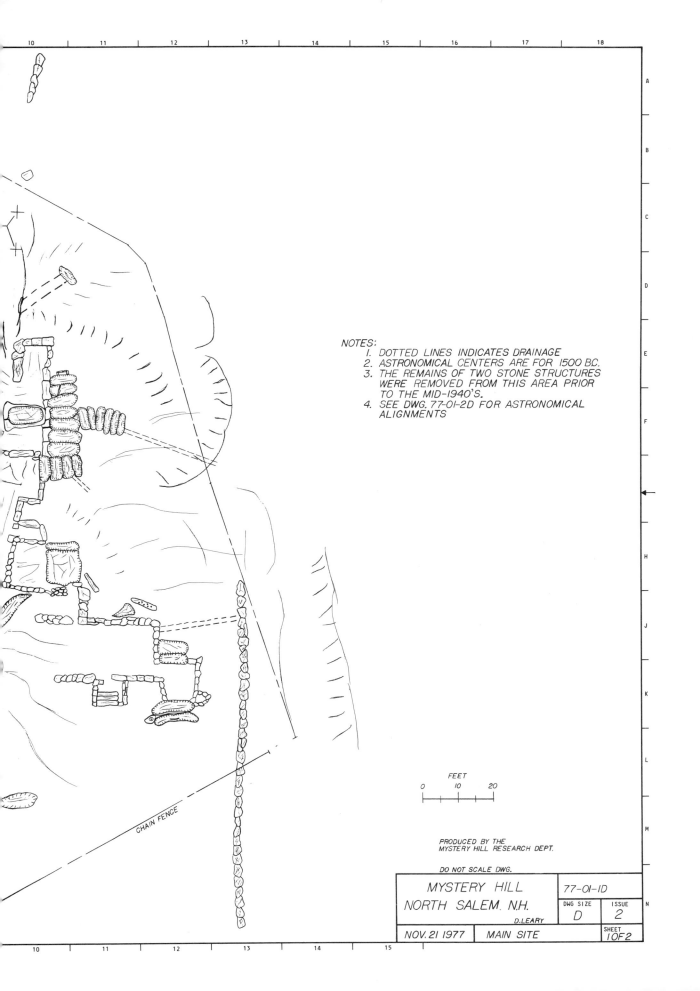

NOTES:
1. DOTTED LINES INDICATES DRAINAGE
2. ASTRONOMICAL CENTERS ARE FOR 1500 BC.
3. THE REMAINS OF TWO STONE STRUCTURES WERE REMOVED FROM THIS AREA PRIOR TO THE MID-1940'S.
4. SEE DWG. 77-01-2D FOR ASTRONOMICAL ALIGNMENTS

FEET
0   10   20

CHAIN FENCE

PRODUCED BY THE
MYSTERY HILL RESEARCH DEPT.

DO NOT SCALE DWG.

MYSTERY HILL	77-01-1D	
NORTH SALEM. N.H.	DWG SIZE D	ISSUE 2
D.LEARY		
NOV. 21 1977 MAIN SITE		SHEET 1 OF 2

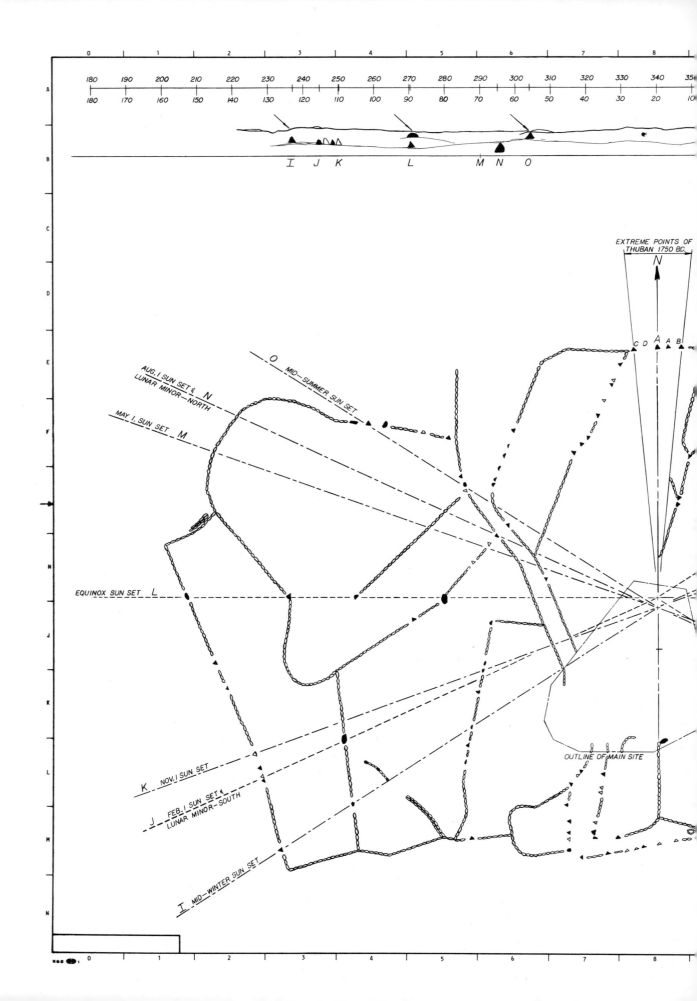

EXTREME POINTS OF
THUBAN 1750 B.C.

N

AUG. I SUN SET &   N
LUNAR MINOR—NORTH

O   MID—SUMMER SUN SET

MAY I. SUN SET   M

EQUINOX SUN SET   L

OUTLINE OF MAIN SITE

K   NOV. I SUN SET

J   FEB. I SUN SET &
LUNAR MINOR—SOUTH

I   MID—WINTER SUN SET

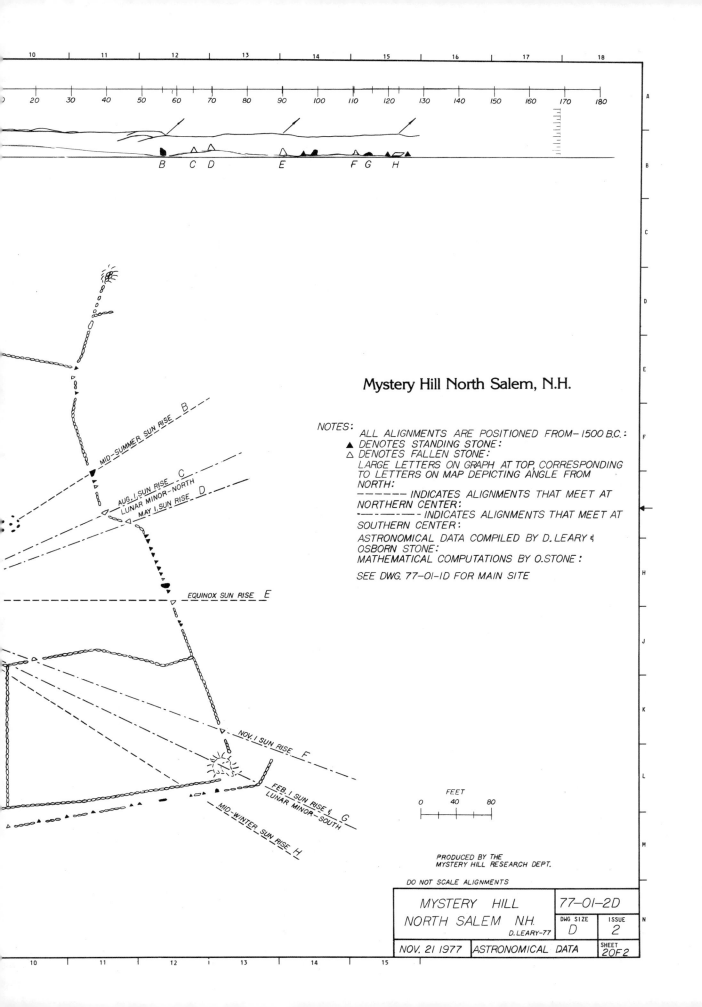

81

Mystery Hill North Salem, N.H.

NOTES: ALL ALIGNMENTS ARE POSITIONED FROM – 1500 B.C.:
▲ DENOTES STANDING STONE:
△ DENOTES FALLEN STONE:
LARGE LETTERS ON GRAPH AT TOP, CORRESPONDING
TO LETTERS ON MAP DEPICTING ANGLE FROM
NORTH:
–––––– INDICATES ALIGNMENTS THAT MEET AT
NORTHERN CENTER:
–·––·–· INDICATES ALIGNMENTS THAT MEET AT
SOUTHERN CENTER:
ASTRONOMICAL DATA COMPILED BY D. LEARY &
OSBORN STONE:
MATHEMATICAL COMPUTATIONS BY O. STONE:

SEE DWG. 77–01–1D FOR MAIN SITE

MID-SUMMER SUN RISE   B

AUG. I. SUN RISE   C
LUNAR MINOR-NORTH
MAY I. SUN RISE   D

EQUINOX SUN RISE   E

NOV. I SUN RISE   F

FEB. I SUN RISE &   G
LUNAR MINOR-SOUTH

MID-WINTER SUN RISE   H

FEET
0   40   80

PRODUCED BY THE
MYSTERY HILL RESEARCH DEPT.

DO NOT SCALE ALIGNMENTS

MYSTERY HILL	77–01–2D	
NORTH SALEM N.H.	DWG SIZE	ISSUE
D. LEARY-77	D	2
NOV. 21 1977 ASTRONOMICAL DATA	SHEET 2 OF 2	

82

65

65 *Sunset photographed December 21, 1970 by Robert E. Stone. Sun silhouettes winter solstice monolith.*

Psychic Reading on Mystery Hill

It is hard to deny that certain measures among these people seem akin to behavior of today; however, fierce competition existed even then.

At the far right of the mound, there is an underground exit. Underground tunnels suggest the use of primitive escape and entrances. It is so.

Further along at the entrance there remains trace of battle near the floor to the left. Kneel, closely examine crystalline structure — Semitic — a clasp for holding ajar a large stone door.

Mound built in 1532 B.C. by warlike inhabitants. From then until 1200 B.C. it was used primarily for storage of stolen and hoarded goods. Later reconstructed and became a temple for worship of Venus.

Q. How often frequented?

A. Occasionally by many, but the major use came later in the 10th century A.D. [B.C.?] Arriving Spaniards [Iberian Celts?] forced the inhabitants of a community underground. 30,000 to 40,000 Spanish invaded America.

Now let me repeat; watch openings. Parapet on right — forecast seasonal changes. Look to left of entrance for signs of former occupations.. Underground caves, caverns. You will be instructed.

At 'Mystery Hill' you will find remnants of an ancient civilization, long before this mound. There were buried sheets of papyrus which contained information about stolen goods of nearby tribes. Piecing together the evidence will lead you to consider a rash of possibilities:

First: that warriors of South American origin traversed this country. [Barry Fell sees a South American connection with the Iroquois]

Second: that their original Semitic neighbors fought long and hard to avail themselves of a secret, the rites of passage which existed in the storehouse of knowledge of the South American tribes. (The rites of passage refers to graves; much information was stored in underground tombs — gold disks, devices to attune souls on the way out of the body — these secrets of knowledge were guarded by South American priests. This struggle was over this hardware!) Likewise these tribes tried to contain the fierceness of one who smuggled stolen treasures from their domain.

Bimini

The Bahama Islands

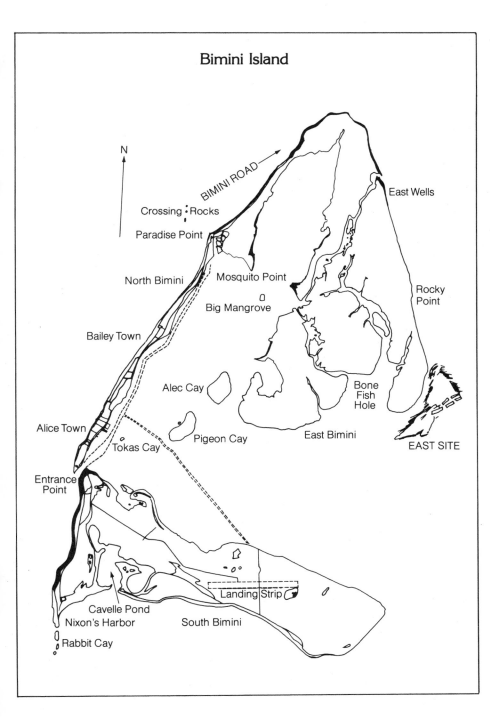

Bimini Island

N

BIMINI ROAD

Crossing Rocks

Paradise Point

North Bimini

Mosquito Point

Big Mangrove

Bailey Town

Alec Cay

Alice Town

Tokas Cay

Pigeon Cay

Entrance Point

East Wells

Rocky Point

Bone Fish Hole

East Bimini

EAST SITE

Cavelle Pond

Nixon's Harbor

Rabbit Cay

Landing Strip

South Bimini

The Bimini site is located off Bimini Island in the Bahamas, about fifty miles east of Miami, Florida, and about 150 miles west of the Bahamian capital, Nassau.

In its overall layout, the site is a reversed "J" measuring approximately 600 meters on its main axis and about 100 meters across. The main axis is oriented roughly North 45° East and the shorter leg opens about seven degrees (to North 52° East). The blocks of which it is constructed are typically about three by four meters in size and about seventy centimeters thick. Ten to fifteen tons is their estimated average weight, although considerable variation in size exists.

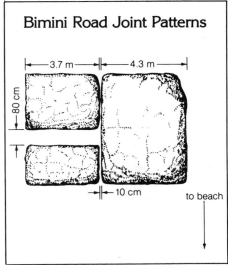

Bimini Road Joint Patterns

3.7 m — 4.3 m

80 cm

10 cm

to beach

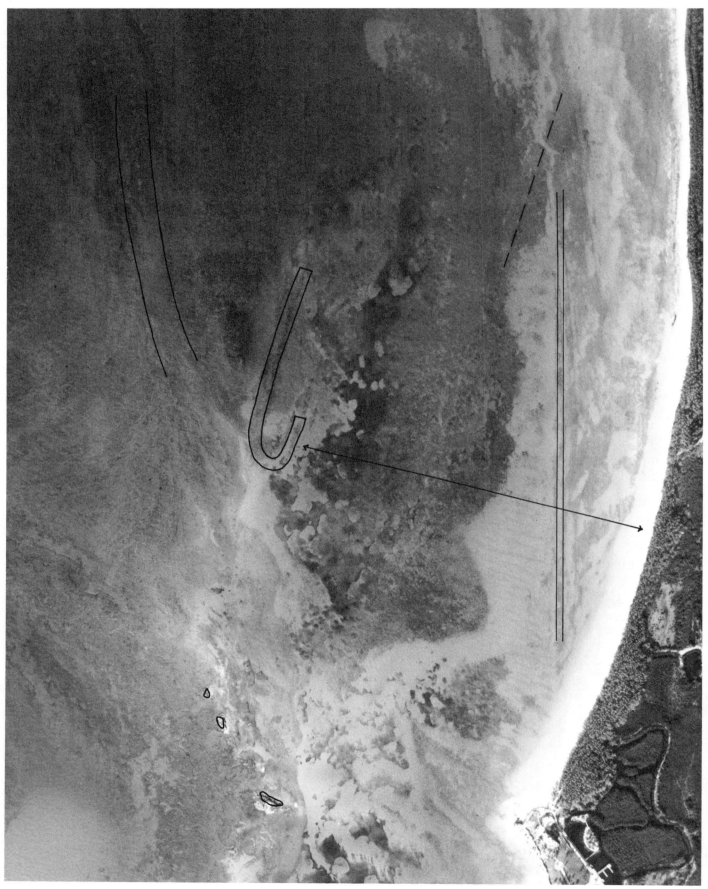

Construction Materials: the megalithic blocks are a sedimentary rock composed of a shell-hash cemented together in a marine environment and subsequently hardened by recrystallization (micritized). The blocks of this site may have been quarried from a homogeneous bed elsewhere and brought to Bimini *or* cut and shaped on or near the site. Trace-element analysis so far does not support the latter possibility. In either case, additional shell-hash blocks with dissimilar cementing has also been made a part of the structure.

Geographical coordinates:
79° 16' 55" West Longitude
25° 46' 18" North Latitude

Historical Background

Known by at least three generations of Bahamian guides as a fishing reef, this underwater site off Paradise Point was first recognized

66 *Looking northeast over Bimini "Road" site off Paradise Point, North Bimini Island. Lower right, Paradise Point; above it, the present beachline. Moving off the beach, several submerged ancient beachlines are seen. A man-made feature, a row of large stones crosses these obliquely; this feature is almost parallel to reversed "J" shape farther offshore — the "Road" itself. Lower left are three coral heads, the Crossing Rocks.*

as a megalithic structure by a Miami zoologist. In 1968 Dr. J. Manson Valentine, who had had a longtime interest in prehistory and archaeology, swam over the huge limestone blocks which lay eighteen feet below him and immediately recognized their implications. So far there is no known connection between this site and the Lucayan Indians found by Columbus on his first landing in the New World. Lucayan culture was related to that of the circum-Caribbean Arawaks but was much more simple; there is no evidence of their having built massive stone constructions.

Between 1968 and the first of my own eight expeditions to Bimini (in 1974), geologists in South Florida took the view that the megalithic blocks off Paradise Point were not the product of human engineering but instead were a part of a natural formation of beach rock. But, when I first investigated the site in 1974, I found a number of discrepancies in the geological description. And, of course, at the time, no artifacts had been found. The entire story of the field work is to be found in my book, *The Stones of Atlantis.* In brief, I found more order than expected, two artifacts, and the evidence which led to two independent lines of reasoning about the origins of the site. Furthermore, a freshwater spring with some radioactivity was found on the sea floor; this suggests the possibility of an ancient healing site. Also, another spring on the island of North Bimini seemed to have healing effects when we investigated it with its discoverer. One

unconventional procedure in the field work was the use of psychics to locate objects and to reconstruct the past through clairvoyance.

The most puzzling aspect of the Bimini site was the discovery in 1957 of a spire or column offshore from South Bimini. When its discoverer, Dr. William Bell, photographed it on the bottom in forty feet of water, energy of some sort appeared around the spire, patterned differently in each of his three photos. None of this was visible to the naked eye. These photos were first published in *The Stones of Atlantis.* The exact location of the spire has been lost, and many unsuccessful attempts have been made to relocate it.

Geological Formation or Archaeological Site?

When we first ran fathometer profiles over the site, I found the ocean floor to be essentially level, not sloping (which is usually the case with beach rock formed *in situ*). I also found hand samples to be much harder than the usual beach rock of the island. Soon I was to find fractures in the marine limestone of the sea bottom which did not coincide with the joints of the megalithic blocks. As I measured these blocks I also discovered significant morphological or structural differences between their patterns and the usual pattern of Caribbean beach rock as described in the geological literature. At length I found that the shells making up

these stones were not always cemented together by the same type of calcium carbonate crystals. Presumably, if the blocks were originally part of a homogeneous sedimentary deposit, they would have a consistent cementing pattern. In fact, between some adjacent blocks, we found sparry calcite crystals on one side, and on the other, aragonite crystals in the cement. One is a blocky form of calcium carbonate, the other a long, thin structure. So far, perhaps, the most promising line of investigation into the origin of these blocks has been nuclear activation analysis to reveal the presence of trace elements. This procedure has so far shown (from cores drilled in 1977) a radical chemical discontinuity between the sea floor and the blocks. One geologist has advised that this condition is not likely if the blocks had originally been deposited at the site.

Archaeology of Bimini

To date, the investigation of this site, probably the most controversial of those included in the present work, has produced only two artifacts. In 1975 I discovered a tongue-and-groove building block fragment which was almost completely buried under the sand. It proved to be a mixture of sandstone and limestone not found elsewhere on the island. It was approximately thirty-four centimeters square and nearly eight centimeters thick. Its flat sides were not parallel: perhaps it had come from a mold. Although it bore a slight resemblance to artifacts of the Olmec culture of Mexico, Mesoamerican specialists have so far not directly related it to any known Mesoamerican culture. At first sight, it seemed to have been fired but investigation at the Brookhaven National Laboratory proved this assumption false. Dating by the thermoluminescent method was therefore impossible.

In the same year as the block was found, one of my divers, Gary Varney, discovered what proved to be a highly stylized animal head worked from marble, another material not native to the island. Its approximate dimensions are thirty-two centimeters high, thirty-four centimeters wide (average), and thirty-three centimeters deep. From its left side, it looks like a cat or a monkey; its right side is severely geometric, a plane shape bounded by a pentagon. Again, it has, so far, been related to no known Meso-american culture. When the head was found, three other worked pieces of marble were found with it. They were basically rectangular. The building block is in the museum in Nassau operated by the Bahamas Antiquities Institute. The head was lifted and delivered to the Commissioner of Bimini Island in 1977.

Tongue and groove block

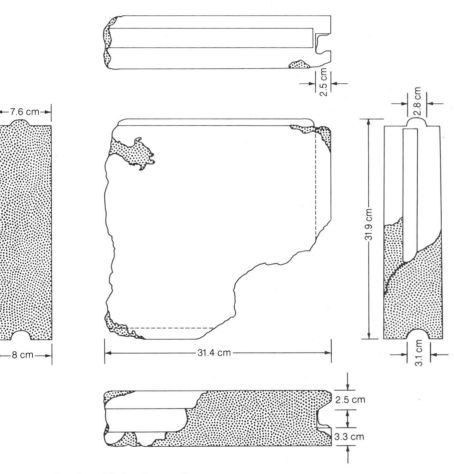

2.5 cm

7.6 cm

2.8 cm

31.9 cm

8 cm

31.4 cm

3.1 cm

2.5 cm

3.3 cm

67

67   *Left side of marble head; roundly modeled, it suggests, to some, a cat or a monkey.*

68   *Right sight of marble head, more severely geometric.*

69   *Front view of stylized marble head found in 1975 by Gary Varney. About 34 cm high, it has marine erosion to a depth of about 7 mm.*

69

Teotihuacán
Mexico

This spectacular Mesoamerican site is located about fifteen miles northeast of Mexico City in a side branch of the Valley of Mexico. At its peak the ancient city was nearly ten square miles in extent. Teotihuacán is dominated by the Pyramids of the Sun and the Moon which are connected by the "Avenue of the Dead," a street misnamed by the Aztecs. The axis of this avenue is oriented approximately North 23° East, and it is over 2,400 meters long (c. 7,874 feet) and forty meters wide (c. 131 feet). The Pyramid of the Moon is at the north end; the Pyramid of the Sun lies to the south on its easterly side. Extensive residential areas, a network of covered aqueducts, public baths, theaters, ball courts and colorful murals were also found here.

Approximate geographic coordinates
19° 41′ North Latitude
98° 52′ West Longitude
Construction material:
Adobe (sun-baked brick)
Lava fragments
Clay and wooden rafters
Tools
Made of a hard, glassy volcanic rock, obsidian.

---

70   Teotihuacán, Pyramid of the Sun, west face; in foreground the Avenue of the Dead.

The Historical Background

The site of Teotihuacán, with its imposing Pyramids of the Sun and the Moon and the intricate temple of Quetzalcoatl, was first visited by Europeans in 1519 in the person of the rapacious conquistador Hernan Cortez. In that century, in the midst of a general devastation of the ancient cultures of Mexico (both by the conquistadors and the Church of Rome), a friar, Bernardino de Sahagun, recognized that a great civilization had existed at Teotihuacán for at least a thousand years and had then become extinct a thousand years before the Spanish arrived.

By the end of the seventeenth century, a brilliant man of the Renaissance, at home both in the arts and in the sciences, and also a professor of mathematics at the University of Mexico, became interested in Teotihuacán. This was Don Carlos de Sigüenza y Gongora who dug there without results, made comparisons between Egyptian and Mexican pyramids, and attributed Teotihuacán to the Olmecs. A believer in the authenticity of Plato's Atlantis, Sigüenza theorized that the Olmec had come from the east (from Atlantis) and were the predecessors of the Toltecs. Today the earliest major cultural horizon at Teotihuacán is called Teotihuacán, the next is labeled Toltec and the latest, Aztec.

More accurate assessments of the site came in the nineteenth century. Commissioned in 1865 by the Emperor Maximilian, a group of engineers led by Ramon Almaraz completed the first survey which was based on astronomical observations. It was, however, to be many years before the full significance of the astronomical orientations of the site would be recognized.

Almaraz estimated the base of the west façade of the Pyramid of the Sun at about 232 meters. In 1925 the base of the Great Pyramid at Giza was established at 231 meters, or 278.65 megalithic yards, a further hint of the earlier-suspected connection between the two ancient cultures separated by the Atlantic Ocean. Working from a nearly-intact stone well-casing which penetrated the Pyramid of the Moon, Almaraz took 80% of the well's width (1.06 meters) as a unit of measure.

In this century an American engineer, Hugh Harleston, Jr., who began working at Teotihuacán in 1972, identified a standard unit of measure of 1.059 meters which he called a "Hunab". Was the original measurement of the well found by Almaraz rounded off? Harleston's recent analysis of the mathematical, astronomical, and cosmic significance of Teotihuacán has been detailed with great care in Peter Tompkins' *Mysteries of the Mexican Pyramids* (1976). Harleston's

90

idea that the basic unit of measurement was the twelfth root of the number two is, perhaps, a modern mathemetics rather than that of the ancients. There is no doubt in my mind that common units of measure were in use throughout the ancient world. However, particularly for their construction projects, the evidence so far seems to favor the idea that the ancients used geometry rather than complex mathematical computations. Perhaps our own more complex mathematics can be viewed as but one of many possible ways of describing the lengths, proportions and geometric shapes found universally in the cosmos — *and* known in other ways by the ancients.

The Archaeology of Teotihuacán

The earliest date of occupation at this site may have been before the eruption of a nearby volcano, Xitli, about 4000 B.C. Some have held that the city flourished as early as 1500 B.C. The conventional date, however, is about 150 B.C. Teotihuacán was one of the largest pre-industrial cities in the world and the largest urban site in Mesoamerica. Its maximum population has been estimated at about 200,000 and the height of its use as a religious center at about 500 A.D. About 750 A.D. the culture suddenly collapsed. Evidence of burning in all temples

and public buildings has led to the idea that a great fire was responsible for its demise. Some have speculated that the fire may have resulted from some unknown cataclysm. Toward the end of the ninth century, many other Mesoamerican cultural centers, including Tikal, Uaxactun, Copan, and Palenque, were also terminated.

The sites of the various cultural phases at Teotihuacán encompass an area of ten square miles. Within this area, a central district of four to five square miles shows the results of extensive planning, including a grid system based on 187 feet (57 meters). About 500 craft workshops were found as well as some 20,000 residential compounds. The Teoti-

71 *Looking northwest from the Pyramid of the Sun to the Pyramid of the Moon in the morning light.*

huacán culture was the dominant force in early Classical Mexico.

After a hiatus of a century, following the destruction of Teotihuacán in 750 A.D., the Toltec people began moving in. Three centuries later the Toltecs themselves were replaced by the Aztecs. Prior to the Teotihuacán period, about five other cultures have been identified.

The Pyramid of the Sun

Conventional dating of this structure is about 100 A.D. This enormous dirt pyramid is estimated to contain over 35 million cubic feet of fill. In the reconstruction by Batres from 1905 to 1910, its original dimensions were altered by peeling away the dirt surface and restabilizing the brick surface thus uncovered. The final dimensions were as follows: the north-south axis of the base, 225 meters (c. 738 feet); the east-west axis of the base, 219 meters (c. 719 feet); the height, 62 meters, (c. 203 feet). The original dimensions have been estimated as 740 x 740 feet on the base with a height of 240 feet. Hugh Harleston believes the base was once 231 meters (c. 758 feet). This has led Peter Tompkins to speculate that the Pyramid of the Sun was once the same dimensions as the Great Pyramid of Egypt; 231 meters equals 750 ancient geographic feet or 500 cubits. Without better data on the original measurements, this is far from convincing.

In 1906 an archaeologist working with Batres found a thick sheet of mica covering the top of the fifth level of the pyramid; this material was lost in the reconstruction. Its presence suggests that perhaps some now unknown energy property of this pyramid may have once been utilized by the priests as is claimed for the Great Pyramid at Giza. In the case of the Mexican pyramid it would be based, of course, on the electrical insulating properties of mica instead of on the effect on consciousness of the geometry of the Great Pyramid at Giza.

In 1971, a heavy rain caused a depression in front of the Sun Pyramid. When cleared, ancient steps into a natural cave were revealed. Winding over 101 meters (over 330 feet) through twenty adobe walls which blocked its tunnel, the cave led easterly to a cloverleaf termination. When explored, there was no running water present; but broken pieces of drain-pipe carved from rock suggested an ancient channeling of underground water. One writer believes that this sacred cave may have determined the original siting of the Pyramid of the Sun. Like the main façade of the pyramid, the cave opens to the west. In the religion of Mesoamerica, the

---

Teotihuacán Cultural Sequence

Patlachique Phase (150 B.C. to 1 A.D.)
Widespread agriculture supports urban development including obsidian workshops making arrowheads and knives. Also develops importance as a ceremonial center. About 10,000 inhabitants.

Tzacualli Phase (1 to 150 A.D.)
City reaches maximum area of twenty square kilometers with about 30,000 people. Many ceremonial compounds are built as well as the Pyramids of the Sun and Moon.

Miccaotli Phase (150 - 200 A.D.)
City expands to south and east; some of Northeastern sector abandoned. Monumental character of city (based on Avenue of the Dead and the Citadel) emerges. Both major pyramids nearly completed and Temple of Quetzalcoatl begun.

Tlamimilopa Phase (200 - 450 A.D.)
Period of greatest magnificence: Citadel completed; over 400 obsidian workshops. Plaza of the Moon, platform on Temple of Quetzalcoatl, mural of mythological animals and multi-family stone dwellings.

Xolalpan Phase (450 to 650 A.D.)
Teotihuacán's influence over Mesoamerica at its maximum.

Metepec Phase (650 - 750 A.D.)
Finest murals and ceramics during this period which ends in the destruction of the city. Evidence of large fire in center of city.

cave was a very powerful symbol. It stood for creation and life itself. When a spring was added, it became the womb of the earth. Often the cave was the location of oracles, sacrifices, rites of passage and graves.

In the 1950's, Geoffrey Hodson, a sensitive, received a series of clairvoyant impressions on top of the Pyramid of the Sun; he saw the ceremonies once held on the pyramid. According to Hodson, the priests who conducted ceremonies were descendants of the Atlantean priesthood. The ceremonies that he describes involved an understanding of earth energies and cosmic energies which few people have even today. The priest's objective was to evoke energies from the earth and the body, energy which the Hindus call Kundalini, as well as to draw upon forces from the sun and "higher planes". Hodson claimed that the priests were in contact with intelligences on the sun, Mars, and Venus. He saw three ceremonies: one with the sunrise, another by high noon, and the last at sunset. Although modern theories do not see it in this light, the type of sun-worship here was actually on a mental level. The priests attuned themselves to the several energies already enumerated and in the process added to their own energies. Many people in that day could see the aura. These ceremonies enhanced the priests' auras (by adding to their body

energies), the result being a reinforcement of priestly authority.

The Pyramid of Quetzalcoatl

Located within a structure misnamed by the Spanish, the "Citadel", and usually dated between 150-200 A.D., the Pyramid of Quetzalcoatl was excavated, beginning in 1919, by Manuel Gamio. While excavating a mound within the Citadel, Gamio first found one pyramid and then, behind it, another, much more impressive in its stonework. It had a base of 4,037 square meters surmounted by six tiers to a height of twenty-two meters (c. 72 feet). Each tier carried fine, sculptured heads representing Quetzalcoatl and the Rain God, Tlaloc. Later, Harleston established that the seven levels of this pyramid may, like the Babylonian ziggurats, represent a model of the earth, the length of each step representing a mathematical basis for a mercator-like projection of the earth.

Several writers have seen a possible Hindu influence in this pyramid. In the background of the sculpture on the tier-faces are various sea shells. Emily Vokes says that this background contains a chank (*Xancidae*) shell, a conch (*Turbinella Angulata*) closely related to the sacred chank of India. The West-

Indian chank is more conical; the Indian has a nipple-like apex. The Sacred Chank is prominent in Hindu mythology, religion and art. Other observers have identified the lotus plant, the celestial tree and other Hindu motifs.

72

72 *Pyramid of Quetzalcoatl, south face.*

73 *Older temple of Quetzalcoatl behind pyramid. Note sophisticated masonry of stairs to right. This is the oldest part of the complex. At left, two panels of stonework carry feathered serpent motif. At right end of the two panels (center of photo) are three shells. Two of each group represent the chank, thought to indicate possible Hindu influence.*

Geophysics at Teotihuacán?

According to Harleston, the "Avenue of the Dead" was once a series of reflecting pools like those in Washington, D.C. Their function was to generate standing waves in response to earth tremors — to detect seismic activity. Much circumstantial evidence suggests that the early recognition of catastrophic earth changes may have been the most important reason for the ancients' interest in the heavens. The use of pools for seismic detection is consistent with this concept.

Mathematical Analysis of Teotihuacán

In 1972, Hugh Harleston decided to investigate Teotihuacán to see if its measurements held any secrets. Because of the uncertainty and inexactness of existing measurements, Harleston decided on a mathematical strategy: he would analyze the proportions of large measurements to reduce the percentage of error. He began with the distance between the centers of the sun and moon pyramids, about 800

74 *Pyramid of Quetzalcoatl, reconstructed to four tiers, with older temple under mound (upper left).*

Archaeoastronomy at Teotihuacán

A survey by J.W. Dow produced a very interesting orientation: a street at Teotihuacán, in its easterly direction, was oriented to 106.9° at the conventional date of construction; the street points toward the rising of Sirius or the Egyptian Dog Star, Sothis. At the heliacal rise of Sirius, the Egyptians began their calendar; one such orientation is found at the Temple of Isis at Denderah. Allusions to Sirius form the basis for one of the more plausible extra-terrestial theories, an idea put forward in the book, *The Sirius Mystery*, by Robert K.G. Temple. Temple tells us that the traditions of the Dogon people of Africa included two unusual elements. First, they believed that they were visited by blue-skinned men from the star Sirius. Secondly, they have a tradition of a dark companion to Sirius, a star we have only recently discovered.

The other end of this street points to 286.9° which is the setting of the Pleiades at the time of the site's construction. This interest in the Pleiades is not unique to Teotihuacán; it is, I discovered, a worldwide concern among ancient people. New information on this relatively insignificant star-cluster was brought to my attention during the research I reported in the *Stones of Atlantis*.

In Hugh Harleston's mathematical analysis of the proportions of the "Avenue of the Dead," its north-south axis appears to represent a scale model of the orbital distances between the bodies of our solar system including Pluto (discovered in 1930) and Neptune (discovered in 1846).

How could the ancients have known the proportions of the solar system without the aid of the telescopes of our own era? In the 1950's the sensitive, Geoffrey Hodson, besides recapturing the ancient ceremonies, also received, through paranormal means, an understanding of the ancient awareness of astronomy. In the series of clairvoyant impressions he gathered while on the top of the Pyramid of the Sun, he realized that the priests of Teotihuacán had observed our solar system clairvoyantly and could even feel the various astrological relationships (such as squares and conjunctions) with their bodies. Thus, at the frontiers of what we today call the paranormal, psychology and physics became parts of a unitary field of cosmic energy for the ancients. With this advantage, they could have known the spacing of the solar system and, furthermore, working from this knowledge, could have easily arranged significant astronomical sightings. In fact, at Teotihuacán, observations of all major solar phenomena (sunrises and sunsets at the equinoxes and solstices) and possibly even the lunar extremes (northward and southward at 18.61 year intervals) are provided for by sighting arrangements from the central complex to outlying pyramids (and other structures) within a two-kilometer radius.

Many commentators have had difficulty in trying to explain how it is that we find significant astronomical alignments at megalithic sites. This is particularly true of those who start with the assumption that the builders began in total ignorance of the true motion of heavenly bodies. Thus, the ancients would have needed hundreds of years of observation and a continuity of records which moderns find improbable in people whose minds they consider primitive. However, if the ancients had come to know the solar system clairvoyantly, an observational astronomy could have developed much more rapidly — *in effect* from a viable theoretical basis.

meters which he divided into the approximately 2,400 meters of the north-south axis of the whole site. The result, of course, was the number "3". This he applied to the fifty-seven-meter spacing of the city's streets: 57 m divided by 3 = 19 m. This result proved to be a length which seemed to fit many structures. He then divided 19 m by 3 which gave 6.333 m; then once again: 6.333 m divided by 3 = 1.059 m, which also happens to be the twelfth root of 2. Harleston found that 1.059 could be used throughout the site to produce whole numbers, that it was, indeed, a common unit of measure. For example, the base of the Temple of Quetzalcoatl was 60 of these units which he called "Hunabs". 60 Hunabs x 1.059 x 100,000 = 6,354,000 meters, a figure very close to the polar radius of the planet. This result led Harleston to feel that other earth-commensurate dimensions might be found at Teotihuacán. Incidentally, the area of the temple of Quetzalcoatl $(60 \times 1.059)^2$ = 4,037.33 square meters is very close to the English acre (4,047 square meters). It is also very close to the base area of the ziggurats of Babylon.

Before Harleston finished, he believed that, in addition to having found the basic unit of measurement at Teotihuacán, he had also located Pythagorean triangles in the layout of the Citadel surrounding the Temple of Quetzalcoatl, that he had

found proportions equal to pi, phi, and even the speed of light. With Peter Tompkins, I doubt that the builders of Teotihuacán actually used our mathematics. Their results, however, could have been produced more directly by geometric expressions of cosmic awareness which they might have achieved in an altered state of consciousness.

Reasoning from Harleston's work, Tompkins believes that the ancient geographic foot (.308 meters) and the cubit (.462 meters) when divided into the best-established measurement at Teotihuacán, the width of the Citadel, give significant whole numbers. One measurement of the Citadel is 399.48 meters; Harleston's is 400.302. The first measurement produces results of 864.68 and 1297.01; the second, 866.45 and 1299.68. The significant whole numbers are 864 and 1296, which, among other numbers, occur again and again in the ancient world. This length (whether in expressed feet or cubits) was used in the ancient world to compute the circumference of the earth. The reader will have to decide for himself as to the closeness of fit of these numbers when applied to Teotihuacán.

Recent Psychic Impressions of Teotihuacán

Some years ago at Teotihuacán, the residual energies of the site were so powerful that, when the sensitive Anne visited, the hair on the back of her wrists stood up as if in the presence of static electricity.

In a recent psychic reading Anne described early papyrus records sealed in some type of container which was later opened and destroyed by one of the conquerors of Teotihuacán. According to the reading, these records told of the flight of the Maya from Brazil — driven before conquering people. Evidently, some Maya were already in Mexico at the time of the migration. Interestingly enough, some Mesoamericanists with whom I have discussed the idea do not balk at the possibility of migrations from the Amazon Basin to Mesoamerica. In Anne's psychic account, it was the Olmec people who drove the Maya north to Teotihuacán. With reference to archaeological fact, several early, classic Maya pottery fragments were found in the city's outskirts. Of course, this was much later than the period claimed in the psychic material.

Anne's account of the Maya puts their development in the period 8000 to 6000 B.C. Just a few years ago this would have been a far less plausible dating. As we noted in Chapter One, in Belize, formerly British Honduras, dates for the Maya have recently been moved back from a previous dating of 900 B.C. to 4000 B.C. The Toltecs, according to Anne's reading, were the conquerors of the Maya as early as the sixth century B.C. Usually the Toltecs are thought not to have been influential in Mesoamerica until their military ascendancy around 1000 A.D.

"At Teotihuacán the solstices and equinoxes were held in esteem — also Venus and Mars — earth's magnetic gravity (sic); observed; poles' reversal threatened." (Anne)

Harleston, as already seen, established a very complex series of alignments to observe the solstices and equinoxes at Teotihuacán.

Ciudad Blanca

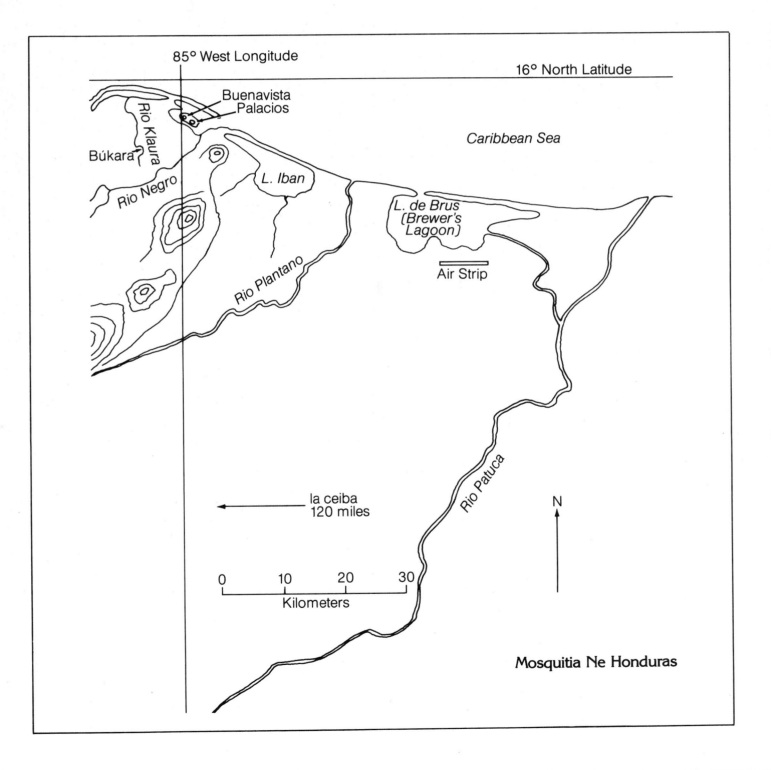

85° West Longitude

16° North Latitude

Caribbean Sea

Buenavista
Palacios

Rio Klaura

Búkara

Rio Negro

L. Iban

L. de Brus
(Brewer's
Lagoon)

Air Strip

Rio Plantano

Rio Patuca

la ceiba
120 miles

N

0   10   20   30

Kilometers

Mosquitia Ne Honduras

On December 3, 1976 the eighteen-man survey party flew into La Ceiba, Honduras, from Miami. We landed in the midst of a tropical downpour which was to soak the port town for two days. While we waited out the rain, I got a full briefing from my roommate, the Honduran anthropologist, Professor Francisco Flores. We were staying at the "Gran Hotel Paris." The hotel's contemporary appearance did not prepare us for its unpredictable plumbing or the water which appeared to have come directly from a muddy river. Professor Flores told me that where we were headed, the Mosquitia, was one of the least explored territories of Central America. The region consists of grassy coastal plains, lagoons and beaches which quickly give way inland to a dense tropical rain forest. The jungle is criss-crossed by many streams; there are frequent rainstorms, and wildlife abounds. Jaguars, bands of howler monkeys, the frenetic army ants, and the presence of nineteen of the world's twenty-six highly poisonous snakes — including the fer-de-lance — make it a territory to respect. It is not surprising that the Mosquitia is one of the last Central American regions to be explored.

Our quest was the legendary lost city, La Ciudad Blanca. Beginning in the sixteenth century, the Spanish invaders of Honduras were told of the mysterious white city lost in the rain forests of the interior. Since that time, hunters and explorers have often claimed to have seen a white-walled city in the largely unexplored Mosquitia of northeastern Honduras, an area of 16,000 square miles. By 1856 the persistent legend of the white city had led to the Honduran publication of a romantic engraving of the mysterious city. A 1954 government map located La Ciudad Blanca (with a red question mark) near the Wampu and Platano Rivers. The Miami-based International Explorers' Society began to study the legend in 1973, and the results of their research led the organization to field the present expedition.

The IES advance work in Honduras included a period of aerial reconnaissance, some of which was assisted by a psychic, Karen Getsla, who had helped me on Bimini and in Bolivia. After zeroing in on some promising areas, the IES fielded a small ground party for sixty days. Their findings were to put us into the target area. The present project was supported by the Standard Fruit Company, Esso Standard Oil and Transportes Aereos Nacionales, a Honduran international airline.

From time to time, when the rain let up, I explored the banana port with its cantinas, banana boats and Indians in from the jungle to shop. Back in the hotel lobby I met a local resident who had picked up malaria on his arrival ten years earlier. This confirmed my suspicions. I immediately picked up "Camoquin", one of the current preventatives. Even so, a week later in Miami, I went through forty-eight hours of alternating fevers and chills. Still later, blood tests gave no clue as to the cause.

Finally, the rain let up and we loaded a ton-and-a-half of supplies and equipment (including the gear of an ABC TV crew) into an old DC-3 twin-engined transport. After a short flight from La Ceiba, we landed on a dirt strip at Brus Lagoon, some miles from our base camp at Palacios. There the dirt strip was too wet for our weight. Left late in the afternoon at a totally deserted strip, we pitched tents and made fires for the evening meal. A large tropical moon shone on the savannah; off in the distance a thunderstorm flickered harmlessly — for the time being.

Just after supper was over and before the dishes were cleaned up, the storm hit. Unfortunately the new tents were not completely waterproof, and the sleeping that night was wet. The few of us who had slung hammocks under a tin shed roof were the only dry ones. In the morning a new tent-mate was found, a tarantula the size of a coffee cup. Harmless, he was still impressive. Nearby, wild boars rooted peacefully.

The next morning, waiting for a small six-place single-engine plane to relay us to Palacios, we dried our gear in the sun. Finally our plane came; its pilot had the reassuring name of "Captain Crash." His engine hour-meter registered over 10,000 hours! One could imagine the maintenance it had had. Over the base camp strip, we made a pass to clear the children and livestock, another to try the wind, and then landed. After stowing our supplies in one room of a concrete-block schoolhouse, we set up our tents. My tent-mate was the distinquished Mayan expert, Dr. Edwin Shook, who listened graciously to what must have seemed bizarre opinions about prehistory. It was a good beginning apprenticeship in dirt archaeology.

Palacios lies 150 miles east of La Ceiba on Laguna Bacalar. In one house there is a battery-operated radio-telephone. This equipment, a sign ("LANSA"), and the grass airstrip are the principal evidence of connection with the outside world. LANSA's DC-3's arrive from La Ceiba only when there is a need. No schedule exists. The setting is lush. In fact, at night, the houses, standing on posts silhouetted by a full moon over the lagoon remind one of a Conrad novel. One evening, in such a house we had a simple dinner (in shifts) of rice, yucca, beans, and tortillas. The drink was water from the brackish lagoon filtered through a hollowed-out coconut log set into the bank. Outside were palms and

large breadfruit trees. Beneath us we could hear the large hogs rooting in the dirt. A single kerosene lamp lit our dinner table.

The livestock of this tiny community included goats and cattle as well. The racial mix of the population is Mosquito Indian, African, Carib and white. The languages are Mosquito and Spanish. Historically, the locale was first settled in 1699 by an English logger, William Pitt. It was called the Black River settlement and included two earthen forts. Some of the cannon are still to be seen.

A six-place gas turbine helicopter arrived from Guatemala to complete our logistics. The next morning we were lifted into our first site, Aguacate, thus saving a day's march through jungle, swamps and rivers.

As we were lifted by helicopter to our first objective, I speculated over what we might find. The principal archaeological exploration of the Mosquitia dates from 1933. In February of that year, William Duncan Strong and others departed from Puerto Castilla for Brus Lagoon and five months on the Patuca River and its headwaters. This survey was a joint Johns Hopkins and Smithsonian project launched to track down reports of great stone cities with carved monuments in the interior. The expedition also sought to learn if, possibly, the Maya culture extended beyond Copan on the western border of

Honduras. No light was shed on either of these questions. The expedition did discover a rectangular stone ruin whose front wall measured one hundred feet in length; this was on the Bonito River. Large mounds were also discovered on the Patuca River at Wankybila, as well as Chorotega-type pottery on the Patuca River. The Chorotega are one of the Central American tribes found at the time of the conquest.

The coastal sites we were to investigate at Aguacate and Búkara were, until now, thought to have no other cultural influences than the Sumo, Paya and Mosquito Indians. There tribes are part of a larger cultural group, the Circum-Caribbean. More generally, these eastern Honduran tribes are thought to originate in lower Central America, while the Mayan influence at Copan in the west derives from the north, particularly Mexico. The ultimate origins of the eastern Honduran tribes is in doubt; possibly, the source was South America. Non-Mexican artifacts with monoliths and stone statues of South American types have been found in *Jicaque* and *Paya* territory but no clear relationship has been established between these tribes and such cultural remains.

The basic Circum-Caribbean culture is a relatively simple farming, hunting, and fishing complex in which no direct evidence of megalithic culture has been found. The

culture-complex includes temple cults with offerings to various deities, mainly celestial (sun, moon and stars, with some evidence of a jaguar cult), a preoccupation with death and ancestors, ceramics with plastic, applied and incised, decoration in zoomorphic (animal-like), anthropomorphic (man-like) and tripod forms. Weaving of cotton, dugout canoes, steep thatched houses — often communal — stone axes, gold objects in all tribes, stone metates (or tripod benches for grinding maize), suggest the cultural level. The lush Central American flora offers these tribes a richly varied diet, the result of hard work in *milpa* (slash and burn) agriculture and fishing with hooks, bows and arrows, harpoons and poison from retenone-bearing plants crushed in the streams. All in all, the culture-complex is sufficiently primitive to make the discovery of artistic-megalithic stonework in the region quite surprising.

At Aguacate (in Spanish, Avocado) our pilot hovered above a swampy field below some thirty-foot high mounds upon which three thatched huts stood. We jumped off and into the mud several feet below, then struggled up the slope to meet the head of the household, Panfilo. He had built his huts on mounds originally built for houses and temples over 800 years earlier.

Before he led us out into the jungle to examine sites he knew, Panfilo showed us some lovely fragments of fine stonework, including a tripod metate fragment with an animal-head adornment collected in his own searches for gold. The whole metate would have been eighteen to twenty-four inches long; this is the usual size. Panfilo also led us to two highly polished basalt cylinders, which would have been taken for manos (or rollers to grind maize on metates) had they not been so large. The largest was 1.04 m long with a middle diameter of 20 cm and ends 14 and 15 cm in diameter! This was a hint of what was to come the next day. In the meantime, we proceeded only a short distance south of Aguacate where we were shown an enormous monolith. It lay partially uncovered in a pit where treasure hunters had left it twenty-five years earlier. At that time a stone sculpture of a jaguar-headed man about six feet tall was taken — likely lost now in some private collection. The monolith we saw was 2.7 m tall (c. 106″) averaged about 75 cm in width (c. 30″) and was at least 1.8 m (c. 71″) thick. Quarrying and moving such a stone was certainly not likely the work of any of the known Circum-Caribbean cultures, such as the Paya or Sumos.

Panfilo cleared the muddy trail ahead of us with vigorous swings of his machete. The jungle foliage has a wild dense green beauty but is full of surprises for the unwary. Brush against the leaves of the thorny palm

76

75 *Stylized owl found at Aguacate in 1976. Composed of a metamorphic rock, it is one meter high and weighs about 250 pounds.*

76 *Back of stylized owl. Similar petroglyphs are found to the south in Panama.*

(Basket ti ti in Belize), and sharp needles penetrate your skin. Another plant when brushed exudes a burning, corrosive acid. Five or six hundred yards further down the trail south of Aguacate we came to the scene of what was to be the real excitement of the day.

We were shown a large altar-stone partly submerged in a pool of water. Panfilo told us he had found it looking for gold a year earlier. The stone measured 2.03 m (c. 80″) in length, and .94 m (c. 37″) wide, except that both front corners had been broken away. Its longest edge was oriented toward 218° (magnetic). In front, to the left, we were shown the top of what was either a support for the altar or a phallic stone. It measured 1.29 m (c. 51″) in length and averaged about 24 cm (c. 9.5″) in width. This led us to begin probing in the mud with our machetes. Rather soon, the machete of the expedition's archaeologist, Dr. Edwin Shook, grated against stone. Digging and bailing the muddy water with a gourd soon exposed the top of a sophisticated stone sculpture! Eventually we were able to lever the stone upwards with a rope and a small sapling cut from the jungle. Our find proved to be a stylized owl with huge eyes. It stood about a meter high (c. 39″) and averaged about 25 cm (c. 10″) in diameter. This approximately 300-pound zoomorphic figure seemed related to stone carvings in Nicara-gua and Costa Rica, yet was superior in craftsmanship. On its back were carvings suggestive of petroglyphs in Panama. Everyone was terribly excited; our first day in the jungle had brought a reward which many archaeologists have never known after years of fieldwork!

Back at Panfilo's compound, his wife baked us fresh tortillas to supplement the canned goods we carried. During the lunch hour we all crowded under the open-sided, thatched cooking hut while a tropical shower passed over.

After lunch we split up. Some were lifted out by helicopter to investigate W.D. Strong's site on the Wampu River; the rest of us began a two-hour march through the jungle to another site, Búkara. In the Mosquito Indian language, this means "out there." In the 1930's it had been a *central* for a fruit company which even built a railway, but all was soon abandoned. Our line of march took us through dark muddy trails of the rain forest, fields of corn and cane opened in the jungle by milpa, and neck-deep swamps where we balanced on knee-deep half-sunken logs to keep our gear dry. Our rest breaks were enlivened by eating raw, fresh corn and chewing sugar cane. Finally, we came to a small, swift river. Some Indians loaned us a dugout canoe to ferry our gear; the rest of us swam, boots and all. The water was cold and refreshing. Finally we arrived at

Búkara, having spent the better part of the afternoon to cover an airline distance of three quarters of a mile. We were now about six miles into the jungle.

At Búkara we found four houses with the usual steep thatched roofs. They were built on mounds thirty to fifty feet high as at Aguacate. However, here the pattern of the mounds was much clearer. Two rows of ten each ran roughly parallel for about 500 meters. The central axis seemed to be about 300° magnetic, looking from the houses at the bend of the Rio Klaura which we had swam. At the houses, the mounds were about thirty meters apart; at the western end, where we would make another exciting find, sixty meters. After sizing up the general layout of the site, we were lifted back to our base camp at Palacios before dark. As we waited for the aircraft, we were given refreshments. Pigs rooting in the mud around the houses did not prepare us for the hospitality inside. The floor was dirt but swept clean; we were given freshly-baked bread and excellent coffee in delicate English china. Our hostess told us of writings on stone in an unknown language in the mountains. In the distance, we heard bands of howler monkeys. At Palacios we found that the other mission (to Strong's site) had been a strikeout. After dinner we celebrated around a large campfire late into the night.

Early the next day we lifted off for more work at Búkara. In the early-morning light the rain forest reflected dazzling light from all of its wet flora. It is a kind of beauty with which some are not comfortable. At Búkara, Francisco, head of the fifteen-person settlement led us to various artifacts in the vicinity. Aside from a granite slab with what looked like drill holes in its edges, the rest was disappointing. The potsherds turned up in planting around the village were red earthenware and very simple in design. We saw no polychrome ware such as is to be seen elsewhere in Honduras. After a time, Francisco led us down the trail, westward to where the mounds opened into what must have been, at one time, a plaza. We soon came to a two-foot-wide trail of warrior ants hurrying to a builtup hill of light earth. Professor Flores, perhaps a bit careless due to his familiarity with the region, was bitten. Immediately, he dropped his trousers and Francisco quickly applied a brown liquid from a small bottle. Their urgency bespoke the consequences of such a bite. Francisco said that, when these ants were really on the march, snakes, deer, and other animals fled the jungle ahead of them.

At length we came to the most exciting discovery: fragments of beautifully carved metates of megalithic proportions. Half buried in the jungle, these graceful objects spoke of a sophisticated culture able to carve metates with legs nearly two meters long (about six feet) from a block of hard metamorphic rock probably weighing at least twenty tons! If the indigeneous peoples had had anything to do with these artifacts, many centuries must have elasped to reduce them to the present cultural level.

Although no megalithic cities were discovered on this expedition, a new Mesoamerican site was found which challenges present archaeological knowledge of the region.

Upon returning from the expedition, I consulted Professor Anthony Aveni's astronomical tables. It seems that the central axis of the mounds at Búkara may have been oriented toward a winter solstice moonrise at about 1000 A.D. This suggests the possibility of a lunar cult.

Geographical Coordinates:
85° 02′ West Longitude
15° 00′ 30″ North Latitude

77

77 Smaller leg from megalithic metate found at Búkara. It is 84 cm long and, like the others found there, is of hard metamorphic rock.

78 Leg, 1.35 m long, from megalithic metate discovered in the jungle at Búkara, December 1976.

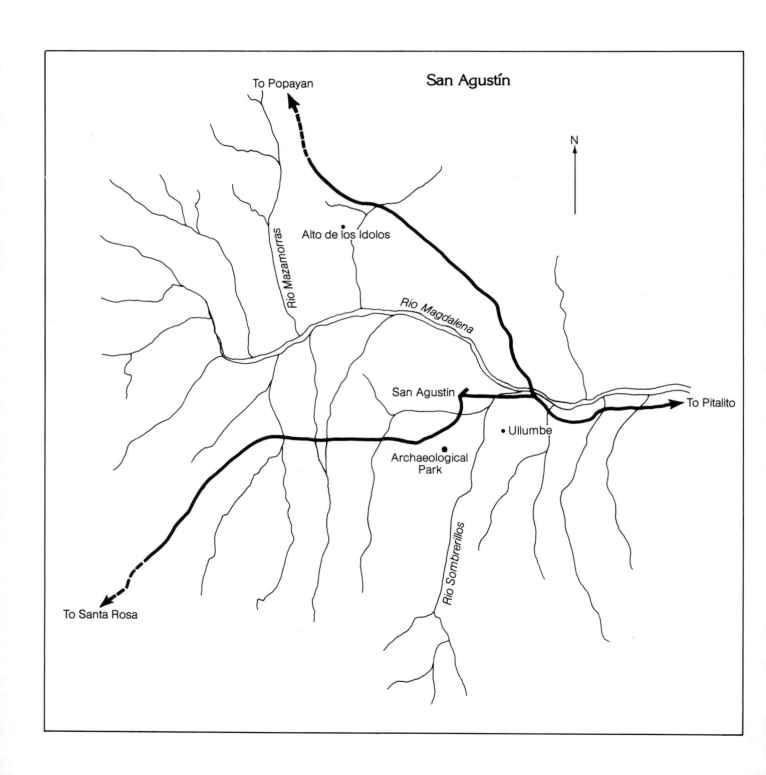

San Agustín
Columbia

One of the least-known cultures of South America once existed at the several dozen megalithic sites of San Agustín in southern Colombia. These sites are located in the vicinity of the modern town of San Agustín about 594 km (369 miles) southwest of Bogota in the lush green of the northern Andes. The location of these archaeological sites is bisected by the Magdalena River which flows north to join others and exit into the Caribbean Sea at Barranquilla, the main port of Colombia. Among the sites of the present work, this is one of the more inaccessible. The elevation is 1,800 meters (c. 5,900 feet). The sites are composed of mounded tombs, dolmen-like structures and monolithic stone sculptures which represent human bodies with feline features (including fangs). Scholars have linked these statues to jaguar shamanism (see "The Jaguar Cult of San Agustín"). Some kind of script (not yet translated) has been found at these sites. The stonework included monolithic sarcophaghi, some of which have lids in the form

Construction Materials:
Local volcanic rock including Micaceous dacite, andesite, feldspathic basalt (hard igneous rocks)
Geographical Coordinates:
1° 52' 54" North Latitude
76° 15' 47" West Longitude

of crocodiles. No crocodiles are found within 1000 miles of San Agustín.

From Bogota to Neiva one may take a beautiful train trip (ten hours) or a bus (six hours) or an airplane. Neiva, located about 150 airline miles southwest of Bogota, is the terminus of the railway and the capital of Huila Department. Another five to eight hours by taxi or bus brings one to San Agustín.

San Agustín began as a small Spanish settlement of the seventeenth century. Today it is a rich agricultural area with a great variety of indigenous plants. Two maize crops a year are usual. The rainy season is June to September with the driest months being December to February. Hot air ascends from the tropical lowlands in the daytime; but the temperature drops sharply at night, the effect of cold Andean winds from the south. This situation leads to abundant but intermittent rainfall.

The archaeological sites of San Agustín lie on either side of the Magdalena River. The main site north of the river is called "Alto de los Idolos." It consists of a large U-shaped hill open to the south with a number of barrows. The western arm of the hill has six large stone slab cists which contain sarcophagi. South of the river lies the other principal site, Las Mesitas, where earth barrows cover stone constructions. The stone chambers at Las

Mesitas have been dated after 425 A.D. The construction is generally quite similar to the megalithic tombs of western Europe.

The monolithic stone figures are top-heavy with over-sized feline heads, squat bodies, and short arms and legs. Some are centrally located in dolmen-like structures. The archaeologist Gerardo Reichel-Dolmatoff places these sculptures between Chavin and Tiahuanaco in style.

The oldest radiocarbon date reported for San Agustín is 555 B.C. It was taken from a trough-shaped wooden coffin at the Alto de Lavapatas site.

79

79 *Ravine of Magdalena River.*

Archaeological History of San Agustín

Because of its isolation there is no mention of the archaeological riches of this locale in the Spanish documents of the sixteenth and seventeenth centuries. In fact no notice was taken until 1758 when a single Franciscan priest, Friar Juan de Santa Gertrudis, wrote a rather superstitious account in which he attributed the stonework to the devil. The first relatively objective report came from Francisco José de Caldas, who visited the sites in 1797. The earliest illustrations of the stone sculptures were the product of an 1851 visit by the Peruvian naturalist Mariano Edwardo de Rivero y Ustoriz and the Austrian Johann Jakob von Tschudi. This and other visits culminated in serious scientific work in this century. The first archaeologist was the German scientist Konrad Theodor Preuss who came from the Museum für Völkerkunde in Berlin in 1913-14.

The first official Colombian excavations of 1936-37 were conducted by the Spaniard Gregorio Hernandez de Alba. Subsequent work was supervised by Luis Duque Gomez, long the director of Instituto Colombiano de Antropologia. Stratigraphic work has also been done by Gerardo Reichel-Dolmatoff.

As Reichel-Dolmatoff points out, the archaeological investigation of the sites surrounding San Agustín has been somewhat one-sided. It has concentrated on the stone sculptures and burial mounds to the near-exclusion of other cultural remains. One consequence has been the lack of a solid basis for a chronology of developmental phases.

Various sites around San Agustín possess an unusual type of grave, over thirty monolithic stone sarcophagi. These are rectangular boxes with some in trapezoidal form (the geometric shape in Inca and some other Bolivian cultures). These one-piece sarcophagi are usually about two meters (c. 6.6 feet) long. They are polished to the extent that no tool marks remain and are covered with a lid adorned with a carved relief. They are usually enclosed in

cists built of six to eight slabs with capstones.

No astronomical significance has so far been seen in these sites. Except for Las Mesitas, no detailed site surveys exist. Also, the sites have been altered by reconstruction.

Some scholars have seen the function of the San Agustín sites to be that of a necropolis centered on a cult of the dead. Reichel-Dolmatoff disagrees, saying that the burial sites represent a relatively small part of the total archaeological complex. Although he does not say so directly, his attention to the evidence for a jaguar cult at San Agustín (see Jaguar Cult) focuses upon the celebration of the life force, not death.

San Agustín Chronology*

The sites span a period of over two thousand years.

Period	Dates equivalent to C-14 dates within the period
Sombrerillos	c.1410-c.1630 A.D.
(Hiatus in Stratigraphy)	
Late Isnos	c.140-c.330 A.D.
Early Isnos	c.40-c.110 A.D.
(large earthworks engineered)	
Primevera	c.20 A.D.
Horqueta	before O A.D.
(sedentary farmers)	

*From Reichel-Dolmatoff's stratigraphic work. *Note:* Sculptures and megalithic structures have not been tied into this chronology. Also, as noted above, there has been but little systematic stratigraphic work at all these sites due to emphasis on monuments and megalithic structures.

80 Closeup of monumental stone figure at San Agustín. Pose is similar to stone figures at Tiahunaco and Easter Island.

81 Two monumental stone sculptures. The figure within the cist (similar to western European structures) indicates phallic aspect of jaguar cult.

82 Dolmens at South Barrow, Las Mesitas.

81

82

The Jaguar Cult of San Agustín

The jaguar motif is widely expressed in cultures of the Central Andes. Aside from San Agustín it is found in the following cultures: Chavín, Paracas, Moche, Nazca and Tiahuanaco. In Mesoamerica the motif is to be seen in the Olmec culture of Veracruz, Mexico, and much of the rest of Mexico and Guatemala.

In addition to evidence of the jaguar cult in cultural remains ranging from Mexico to Chile over a vast period of time, the cult was strongly represented in the recorded mythology of the early people found by the Spanish. The feline cult first appears in the Olmec culture (c. 1200 - 400 B.C.). One Olmec monument represents a jaguar copulating with a woman, the subject of the Ullumbe sculpture at San Agustín. In Colombian archaeology, the jaguar motif goes back to 1000 B.C. At San Agustín, in addition to realistic jaguars attacking human females, the stone sculptures also represent men with fierce feline characteristics, and jaguar-men associated with other monstrous beings.

In American aboriginal cultures the connection between shamanism and the jaguar cult has three main beliefs: (1) the shaman may turn himself into a jaguar as a disguise, either to threaten (or kill) or to benefit another. Shamans may challenge each other through an actual animal combat. The shaman whose animal dies may himself soon die; (2) the shaman can draw on the natural or supernatural power of the jaguar; (3) finally, after his death, the shaman can simply assume jaguar form, the *were-jaguar*.

Reichel-Dolmatoff says that the Chibcha-speaking Paéz Indians near San Agustín retain many features of the aboriginal jaguar cult. According to their beliefs, in the beginning of time, a young Indian woman was raped by a jaguar. Their son was called

84

83 Boulder carving at Ullumbe site showing a jaguar attacking a woman.

84 Jaguar god within the cist. Sculptures supporting the capstone have the alter-ego figure above them.

Thunder-Jaguar; he was an important culture hero. Thunder is the central theme of Paéz myths. It is closely related to shamanism, rain, fertility, and the jaguar spirit. When "voracious little beings" (Thunder's children) appear to shamans in visions, they display male organs conspiciously. They also are supposed to steal women. The Paéz shaman is believed to be able to turn himself into a jaguar. The Colombian Indian shaman is credited with great creativity and sexual energy to be used for the good of his people. In this cult there is a deep awareness of the life-force and its implications. It is the basis of continuing life but, unless directed, it becomes destructive. The jaguar symbolizes this same creativity and power in nature; but here it is uncontrolled. The jaguar thus symbolizes the male procreative energy which becomes destructive if the individual does not come to terms with it. Sexual power can thus be seen as an ambivalent force which the shaman masters within himself so that others may do likewise.

Psychic Reading on San Agustín

These ancient statues indicate early advances of primitive men to deal with complexities. Unresolved riddles plagued them. Their worship of stars and earth constituted an advance in understanding. There were noted similarities of structures in rock and mineral formation. Tigress cult in evidence here. Squareness indicates solidarity. They depicted ... huge complex in which statues signified results of early creation. Stones broad-based squat represent solid-earth condition — matter solidified, low expectations. Knowledge of the One Spirit from which all descend was held back at this time. These people were primitive, escaping only to astral levels. Their debates on existence were coarse and unfruitful. They were simply a span of man's development when matter was all. Forlorn, un-awe-inspiring, a period of regeneration was coming. Nothing soaring in their art — only the basic. Other culture — Bering Strait — Eskimos link with. Had traversed North America southward in nomadic bands — short, brown, stocky people. Followed migration of elk and reindeer, later buffalo — arrows — Indian-Eskimos (with oriental slanted eyes). The chain of events — cataclysms — survivors — 7000 B.C.? Drift southward, 660 A.D.

85 *Monumental stone sculpture of fierce jaguar man with erect phallus; jaguar cult has strongly sexual overtones.*

Inca Civilization

A Recent Megalithic Culture

The Inca period represents little more than a century of a long Peruvian prehistory which began over 22,000 years ago (at Ayacucho in the Highlands) and which concluded when the Spanish conquistadors destroyed the empire between 1532 and 1535. The last Inca, however, was not killed until 1572.

The long foreground which would help us to understand the diverse elements from which the Incas wove their incredible cultural fabric practically overnight is just now beginning to be appreciated. Archaeology in Peru has only recently begun to move ahead rapidly. The intensive study of the Virú Valley on the north coast of Peru, beginning in 1946, provided the first impetus. Here a cultural sequence was developed going back to 2,500 B.C. and for a time influenced (perhaps unduly) the understanding of the other prehistoric Peruvian cultures.

Before the Incas led their people into an imperial expansion extending from their center at Cuzco eastward to Lake Titicaca in what is now Bolivia, southward into present-day Chile and northward to modern Quito, Ecuador, many cultures had flourished in Peru. An obsidian mine at Quispisisia supplied other locales within a hundred kilometers as early as 10000 B.C. A flute found on the coast at Paracas dates back to 6000 B.C.; pottery at Valdivia, in Ecuador, comes from as early as 3000 B.C. By about 900 B.C.

the Chavín culture began, and during its span of existence (about 900 years), its influences covered much of the area of present day Peru. On the southern coast, by 400 B.C., the Nazca culture responsible for the mysterious lines in the desert, fine weaving, and excellent ceramics, as well as the Paracas culture with its extraordinary textiles, had emerged. Shortly after (about 200 B.C.), the northern coastal area of Peru saw the beginnings of the Moche (or Mochica) culture which lasted nearly 900 years and, like many other Peruvian cultures, produced fine goldwork and excellent ceramics. Still another Peruvian-wide culture, the Huari, also preceded the Inca, having influence from about 500 to 900 A.D.

As recent as are the origins of Inca culture, they are still shrouded in mystery. Possibly they are descendants of the little-understood Tiahuanaco culture. About 700 A.D. the influences of this culture were widespread throughout Peru. The principal myth described the founders of Cuzco as two children of the sun, Manco Capac and Mama Occlo Huaco who were both brother and sister and husband and wife. Sent by the sun, who had compassion for the barbaric state of the people, the couple advanced from Lake Titicaca with a golden wedge. They were to take up residence where the wedge should sink into the earth without

effort. This occurred at Cuzco. This tradition was the one best known to William H. Prescott, who wrote the first modern account, but he also gives another legend. It "speaks of certain white and bearded men, who, advancing from the shores of Lake Titicaca, established an ascendancy over the natives and imparted to them the blessings of civilization." Prescott then noted the obvious similarity to the Aztec Quetzalcoatl, the "good deity" who came from the east to Mexico. Quetzalcoatl's appearance and mission were identical.

Cuzco, the site from which the Quechuas under their chiefs, the Incas, began their expansion, only dates back to about 1200 A.D. The oldest continuously inhabited city of South America, Cuzco lies at an elevation of 11,440 feet in the Urubamba Basin of the Andes. Cuzco's name means "navel" in Quechua. This city's history becomes verifiable only with the reign of its ninth king, the Inca Pachacuti, who reigned from 1438-1471, and who also began the imperial expansion. His son and successor initiated an incredible road construction program which ultimately built 6,000 miles of road including a run of over 3,000 miles from Quito, Ecuador to Talca, Chile. In an incredibly short time the princes of Cuzco had conquered over 500 tribes and had made themselves masters of over 350,000 square miles of territory. They built over a dozen

major cities from about 35° south latitude in Chile to about 1° north latitude in Colombia, a distance of 3250 miles. By comparison, at the height of the Middle Kingdom in Egypt, its structures from Alexandria to Aswan extended only 625 miles. All of this came to an end when the Spanish conquered them, essentially between 1533 and 1535.

The overriding question concerning Inca culture is the extent to which it was invented and how much was due to the influence of the rich cultural fabric which preceded it. Metallurgy (including fine goldwork), agriculture (including the basic Inca work unit, the *ayllu,* or village), ceramics, masonry and other important elements were inherited by the Quechuas. However, the organization of the basic Andean unit of agricultural production, the *ayllu,* into a large bureaucratic economic structure with complex irrigation systems based on terraced fields, the *andenes,* was novel. The central government at Cuzco taxed the *ayllus* through crop levies and drafted labor quotas to serve the state's needs, the *mita* system. There was no currency system and no "profit" as each family retained only what it needed for consumption. The bulk of production went to the government for storage in warehouses and granaries. Trade and communication throughout the empire were rigidly controlled. Special permission was required for use of the state-constructed roads. The material needs of all were satisfied in times of food shortage by the state granaries. This system has been praised by some as the prototype of the ideal welfare state, but others call attention to the price of such security — a complete loss of personal liberty. Still others have noted that the welfare state concept is not based on the facts, and that

conquered peoples became part of a structure not necessarily administered for their own good. On the other hand, the Inca administration was far in advance of the usual looting of the day.

The overall achievement of the Inca culture is astonishing in the absence of a written language. Various types of information needed for administrative purposes were transmitted by the *quipu,* (from the Quechua word for "knot"). The *quipu* was a main cord from which smaller strings dangled. These latter strings were knotted in a system which apparently required an accompanying verbal comment. One scholar, Nordenskiöld, claimed to have translated astronomical information from the *quipu.*

Inca religion was essentially a solar cult which also paid homage to the moon, various other planets and the Pleiades. Imposition of their religion upon other locales was a stabilizing influence in the empire, as was the practice of recruiting leaders from conquered peoples. A frozen caste system with its dangers was thus avoided.

Perhaps the most original feature of this culture is its architecture. One striking feature is the use of enormous polyhedral blocks forming temple and palace walls like those at Sacsahuaman, a fortress. Walls which slope slightly inward and narrow at the top (as in Egypt) rose abruptly in the fifteenth century without local precedents. The nearest parallels are in the Pacific, on Easter Island and in the Marquesas.

In the short space of about a century, dozens of Inca cities sprang up, roads were built, all as the empire dramatically expanded. Much of the stone work is, of course, megalithic.

Megalithic cultures, however, were found in South America long before the incredible burst of archi-

tectural creativity by Inca builders, which took place in the century before their subjugation by the Spanish conquistadors. In the northern highlands of Peru the Chavín culture (c. 1000 B.C. to 0) was long credited with the invention of megalithic architecture. The major site of this culture, Chavín de Huantar, is found at the headwaters of the upper Marañon River (a tributary of the Amazon) northeast of Lima. From the evidence of trace-element analysis of Chavín obsidian artifacts taken from many Peruvian sites, it is clear that the obsidian originated at Quispisisia (between Lima and Cuzco) and was part of a Peruvian-wide trade carried on by the Chavin culture. Thus its influence would have been felt throughout the country.

However in the 1950's Dr. Frederic Engel discovered and excavated an important pre-ceramic site at El Paraíso. This culture built megalithic structures before 1500 B.C. when the site was abandoned. Located in the Chillon River Valley near Lima, this site is claimed by Engel to be the oldest architectural complex in the Americas. One of its megalithic stone buildings was 1,000 feet long.

In recent years the Colgate University astronomer Professor Anthony F. Aveni and University of Illinois archaeologist, Professor R.T. Zuidema, have been investigating possible sites around Cuzco to recover the astronomical towers reported by the Spanish chroniclers.

Professors Zuidema and Aveni also investigated the Intihuatana and the Temple of the Three Windows at Machu Picchu to determine if significant astronomical orientations exist. Professor Aveni tells me that a possible winter solstice sunrise orientation exists at the Temple of the Three Windows.

The highlights of Peruvian Archaeology

1553   Pedro de Cieza de León, soldier with the Spanish conquistador Pizarro, observes the Incas and writes first contemporary account of ruins and antiquities: *La Crónica del Peru*, 1554.

1847   William H. Prescott's *The History of The Conquest of Peru*. Pioneer work by the blind Harvard historian which draws upon many unknown documents in Europe.

1877   E. George Squier's *Peru: Incidents of Travel and Exploration*. Lincoln's representative to Peru and a pioneer "dirt" archaeologist who excavated at Pachacamac.

1896   German archaeologist, Max Uhle, begins first stratigraphic work in the New World (at Pachacamac), thus initiating modern archaeology in Peru. He saw four cultural periods: (1) Pre-Tiahuanaco (2) Tiahuanaco (3) Post-Tiahuanaco (4) Inca.

1911   Yale historian, explorer, and archaeologist, Hiram Bingham discovered Machu Picchu, later told the exciting story in *Machu Picchu: A Citadel of the Incas*, (1930). Bingham thought he had found the legendary Vilcabamba.

1920's-1930's   Alfred L. Kroeber, Wendell C. Bennett and Julio C. Tello the major investigators.

1931   Shippee-Johnson aerial survey revealed vast numbers of previously unknown sites.

1946   Institute for Andean Research sponsored Virú Valley project which revolutionized Peruvian archaeology. Gordon R. Willey and others worked out a chronology back to 2500 B.C. in this valley, a development which hinted at the vast period of unknown Andean prehistory. This project initiated the truly systematic work which has since gone on.

1948-49   Additional aerial photography under the supervision of Paul Kosok identified nearly 1,000 pyramid sites in Peru.

1964   The Espiritu Pampa expedition by explorer Gene Savoy made a preliminary survey of what Savoy believes is the real Vilcabamba, the last refuge of the Incas.

Inca Archaeoastronomy

Prescott said that the Incas used a twelve-month lunar calendar with weeks of 7, 9 or 10 days. This lunar calendar was corrected by solar observations taken by means of eight towers built around Cuzco by the ninth king, Pachacuti. These towers, no longer in existence, let Inca astronomers observe the solstices. Their year began with the winter solstice. Prescott also says that a solitary gnomon was used in a circle within the great temple (the Coricancha?) to determine the equinoxes which were celebrated with great rejoicings. Exact knowledge of the Inca calendar, unless yet to be found in the knotted quipus, is probably lost forever. The winter solstice was apparently sacred to the sun, and there was a ritual of new fire to celebrate the days which would subsequently lengthen. The summer solstice (southern hemisphere) in December was the time of puberty initiations for boys of noble rank.

According to John Howland Rowe in *Inca Culture at the Time of the Spanish Conquest* (Vol. II of *Handbook of South American Indians*) the Inca also observed and worshiped the Pleiades as divinities of the sowing of seed and the controling of seasons. Writing in 1946, Rowe doubted that they observed either the equinoxes or solstices. A Swedish scholar writing in the 1920's, Erland Nordenskiöld, said that the quipus recorded the days for the synodic revolutions of Jupiter, Mercury and Venus.

El Panecillo
Ecuador

The high moutain valley in which Quito nestles is surely one of the most spectacular locations for a capital city to be seen in the New World. At 2,850 meters (c. 9,350 feet), despite its near-equatorial location, a climate is found much like early fall in Colorado. It is the second highest capital in the world. Of course, I was lucky to arrive between the rainy seasons which are February to May and October to November. Looking up the wide modern avenues in central Quito, one sees mountains which rise another 4,000-5,000 feet.

One of the northern outposts of the Inca empire was found in Quito. This Inca city is now represented only by a watchtower (or observatory) located on Cerro Panecillo 183 meters above the city and to the southwest of its center.

Ecuador has another important Inca city with extensive stone structures. It is Incapirca which lies to the south in Cañari province. This was named after the tribe which immediately sided with the Spanish conquistadors to attack the Incas. Today's Ecuadorian intellectuals often come from this province.

On the coast of Ecuador is found the site of the Valdivian culture which may possibly have been influenced by the Japanese Jomon culture about 3000 B.C. About ninety miles south southwest of Quito is the mighty volcano, Chim-borazo, whose 20,702 feet make it the highest in Ecuador.

Due to the limited work in English on Ecuadorian archaeology, anyone but a specialist will be greatly helped by the excellent guided tours (available in English) of the modern archaeological museum located on the fifth floor of the Banco Central in Quito. Either a bus or taxi will take you up hill to El Panecillo from which a spectacular view of the city can be had. This is an archaeological site on which the visitor must fend for himself. Even the museum staff had little to say about it.

The so-called watchtower (or observatory) is constructed like a beehive of thin bricks and mortar. Inside, it is plastered and its internal dimensions are roughly twenty feet in height and ten feet in diameter with an eighteen to twenty-four-inch opening at the top and a seven-foot-high tunnel leaving it. The tunnel is excellent Inca masonry done with andesite. Set into the hillside it is surrounded with a retaining wall of fine Inca masonry, also done with andesite.

It was rebuilt by the Inca prince, Huayna Capac who shortly after became the eleventh Inca (1493-1527).

86 Beehive structure on El Panecillo constructed of brick and surrounded by a retaining wall of the usual fine Inca masonry of andesite. Said to be an Inca watchtower, it is more likely a type of observatory.

Construction Material
Brick and mortar
plaster
andesite (a granite-like igneous rock)
Geographical Coordinates
0° 15' South Latitude
78° 32' West Longitude

87 *Andesite masonry tunnel entering the structure underground.*

88 *Detail of brickwork and masonry retaining wall.*

Archaeoastronomy at El Panecillo

An Ecuadorian history (in Spanish) gives us the little that is known of the functions of this site: "The Temple of the Sun which occupied the little flat place of the summit of El Panecillo was a square shape of carved stone with enough perfection, with a pyramidal covering and a great door to the east, through which the first rays of the sun struck the sun's image in gold. There was not much wealth or adornment with the exception of the vases which served for the sacrifices ... nevertheless this temple was very famous for its adjoining astronomical observatories." These observatories are described as two tall gnomons to observe the two solstices for the principal festivals of the year.

It is possible that the beehive structure was also an observatory. In a preliminary survey I found that its tunnel pointed roughly towards an azimuth of 27°. Later, consulting astronomical tables, I found that the tunnel at least was oriented towards the rising of no principal astronomical body at this latitude in about 1500 A.D.

While inside the structure, however, I observed the sun's light projected within (see photo). This led me to speculate that possibly this structure could be used for equinox observations of the sun. It is also the type of structure which could be employed for meridian transit observations of stellar bodies such as the Pleiades, which were worshipped by the Inca.

89

89 Solar motif at tunnel entrance inside the structure.

90 Off center, the disk of the morning sun projected through circular opening in top of beehive structure.

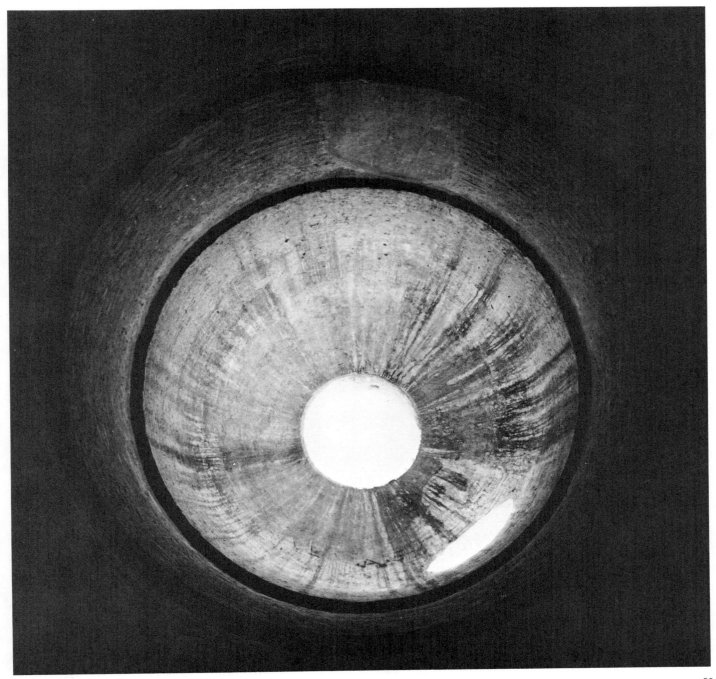

Sacsahuaman
Cuzco

91

This memorable city is reached by a short but dramatic flight over the jagged, snow-covered Andes from Lima. Even the experienced traveler will be surprised at the procedures for landing modern jets in the high mountain valley. Aeroperu's Boeing 737 pitched down like a fighter aircraft to go into its landing pattern. We were lucky; the day was clear. Earlier in the year one of my associates had been aboard when the plane to Cuzco had dipped down through the clouds — into the wrong valley — then climbed out. Many passengers were grateful for the airsickness bags.

The first day in Cuzco should be taken cautiously. The altitude, 3500 meters (c. 11,440 feet), may induce the *soroche* (altitude sickness) for lowlanders. It can be severe, including migraine headache, palpitation of the heart, nausea, and blackout. Two common local remedies are available: coca tea (from the Peruvian coca bush, the source of

91 *The author standing in front of 440-ton megalithic stone in first wall of three-tiered fortress of Sacsahuaman. Interlocking masonry, more massive than usual, is typical of Inca stonework.*

92 *One of the massive entrances at first level. The author's wife, Joan.*

92

cocaine) and oxygen. Both can be found in the hotels. Rest is at least as important, and be careful with alcohol.

The city, laid out by the Inca Pachacuti, is a charming blend of Inca stonework and Spanish colonial architecture. Religious festivals, the local Indian markets, and the archaeological museum on Tigre Street, make Cuzco a fascinating place to begin an acquaintance with Inca culture.

The megalithic ruins of Sacsahuaman, an engineering achievement without parallel in the New World, lie within walking distance of Cuzco. Located several hundred feet above the city, the site also provides an excellent view of Cuzco.

Sacsahuaman is an enormous zigzag fortress of stone over 1500 feet long and sixty feet high. Its megalithic blocks, the largest of which is estimated at 440 tons, form three tiers of walls which face a flat field. Behind the fortress the hill falls away steeply. The stonework, in addition to its incorporation of such huge blocks, is the typical polygonal Inca masonry, whose jointing system seems admirably suited to withstand earthquakes. Typical blocks of the local gray Yucay limestone average ten to twenty tons. Andesite was also used in the structures. Its nearest sources are two quarries, one nine and the other twenty-one miles away.

93

Construction was begun about 1438 A.D. by the ninth Inca, Pachacuti, ("Earthshaker") and continued for about seventy years. After 1471 the project fell to Pachacuti's son, the tenth Inca, Topa Inca Yupanqui ("Unforgettable"). The *mita* (Quechua word for "a turn") labor force is believed to have numbered about 30,000 men. The scope of the project approaches that of the Egyptian pyramids.

Above the fortress are the foundations of three towers one of which housed the Inca. One tower included a reservoir fed by a siphon arrange-ment which ran two miles away to the nearest water source. The capacity of the reservoir has been estim-ated at about 12,500 gallons. This is an excellent example of Inca hy-draulic engineering.

Across the grassy plain in front of the fortress is a natural geological formation, the Rodadero, said to have been used as a slide. Near here was once the entrance to an under-ground maze, the *chincana* (a Quechua term for labyrinth). To avoid problems with this extensive underground structure, the authori-ties sealed off the entrance.

Construction Materials
Yucay limestone and block andesite
Geographical Coordinates
13° 31′ 30″ South Latitude
71° 58′ 30″ West Longitude

93   *Foundation of one of the large towers above Sacsahuaman. Called Muyumarca, it may have included the large reservoir along with the residence of the Inca.*

Ollantaytambo

Sixty-eight kilometers out of Cuzco, on the road towards Machu Picchu, are found the remains of Ollantaytambo, once a walled city serving as a border citadel for the Inca. It was here in 1536 that Manco Inca held off Hernando Pizarro. The structures of this site are built over *andenes*, or agricultural terraces. This complex was started by Pachacuti using Colla (Aymara) Indians from near Lake Titicaca. This may explain the presence of the stepped motif of Tiahuanaco on one of the six largest stones which average about fifty tons. The largest of these (on the right end) is 4 meters (c. 13.1 feet) high, 2.1 meters (c. 6.9 feet) wide at the base, 1.9 meters (c. 6.2 feet) wide at the top, and 1.7 meters (c. 5.6 feet) thick. Nearby is an incredible stone block of the same material, a diamond-hard red porphyry. This latter block is 6 meters (c. 19.7 feet) long and has a cross section of 1.5 meters (c. 4.9 feet) and 1 meter (c. 39 inches). Its bottom surface has the smooth polish found in the best Egyptian sculptured granite. Such a stone would weigh over 24 tons. The stones for Ollantaytambo were quarried across the river 200 feet below and about 3,000 feet up the opposite slope. A 250-ton stone from this quarry lies at the bottom of the river.

One stone is cut for a Tiahuanaco-style clamp, and the globular pottery of Tiahuanaco has been found here.

94

Construction Material
Red porphyry - a fine-grained igneous rock with large feldspar crystals.
Geographical Coordinates
13° 15′ South Latitude
72° 16′ West Longitude

94 Six massive slabs of red porphyry; fourth from left has the Tiahuanaco stepped motif.

95 At Ollantaytambo, the Tiahuanaco motif is found on one of the six huge monoliths. This stepped motif is similar to the Egyptian hieroglyph for "the exalted one," or God. At Tiahuanaco and in Egypt this motif is found in a horizontal rather than vertical position.

95

96

96 Typical Inca stonework; the protuber-
ances are thought by some to have been
left as aids in levering the massive stones
into position.

97 Another Tiahuanaco influence: a
keyway cut into stone to carry metal
clamps for stability in earthquakes.

97

Machu Picchu and Vilcabamba

98 *Machu Picchu; in the background, Huayna Picchu (New Peak) has a trail to the top where other Inca works are found. Toward lower right, the horse-shoe shaped watchtower (or Torreon).*

98

126

The ruins of Machu Picchu, partly because of their breathtaking location on a narrow ridge about 450 meters (1,500 feet) above the rapids of the Urubamba River, inspire a deeply emotional response from many visitors. Located about sixty-seven miles down river from Cuzco, the site is reached first by a three-and-a-half-hour train trip, then by a fifteen-minute bus trip up an incredibly precarious switchback road.

In 1911 the American explorer-archaeologist, Hiram Bingham, later Yale Professor and United States Senator from Connecticut, was searching for the legendary Vilcabamba, the fabled city of refuge for the Inca survivors of the Spanish butchery. On July 24 of that year, he found the present site called Machu Picchu (meaning "Old Peak"). The steep pinnacle in the background of the usual photo of the site is Huyana Picchu ("New Peak"). Until 1963 Machu Picchu was accepted as Vilcabamba. In that year, G. Brooks Baekeland and Peter R. Gimbel led a parachute expedition into the unexplored Cordillera Vilcabamba and re-opened the question. The next year a member of the Explorers Club, Gene Savoy, explored a site at Espiritu Pampa (Plain of the Ghosts) about fifty miles northwest by west of Machu Picchu. His evidence certainly suggests an Inca site. Furthermore, it is one which

shows a Spanish influence (in the use of tiles). The Inca that ruled Vilcabamba, Manco II, had Spanish prisoners who could have been responsible for this innovation; the Inca themselves had worked with clay for centuries. Bingham had seen this site earlier but had been unable to explore it.

My guide at Machu Picchu described yet another Vilcabamba, apparently discovered about 1967. Professor Edmundo Guillen had, I was told, been working on this site since then but had published no results of the project, not even photos. *This* Vilcabamba is located forty kilometers by rail beyond Machu Picchu and then twenty kilometers more by trail.

Machu Picchu itself raises a multitude of questions. Extensive archaeological investigation by modern procedures had to wait until about 1975 when UNESCO assistance began to fund the work. The site is not dated. Presumed to be an Inca site, its function is not clear. Skeletal remains on the site suggest a ratio of ten females to one male among the inhabitants. This has led some to regard Machu Picchu as a sanctuary for the "Nustas" or Virgins of the Sun. A royal Inca trail leads over the mountains toward Cuzco. It has been suggested that the site may have been built before Cuzco.

Machu Picchu seems to have provided independently for the

subsistence of 1,000-1,250 people. A system of fountains and stone aqueducts existed in the city, the latter feeding the hanging terraces (or *andenes*) where maize, vegetables and varieties of potatoes were grown. There are also baths, temples, palaces and about 150 houses with steep gables and thatched roofs. The basic construction material is white granite, some blocks up to 3.7 meters (12 feet) in length. Evidence of local quarry-work, including splitting with wedges, is still in evidence. It is believed that stone hammers and bronze chisels (including beryllium-hardened surfaces) were also used. As usual with Inca architecture, large polygonal blocks were used in the walls of important buildings, and much was done to incorporate shapes from the living rock.

Strong astronomical orientation possibilities exist, particularly with possible backsights and foresights in the Temple of Three Windows. The famous Intihuatana, or Hitching Post of the Sun, is said to be corrected vertically for the local latitude. This hints at an equinox observation. Its complex shape could, however, serve other astronomical functions. This particular Intihuatana is the only such device which was not destroyed by the Spanish.

Machu Picchu, of course, is presumed to have been related to the religious practices of the Inca's solar cult, and two interesting features of

99 *Watchtower (or Torreon). Dr. J. Manson Valentine has photographed a rectangle of sunlight falling on the carved stone mass within at the time of the winter solstice.*

100 *Piece of white granite illustrates quarry technique using chisels and wedges to split stone.*

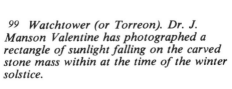

99

100

101

102

this site exist which may have implications for altered states of consciousness for those in a meditative state. The first fact is that the site is located on a geological fault. Often what are sometimes extreme magnetic anomalies are found in such locations. My own research has shown a connection between magnetic anomalies and the sensitivity of psychics. The second fact is that the ridge upon which the site is built

103

faces to the east in a huge horseshoe-shape surrounding a bend of the Urubamba River. I was unaware of this feature of the terrain until a chance flight over the site. This topography may have subtle effects on altered states of consciousness.

Construction Material
White granite
Geographical Coordinates
13° 09′ South Latitude
72° 33′ 20″ West Latitude

101 Presumed to be a royal tomb cut from the living rock under watchtower.

102 Despite interlocking Inca masonry's resistance to earth movements, this joint in Temple of the Three Windows shows the technique is not proof against earthquakes.

103 Temple of the Three Windows. In the foreground, the standing stone represents a possible backsight for solar observations; the foresight would be one of the windows.

104 View through one of the windows.

106

105 Temple of the Three Windows; detail of corner masonry. Technique is very similar to that found in the Valley Temple at Giza.

106 Remarkable granite masonry in a corner of Valley Temple, Giza.

107 The Intihuatana (or Hitching Post of the Sun), the only such device remaining intact. Its complex geometry, said to be corrected for the latitude of the site, is not yet fully understood.

105

Psychic Reading on Machu Picchu

Anne's 1976 readings on Machu Picchu again give hints of extra-terrestrial influence in the past: "The elevation here is extremely important because extra-terrestrials need a landing place facing the sun. Winter rays of sun on slopes possible reason for alignment of the site ... rainforest surrounding this site ... terrain here pushed up considerably — earth upheavals at the time of the Liman (?) conquest." Anne gave the original occupancy of the site as 11000 B.C. Of the Temple of the Three Windows she said, "archway over terrace below, sightings of solar positions, eclipses. Three windows next to causeway. Exact position important because was situated east-west (Equinox). The positions were then of vernal equinox and subsequent seasonal changes. (Implied are earth changes which invalidate present orientation for astronomical purposes). (In reference to the Intihuatana) watch out for duplications. Past information partly correct. Primarily to gauge sun's speed during the day. (No significant stellar functions?) Stellar positions more related to three windows. Moon's path illuminated the dial somewhat. It wasn't as important. Speed of the sun was considered of great significance and the day's beginning and ending marked in those times as has often been mentioned. The years varied from present time. (Many have speculated from the evidence of ancient calendars etc. that the length of the year has not always been the same.)

A second reading on Machu Picchu continues: "As has been given, earlier times (saw?) land upheaval, then subsequent disasters. After this some reconstruction of this site. On Machu Picchu then were erected fine instruments for detecting solar eclipses in advance by several hundred years. These times were strategically geared to ratios, and the understanding of numerical relationships formed the basis for many treatises. Now, limited viewpoints on every hand show demise of cosmic memory of man. Astrology had an important place here and astronomy. (Machu Picchu an Inca site?) No, far from this. This race was pre-mixture of Caucasian and Mongoloid, Asiatic, and had features in common to each. They preceded the Incas by several thousand years. They were devoid of Negroid characteristics. Wisdom excelled. Many of forerunners of science today began here and are carrying on their inquiries.

The construction was cemented by limestone and mud. The purpose of the site was an enclosure for beings advancing mathematically ... mathematics was knowledge primarily for chosen few for it exemplified far-reaching principles of the universe. (cf. Hugh Harleston's work at Teotihuacán, Mexico) Nuclear housing attached to jet propulsion units, now regarded as archaic. Use of nuclear devices here aided in the formation of galactic commerce, space travel primarily. Which one of you would understand. Space's laws = energy = action. Space brothers warning you even now of misqualified use of energy. Please understand. These formulas must be observed. Until man reaps all energy from actions, no progress can be made; so with individuals and continents. Global destruction imminent. (But Machu Picchu group?) Pre-Incan priests attempt here to regain footing, intelligent use of energy before more earth destruction. Aligning of planets foretold of energy patterns, suggested planting schedules and growth rates. We are through."

Psychic Reading on Vilcabamba

"Gene Savoy *did* discover the northeast section of Vilcabamba which was once a scene of great beauty with towering stone walls and great arches like a monastery. I see two men about forty feet apart shaking something metallic between them making a sound of increasing frequency to aid in levitation of stones. Nearby men with ropes are lifting large stones from all direction. Sound aided lifting. Frequency increased with lifting until highest frequency coincided with highest lift and final placement of stones."

He said, "that's the stuff the Incas used for shaping stones. The juice will soften up rock till it's like paste" *(Lost Trails, Lost Cities).* He seemed to think that the plant might be found on the Pyrene River in the Chuncho country of Peru. His son, who edited the book, described an incident in which an ancient piece of sealed pottery was dropped on a rock in a scuffle. Subsequently the rock was found to be softened.

In a 1976 reading, Anne gave a name for the plant: Caochyll. She saw it as having sparse leaves with reddish veins and standing about three to four feet high.

Shortly after this, Anne was shown a new technique for clairvoyance by the chemist Dr. Marcel Vogel, senior scientist for IBM in San Jose and himself a gifted sensitive. The new procedure limits the sensitive to specific topics without as much emotional involvement which can be heavy in prehistory. Here is her account:

"I asked for the architect who designed the last site David was at (Tiahuanaco) to show me how the stones were cut. Holding a tiny crystal which Marcel Vogel had just handed me, I saw a ten-ton andesite stone with razor-sharp edges which lay on the ground at Tiahuanaco. I saw a sheet of gold but said nothing, not understanding its significance. Vogel said, 'So that's how they do it.' He had also seen, as he explained it, how a solar battery was used. Another metal was sandwiched with the gold to generate a small current. I saw forms around the edges of the stone over which the gold was placed. A paste of the plant acid was activated by the solar battery to melt the stones into the forms! It was an electrochemical method."

Inca Technique for Softening Stones

Note: Writing in *Across South America,* (1911), Hiram Bingham alluded to a favorite Peruvian story he encountered in his travels; that of the plant whose juices softened rock so that it could be worked into tightly fitted masonry. Later, the British army officer and explorer, P.H. Fawcett, lost in the Mato Grasso of Brazil in the twenties, describes the plant as being about a foot high with dark reddish leaves.

Tiahuanaco

109

Flying east from the Pacific over the breathtaking snowy peaks of the Andes, you come to the highest navigable water in the world: the 3,200-square-mile Lake Titicaca located between Peru and Bolivia at an altitude of 12,500 feet. About the size of Lake Erie, its surface traffic includes hydrofoil vessels and two steamers built in England in the last century. Its present fauna (including a kind of sea horse), its salinity, and

the tilt of an ancient beach-line have led some to speculate that the lake was once connected to the ocean. Later, in the recent geological past, it was then raised by the same forces as the Andes themselves. These questions about Lake Titicaca's past are underscored by the presence nearby of a mysterious archaeological site called Tiahuanaco.

Located high on the arid, wind-swept *Altiplano* about twelve miles

south of the lake and about sixty miles west of the Bolivian capital, La Paz, Tiahuanaco contains the puzzling remains of an ancient culture whose stunning megalithic structures pose difficult questions about the builder's technology. Around Tiahuanaco, more or less oblivious

109 Craft built of fresh-water reeds on Lake Titicaca gave Heyerdahl the inspiration (and part of his evidence) for a cultural link between Tiahuanaco and Easter Island.

to these remains, the Aymara Indians carry on a subsistence-level farming.

When the Spanish conquistadors and their priests first encountered Tiahuanaco in the sixteenth century, they made every effort to destroy the pagan shrine. Three centuries later, in 1864, when E. George Squier visited Tiahuanaco he was deeply impressed by the ruins; he called them the Baalbek of the New World. About the same time Augustus le Plongeon, a man whose unconventional theories about the Maya outraged the archaeological establishment, recognized that the strata of seashells in the vicinity of Tiahuanaco hinted that the site had once been at sea level. Much later, H.S. Bellamy said the same. Around the turn of the century, Bolivian engineers who were building the railways broke up many of the megalithic stones as ballast for the roadbed. Today, after restoration by the chief Bolivian archaeologist, Carlos Ponce Sanginés, the main site is far more impressive than when first seen by Squier. The sombre entrance to the Kalasasaya with its huge monolithic red sandstone steps and the twelve-ton monolithic Gate of the Sun within are the most impressive elements.

What I, personally, found most dramatic, however, was a part of Tiahuanaco infrequently visited, the Puma Punku, or Gate of the Puma. Here, seemingly thrown about like children's toys, are huge blocks of red sandstone and andesite. Some of

110

110 *Monolithic statue from Tiahuanaco. One of the huge figures found by Heyerdahl on Easter Island had the same pose, reinforcing his theory of a link between the Andes and Easter Island.*

111 *Keyways to hold copper (some say silver) clamps to secure stonework from earthquake damage. When Spanish invaders removed the metal, subsequent earthquakes leveled the structures.*

112 *Main entrance to principal temple at Tiahuanaco, the Kalasasaya. When Bolivian archaeologist, Sanginés began restoration in 1950's, only the two standing stones and stairs were intact.*

111

112

the sandstone blocks are up to twenty-seven feet long and weigh at least 200 tons. The nearest source for this sandstone is twenty kilometers southwest of the site. Also found at Puma Punku are many precisely shaped blocks of andesite, a hard granitic rock whose nearest source lies twenty kilometers to the north. The andesite is shaped so carefully that it resembles a machinist's work

with its straight, true edges and countersunk geometric shapes. At Tiahuanaco, straight lines, plane surfaces, and geometric shapes are executed with the same artistry that the Egyptians used for their rounded, modeled statuary of granite. The evidence for considerable engineering knowledge and great skill in working stone is strong.

There are two schools of opinion

about the cultural origins of this site. The first is called by conventional archaeologists the romantic school. For the romantics, Tiahuanaco was the Garden of Eden, the site of the beginning of human life on this planet. A modern variation on this view dates the site as old as 12,000 years ago and claims it to have been the earth-base of ancient astronauts. In conventional archaeological

115

113

113 *Gate of the Sun (or Gate of the Weeping God) now located within the Kalasasaya. Before being broken by an earthquake it was a single piece of andesite weighing about twelve tons.*

114 *The weeping god, closeup.*

115 *This block near the Kalasasaya is of very hard andesite, a form of granite. The double cruciform shape, a variation of one of man's most ancient symbols, let into this stone seems almost to have been machined.*

116 *The site known as Puma Punku (Gate of the Puma) near Tiahuanaco. The two massive sandstone blocks (center and right) range between 200 and 300 tons. This type of sandstone is found no nearer than 20 kilometers.*

114

116

opinion, Tiahuanaco was long held to be a ceremonial center — dating from about 600 to 1000 A.D. Recent Bolivian archaeology (based on carbon-14 dating) puts the first period of Tiahuanaco back to 1700 B.C.; the second period to 360 B.C.; the third period, the era during which the semi-subterranean temple was constructed, from 133 to 374 A.D., and terminates the fifth period at about 1200 A.D.

In Inca legends, as we pointed out earlier, the male and female founders of Inca society came to Cuzco from the Island of the Sun on Lake Titicaca. They were Manco Capac and Mama Occlo Huaco, brother and sister, husband and wife, and children of the sun. Because of this legend, Peruvian archaeologists have pursued the possibility of ancient connections between Tiahuanaco and the pre-Inca cultures. The political division between Bolivia and Peru is a modern one; ancient Peru encompassed both countries. The Incas are, of course, Quechuas. Modern Bolivian archaeologists such as Carlos Ponce Sanginés hold that Tiahuanaco was the work of the Aymara. As Ponce Sanginés interpreter said to me, "Here, you know, it was all the work of the Aymara." If so, perhaps, as the great German naturalist Baron Friedrich Heinrich Alexander von Humboldt speculated in the nineteenth century, the primitive cultures Europeans found in various parts of the world were the remnants of more evolved civilization earlier devastated by violent earth changes. The circumstantial evidence at Tiahuanaco makes this a real possibility.

Modern archaeology begins at Tiahuanaco around the turn of the century with the work of Arthur Posnanski. Thirty years of patient investigation led Posnanski to claim

Tiahuanaco (after Posnansky)

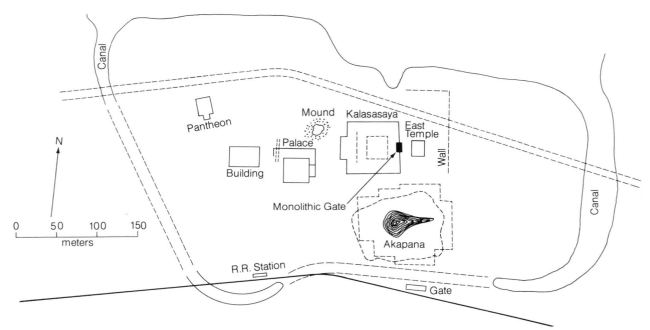

117 *The weeping god of the Gate of the Sun surrounded by running (or flying?) figures.*

an age of 10,000 to 12,000 years for the site, an age usually rejected by archaeologists today. Another prominent archaeologist who added to our understanding of the site was Wendell C. Bennett who began work in 1932. In excavating the semi-subterranean temple of the site, he found the largest known Tiahuanaco sculpture, the 7.3-meter high red sandstone monolith now in front of the city stadium in La Paz. Bennett also found the smaller monolith with the beard which now stands in the semi-subterranean temple. The major work at Tiahuanaco was directed by Ponce Sanginés who began a complete excavation and restoration of the site in 1957.

Writing in *Pre-Columbian Cities* (1973), Jorge E. Hardoy describes Tiahuanaco as the "first large planned complex in South America" and though, for him, it lacks the impressiveness of Mexico's Teotihuacán, it is similar to the Mexican site in such crucial design elements as "the rectilinear direction of the composition" and "orientation to the cardinal points." Whatever Ponce Sanginés believes about the culture responsible for Tiahuanaco, Hardoy gathered the impression from Sanginés' work that the culture had come from elsewhere. Hardoy puts it this way: "Ponce Sanginés describes the culture as appearing suddenly, already formed and vigorous from its very beginnings, which suggests that its origins were not local but foreign."

142

119

118 *Closeups of heads set within wall of the semi-subterranean temple. All racial types are represented. Not all are humanoid.*

119 *Corner detail of the Kalasasaya. More than two hundred of these massive mono-* *liths outlined the rectangular area of the temple; some are four meters high. Many of them evidently carried inscriptions at one time, but the priests with the sixteenth-century conquistadors defaced them.*

Psychic Impressions at Tiahuanaco

At Tiahuanaco many visitors gather the impression that it is the most mysterious and inexplicable archaeological site of the New World. It should not, therefore, be surprising that psychic impressions of its past contain some bizarre elements.

Karen Getsla, who had assisted me with the Bimini project, flew to Bolivia with me to give on-site impressions at Tiahuanaco. Her experience there was so emotionally powerful that it led me to question the advisability of taking sensitives into the field.

At the entrance to the site, the semi-subterranean temple was ahead of us to the south. On its walls are tenoned limestone heads which reflect great racial variety; not all humanoid. To our right (looking west) was the great Kalasasaya, a rectangular enclosure about 443 by 427 feet, surrounded by red sandstone monoliths set into masonry. The monolithic stairway of the Kalasasaya faced us. Behind the semi-subterranean temple lay (further to the south) the Akapana, a great earthen mound about 650 feet on a side and about fifty feet high. Within it was a central depression, and a stone drainage structure had been found leading from this depression.

When I asked Karen about the original culture of Tiahuanaco, she saw a very, very small people with the group numbering no more than 100 to 150 people. "You are talking about one of the most holistic cultures I have ever [tuned into], one in which there were no important numbers because they were all important . . . there is such oneness of mind that there is no discussion." Karen saw the Kalasasaya as the location of this original group's "Court of Standards". The first culture at the site was, she said (in understanding) a very high one, yet one which lived very simply and did not require cities or towns. Karen gave no information about their origins. She saw, basically, three cultures: the founding group, a transition culture and, then, later the Inca. Further broken down, she saw a total of five distinct cultures before the Spanish arrival. This is consistent with modern Bolivian archaeology, at the time unknown to her.

Within the Kalasasaya itself (in what Bennett called the inner court) she saw thirteen alcoves representing the various regions — a total of twenty-six presumably occupied by judges representing the regions. Of these alcoves no evidence remains. She said that the Gate of the Sun had been brought to the Kalasasaya from elsewhere (this was later confirmed); she also said that none of the monoliths belonged within, either. She had the impression that the Spanish found the Kalasasaya the best place to bury these pagan artifacts to get them out of the way. If this is correct, inferences from the twentieth-century locations of monoliths within the Kalasasaya would be invalid.

The Akapana, usually believed to be a ruined pyramid, was, she said, "a water supply, not a pyramid . . . [used for its] medicinal properties [and] purification." She noted that the original culture needed only water, not food, and she observed no sign of cultivation. This was just what another psychic, Carol Huff-stickler, had told me about the culture coming into Bimini 30,000 years ago.

West of the main site and south of the present village of Tiahuanaco lies the Puma Punku, its assortment of huge monolithic shapes weighing up to 200 tons a puzzle to all. Karen linked Puma Punku to the transitional culture. She said that an interest in numbers began with this transitional culture and "you will find an interesting astronomical correlation between Tiahuanaco and Puma Punku". "It will require," she said, "the excavation of the hilltop [the mound at Puma Punku which faces away from Tiahuanaco]." The red sandstone of Puma Punku belonged to the first transitional group, and the andesite belonged to the latter transitional group.

When I first read W.C. Bennett's monograph on his 1932 excavation at Tiahuanaco, my attention had been drawn to two monoliths he found within the semi-subterranean temple. In particular, the bearded statue suggested to me the influence of another culture. I asked Karen about these two figures. She had the impression that the two red sandstone monoliths had been added at a later time when the culture realized, "That its emphasis had shifted from spiritual to non-spiritual." The two monoliths (the bearded one and the militaristic figure) side by side then, the bearded one and the largest one at the site (now in La Paz) represented a prophecy of the ultimate downfall of the civilization. The bearded figure is about 8.3 feet tall and weighs about three-quarters of a ton; the militaristic figure is twenty-four feet tall and weighs about twenty tons.

Karen said that the two red sandstone monoliths in the semi-subterranean temple were done by the transition group (the second group) before the arrival of the Inca. In her words, "The bearded one was a person of high spirituality going beyond anything that I have experienced culturally, be it Indian or oriental ... a breakdown in language when I try to indicate how powerful the spirituality was and how the ideal was a 'lived' thing, not something they had to write down in books. It was so well lived that there was no need for documentation or schooling in it. It was tremendously consistent from individual to individual, not requiring record-keeping as to what the rules of the game were about."

Karen saw the juxtaposition of the two statues as a "warning of the deterioration that was coming; warning that it was already within the culture." The two monoliths found by Bennett then, according to Karen, represented a change from spiritual values and simplicity to militaristic power and complexity, from a homogenous group structure to a structured hierarchical society based on power.

Her interpretation of the militaristic monolithic figure focused on the kero (beaker) held in one hand and the bird of prey in the other. For her these two elements highlighted the radical change of consciousness. A cup of water, nourishment, freely offered, contrasted with combat, the bird of prey.

Before my actual visit to Tiahuanaco, I had asked another psychic who had been most helpful at Bimini, Anne, to give me her impressions of the site. In view of the fact that during the last century many have speculated that the human race began at Tiahuanaco, I was, in a sense, prepared. However, Anne's readings evoked in me the same response I'd first had at Bimini with a similar version of prehistory: science fiction. Upon reflection, however, her version was not inconsistent with many presently emerging clues to prehistory.

Here are some excerpts from a series of impressions done over seven months prior to my visit:

"Lake Titicaca represents an advance of beings from other stars whose similarity to man stems from being predecessors."

"The splendor of Tiahuanaco lay in the fact that its achievement ran contrary to what was expected. At first a superior race were guardians of secrets of accomplishment brought here from Mars. Reservoirs to sustain life-form were necessary to the experiments. These stellar beings composed from earth the materials necessary to sustain life. Their achievement lies in the fact that, until this time, no minerals were known. Here, minerals were mined and collected and the properties assigned to each."

"... the Titicaca experiment left much to be accomplished. The temple was destroyed by wind storms of the solar eclipse, beings disseminated through the earth from this point." Anne also had the impression of a major geological change at 25,000 B.C. — the uplift speculated upon by many observers?"

Her readings suggested a stunningly long sweep of prehistory:

"The early progenitors spent four billion years readying the planet. At Tiahuanaco they spent 200,000 years. They left and returned in different groups checking on the experiment. When they came in they were thought of as gods ... migrating tribes occupied such sites at a much later date. Little understanding of significance using them as shelters, feeling something of the holiness of the grounds."

If this were true, it would explain my own feeling that the megalithic structures (and the implied engineering skills) somehow were not compatible with the pottery and other Tiahuanaco artifacts.

Question: "What is the function of the faces on the sunken wall (the semi-subterranean temple) at Tiahuanaco?"

Answer: "These were carved in stone at a time prior to man's history. Their significance exemplifies the root races that will be forthcoming upon the earth. All was known and planned in advance of man's gradual evolvement. Those who carved them were a superior race who undertook to achieve preliminary investigation on behalf of man. Knowing what would be needed within the earth's framework would insure the success of the human organism."

It was this final impression of Anne's which led to speculation on a similarity between the bearded statue and Hindu thought: "At Tiahuanaco the pottery comprises a mixture of cultures. First, on the one hand, you will see the remains of a giant civilization ... on the other hand, you will see remnants of a later people scattered through the land by invaders. The bearded statue belongs to the first group ... the bearded statue represented a man chosen to descend to teach. He was fair. His robe and sandals were similar to those worn by Jesus. He spoke plainly and reminded man of the reason for the descent and the goals of evolution. These goals were to raise the animal appearance to higher levels. Jackals at his feet and head show 'serpent energy' could achieve the reversals of the animal energy [the animals are usually interpreted as pumas; but they actually look like jackals] ... the pottery represents one foot on earth the other in the heavens. Longing to return was intense and evidence of the period."

The allusion to "serpent energy" reminded me of the Hindu Kundalini yoga, its concept of body energies, and the evolution of these energies from body center to body center (the so-called chakras). For the mainstream of western science these are metaphors. In an university-based Kirlian project of my own, I found that practised meditators could influence Kirlian photos of their fingertips by concentrating on the various chakras. Whatever the reality of the chakras, eastern tradition includes body and hand positions to facilitate alteration of the individual's energy patterns. In a characteristic pose the left hand covers the solar plexus area, the right, the heart area. This is exactly the pose of the bearded monolith. Was there a worldwide tradition upon which both the Hindus and those at Tiahuanaco drew?

It is interesting to us that, in Mexico, at the Teotihuacán temple of Quetzalcoatl, another investigator has recently speculated on possible evidence of Hindu influence.

During one of my visits to Tiahuanaco, I talked with the caretaker, Jose Zuñaga, who gave me a clue that seems to bear on the question: were the Aymara Indians the builders of the megalithic site? In Aymara, I was told, "Kalasasaya" means "standing stones"; "Akapana" means "hill". This suggests to me that the Aymara first saw the site essentially in the ruined condition of 1957, the date when Sanginés began his excavation and restorations. At that time, the Kalasasaya resembled a rectangular pattern of standing stones, the intervening masonry, now reconstructed, having been torn down through the centuries.

Both Zuñaga and Ponce Sanginés gave me clues to the astronomical possibilities of the site. For one thing, reminiscent of ancient Egyptian geography, the towns of Pajchire, Tiahuanaco, and Wankani all lie on a meridian. There appears also to be an equinoctial sunrise alignment through the monolithic gateway of the Kalasasaya, over the semi-subterranean temple and, far to the east, over the snowcapped Illimani 100 kilometers distant.

120 *View within semi-subterranean temple.
In the foreground, the bearded monolith of
red sandstone found by Bennett; in the
background, the temple wall with its many
sculptured heads; above, the main entrance
to the Kalasasaya, a monolithic statue
within.*

121 *One of the militaristic statues carved
in andesite standing within the Kalasasaya.*

120   121

122

123

124

125

122 *Side view of bearded statue. The animals above are said to be pumas but, in the author's opinion, are more like jackals, which are not indigenous to the region. The snake which curves upward parallels Hindu teachings about what is called Kundalini energy, the raising of which is thought to affect creativity and spirituality.*

124 *Serpent and egg motif.*

125 *Front view of bearded statue. In terms of Hindu psychology, his right hand covers the solar plexus chakra; his left, the heart chakra. The entire pose is in marked contrast to the other usually militaristic sculptures; even the beard is out of place in the Andes.*

123 *Closeup of jackals at head of bearded statue.*

150

126   Row of moai, re-erected in 1960.

4

The Pacific

In comparison with the Old World, the archaeology of Oceania is really in its infancy. Until Heyerdahl's expedition to Easter Island in 1955-1956, for example, no real excavation by modern archaeological methods had been done. It was only after World War II that many parts of the Pacific were actually linked with the rest of the world. Military operations in the Pacific followed by postwar affluence and the jet age were the major factors. Even today, distances are vast, and substantial expeditions thus require the logistics support possible only from ocean-going vessels capable of sustained independent operation. Fifty tons of displacement would be spartan — 500 tons more effective. Already the expedition has become an expensive operation. It is also important to realize that some pioneer anthropologists have been killed during their field work in the Pacific. Not all found the hospitality accorded Margaret Mead on Samoa. This was the case, for example, with Deacon on Malekula.

Many of the world's archaeologists, strongly committed to the European model of civilization, have preferred to seek out the archaeological roots of that civilization in the Old World. Next in interest come the pre-Columbian cultures of the New World, attractive because of highly evolved social structures. Serious interest in the relatively simple Stone-Age cultures of the Pacific has, until recently been the by-product of an emotional attraction to the romantic South Sea Island peoples. Writers like Herman Melville, with exotic stories about island sexual mores, have been the impetus for a number of field projects in Oceania.

The huge area of the Pacific Ocean certainly adds to the difficulties of archaeological field work. Oceania includes some 25,000 islands scattered over about 3,000,000 square miles. Once off scheduled airline routes, the traveler steps out of the conveniences of the jet age and back into the slower island rhythms.

Man's earliest presence in the Pacific probably was at Modjokerto, East Java. Here the Djetis bed has yielded fossil bones of a *Homo erectus* child *(Pithecanthropus modjokertensis)* dated 1.9 ± 0.4 million years. This date was established by the potassium argon method. From here, according to the usual view, migrations went forward to Australia, then New Guinea, afterward to Melanesia by about 4000 B.P., Micronesia by about 3500 B.P., into western Polynesia by 1140 B.C. at Tonga, and, subsequently, to either the Society Islands or the Marquesas by about 300 A.D., to Easter Island by about 500 A.D. and finally reaching Hawaii about 650 A.D. The evidence upon which this pattern is based, however, is so slender that the sequence will doubtless be revised again and again.

An alternative point of view is that of anthropologist Robert C. Suggs who worked in the Marquesas during the fifties. He puts the origins of Polynesia in South China about 2200 B.C. In his opinion, the migrations probably went both ways, through the Philipines and Indonesia.

As will be seen in the Easter Island section, Thor Heyerdahl has a different view of Pacific migrations. He believes that the Pacific was probably first settled from southeast Asia but that later another migration originated in Peru, passed through Easter Island and then went on to the Marquesas.

Whichever way it went, megalithic cultures have left their traces in many parts of the Pacific. Sites on New Guinea, New Caledonia, and Fiji are thought to date as early as 1000 B.C. Other sites are found in Indonesia (Nias, Timor, and Sarawak), the northern Celebes, the Trobriand Islands, the Carolines (Ponapé), the Marianas (the Lat'te culture: Guam, Rota, Saipan, Tinian), the New Hebrides (Malekula), Tonga (Tongatabu), the Marquesas, and Easter Island. Did megalithic culture develop along the route from Southeast Asia as the settlement dates suggest? And, if so, did Polynesians then originate the megalithic cultures of Peru? Or, was megalithic culture spread from Peru to Easter Island and then on to the west as in Hyerdahl's theory? The

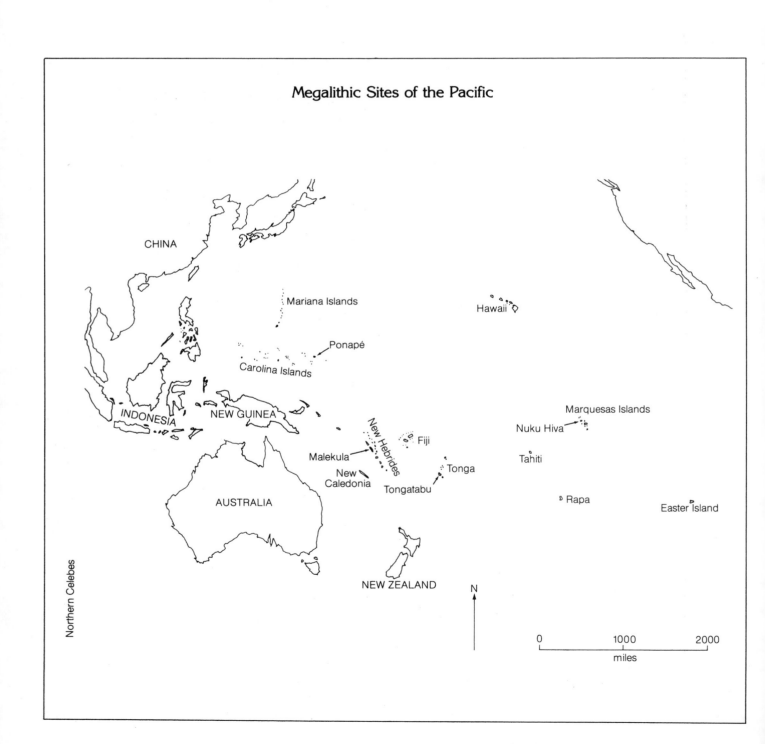

Megalithic Sites of the Pacific

CHINA

Mariana Islands

Hawaii

Ponapé

Carolina Islands

Marquesas Islands

Nuku Hiva

INDONESIA

NEW GUINEA

New Hebrides

Fiji

Tahiti

Malekula

New
Caledonia

Tonga

Tongatabu

Rapa

Easter Island

AUSTRALIA

Northern Celebes

NEW ZEALAND

N

| 0 | | 1000 | | 2000 |

miles

full answer to this intriguing puzzle may never be known.

One thing, though, is certain. Migrations throughout the Pacific area certainly took place. Seasonal changes in the directions of ocean currents and winds made possible voyages all over Oceania, depending upon the time of year. Sailing with spritsails rigged on huge double-hulled canoes built of pegged and lashed planks with a platform between (like modern catamarans), reading star maps of coconut hulls or networks of sticks and shells, and drawing upon an uncanny sense of direction, these ancient navigators were superb voyagers.

Nevertheless, the environment of the Pacific, despite its beautiful and often fertile islands, can be quite hostile to man. Tectonic and volcanic activity have both destroyed and built islands. Typhoons frequently destroy trees, crops, sometimes even the thin soil covering the lower coral islands or atolls. Famine soon follows, and migrations become a matter of survival. Migrations are also spurred by defeat in war, an oppressive ruler, or even a great love. These and other motives are recounted in the legends of the Pacific.

In these circumstances it is easy to understand cultural regression, especially if a particular culture should happen to lose control of the delicate balance between an island's food resources and the birth rate of its population. Many other factors, including the diseases brought by western seamen who reached the Pacific by the sixteenth century, have led to the same consequence. Whatever the causes, encountering a culture which has lost its vitality is frustrating to the field worker. Lacking a written history, he hopes at least to gather an understanding of the culture through local informants. Reading John Layard's work on Malekula in the New Hebrides, one gets the impression of a people maintaining cultural practices taken over from others and not fully understood.

From the point of view of our present topic, the archaeological literature gives the idea that prehistory in Oceania is based on very scanty evidence, mainly ethnological. The major emphasis seems to be on language and all cultural materials *except* megalithic structures. Furthermore there seem to be few site-surveys in existence which are sufficiently accurate for analysis of the astronomical possibilities of megalithic structures in Oceania. Yet Polynesian navigators were quite at home with the night skies, and the Hawaiian calendar began with an astronomical phenomenon familiar to ancient watchers of the sky the world over: the rise of the Pleiades. According to the great Maori anthropologist, Peter Buck, all Polynesians used a lunar calendar. Some also used sidereal and solar calendars, not necessarily the same. Except in the western part of Polynesia, each island group had thirty names for the various phases of the moon from new moon to new moon. In the west, the days of the month were counted numerically or in groups. All but western Polynesia began the new year by the morning or evening rise of the Pleiades. Such calendars and the navigation skills of Oceania imply an observational astronomy which ranges from the system of navigation in the Carolines to solar orientations on Easter Island. The evidence suggests that astronomy in Oceania derived more from navigational needs than, as in other parts of the world, from agricultural requirements.

Except at Easter Island there exists no basis for connecting the astronomy of Oceania with megalithic structures. Although the dating is somewhat uncertain, the oldest megalithic structures in Oceania may be those on the island of Nias found off the northwest coast of Sumatra. Here are reported to exist very impressive megalithic walls, stone stairways, bathing pools, and large, sculptured monuments. Hindu traders and adventurers found these upon their arrival in the fifth century A.D.

Malekula

New Hebrides (Melanesia)

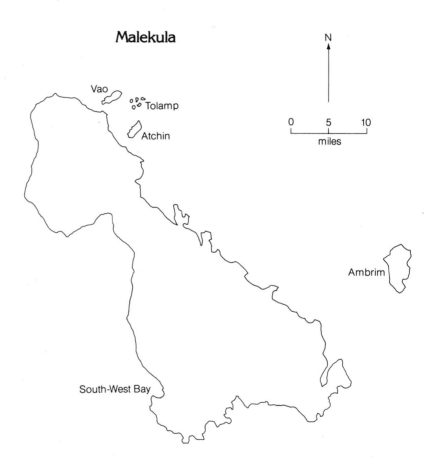

Malekula

Vao

Tolamp

Atchin

Ambrim

South-West Bay

N

0   5   10
miles

The archipelago of New Hebrides is located midway between Australia and the Samoa group. From the New Hebrides it is over 1,200 miles either way. A part of Melanesia, the New Hebrides lie in an area of Oceania believed not to have been inhabited much before about 4000 years ago. The archipelago runs 400 miles northwest and southeast. The islands of this archipelago are mainly volcanic with little coral, since they rise abruptly from deep water. The principal rock is basalt and earthquakes are common. Efate Island in the southeast has had its earliest archaeological site dated at about 350 A.D. Located here, is the capital, Vila, the principal port of call with two excellent harbors and an airport. Thirty miles northwest of Malekula is the island of Espiritu Santo, the location of the nearest airport and a 6,169-foot active volcanic peak. The Portuguese navigator, Pedro Fernandez de Quiros, first sighted Espiritu Santo in 1606. Several others called in the archipelago after this. Finally, in 1774, Captain Cook named the group. The origins of the word "Malekula" are unknown. The island is about sixty miles long and is about 780 square miles in area.

In 1943 Herbert W. Krieger wrote, "The New Hebridean is actually most concerned with obtaining and slaughtering pigs, with problems of social prestige which is dependent of wealth, and with the obtaining and keeping of women." For Krieger this meant that the religion of the New Hebrides was observed in a context of essentially "selfish emotions."

Cannibalism was formerly typical of this group. By the beginning of World War II it was still reported to exist on Malekula. The preferred victim was female, captured and fattened for slaughter. In this century, the pig has been substituted as the ceremonial meat.

Graded classes exist which are entered through initiation ceremonies, important island events involving the consumption of much food, including many pigs. Despite the apparent simplicity of the culture of the New Hebrides, the people observed on Malekula by Layard represent a surviving Stone-Age culture with megalithic elements including altars, monoliths and dolmens, much like European megalithic culture. The culture also uses the labyrinth design as a way of access to their immortal dead. Because of the fact that the Malekulans represent a living culture with megalithic elements, some attention must be given to their major ceremony, the *Maki.*

For this purpose, we shall turn to the work of John Layard, who worked on the small islands offshore of Malekula in the New Hebrides during 1914-1915. He concentrated his efforts on the island of Atchin where he found a living megalithic culture. This was at the time of great interest in world-wide diffusion theories now much in disrepute in conventional anthropological circles (see The Ancient Navigators, Chapter One). In addition to his local field work, Layard became deeply interested in the idea of the Journey of the Dead as it paralleled Egyptian funerary practices and involved megalithic structures. He saw the ceremony as an overcoming of death, as a renewal of life. As Layard put it, "The motivation for the Journey of the Dead is to be sought, not in the fact of death itself, but in the desire for the renewal of life through contact with the dead ancestors who are already leading a life beyond the grave. The juxtaposition of tomb, labyrinth, and portrait statue of the dead, which we find in Egyptian funerary monuments, can accordingly be brought into a direct parallel with the Malekulan variant of the Journey of the Dead."

The immediate origin of the Malekulan megalithic culture was, according to Layard, Indonesia, possibly Nias, off Sumatra.

The most important ceremony Layard found in the Small Islands was the *Maki.* The execution of the High *Maki* was usually spread over fifteen years. It is a ritual rebirth whose symbols include the taking of a new name and the lighting of a new fire. During a period of physical and spiritual isolation, including abstention from sexual intercourse, the "celebrant virtually becomes a child," as Layard put it.

In addition, through this continuing ceremony, he becomes one with his dead ancestors. He honors them with the erection of stone monuments; they (and later, he,) hover about these monuments. The potential wrath of all ancestors, personified in the devouring Guardian Ghost who guards the cave through which his ghost must later pass enroute to the Land of the Dead, is also evoked in the *Maki.* Thus the *Maki* establishes a continuity with one's ancestors (is thus a kinship rite, too) and safeguards one's spiritual future.

Elaborate singing and dancing accompanied by rhythms from gongs (hollowed tree trunks with a long slit), taller than a man, and set vertically in the ground help generate a kind of communal ecstasy that helps the participant to rise above his own personality and achieve a community of spirit with his ancestors, even with life itself. The sounds from these gongs (or drums) are taken to be the ancestor's voices.

A major feature of the *Maki* is the sacrifice of tusked boars whose upper canines have been knocked out to allow the tusks to recurve — as many as three complete circles. Such boars become famous and large fees are charged just for viewing them. At the climax of the fifteen-year-long ritual as many as 200 of these boars may be sacrificed on the dolmen and stone platform at Vao, one of the Small Islands. At death, the ghost of the boar passes to the sacrifices to build up the celebrant's power to face the Guardian Ghost at his own death. Formerly, human sacrifices were used instead of pigs.

The entire *Maki* ritual was, incredibly, purchased piece by piece from the people on mainland Malekula. Some time during the past century white men gave firearms to the Small Islanders who exterminated the mainlanders, the source of the *Maki.* The Small Islanders now bitterly regret their actions, according to Layard.

The megalithic dolmen just mentioned represents the female principle in the *Maki,* the monolith the male. Furthermore the dolmen also represents the cave in the Journey of the Dead which leads the spirit to Ambrim Island, the site of an active volcano. One by one monoliths become the short-hand of a very accurate oral genealogical record.

The concept which Layard finds existing in all megalithic cultures is the idea of a communal effort which, since it is not directed toward a utilitarian end, must stem from a religious view strong enough to justify the considerable effort to erect megalithic monuments. Layard was sophisticated enough to recognize that this impulse might be found in many different cultures and that the only common element might then be the megalithic structures erected by communal effort.

At the mainland village of Tolamp, Layard found a giant monolith which stood twelve feet above the ground. Another at the same location, believed to be erected about 1765, originally stood over thirty feet. The breadth at the base was over three-and-a-half feet. Broken into three pieces, only eight-and-a-half feet of this coral monolith stood at Layard's arrival.

127 *Basalt "log" wall of Nan Dowas.*

Ponapé
Caroline Islands

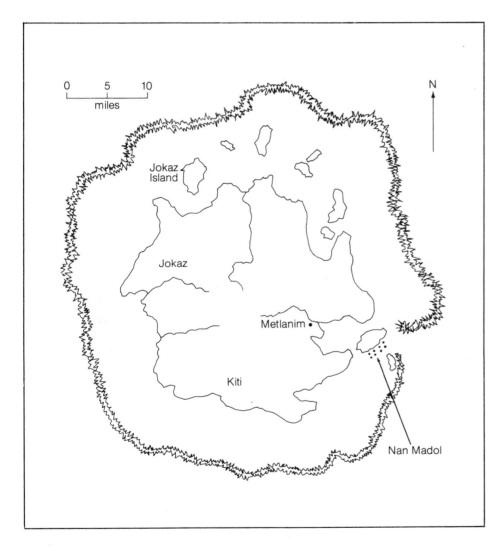

Except for the western part (Marianas, Yap, Palau), very little archaeology has been done in Micronesia. In this respect it is the least-known part of Oceania. Some early radiocarbon dates in Micronesia include a pre-ceramic culture on Saipan (in the Marianas) by 1527 B.C.

Ponapé is the easternmost of the Carolines, which became a part of the United States Trust Territory after World War II. The island rests on a submarine plateau which carries all of the Caroline group. As Peter Tompkins said, "Ponapé is the home of an enigmatic megalithic culture about whose origins and people there is little trustworthy data." N.F. Zhirov, Russian authority on Atlantis, saw Nan Madol on Ponapé as the center of a now-sunken megalithic culture in the Pacific.

Ponapé is a high island with 2500-foot peaks in the interior; its area is about 130 square miles. It was once the Spanish capital of Micronesia. John H. Brandt says that the name comes from "Fanu-Pei" (land of holy stones). The island's population includes Micronesians, Filipinos, Polynesians, Melanesians and Japanese. Its major archaeological site, Nan Madol ("the place of the spaces") is off the southeast coast, near the island of Temwen.

At the turn of the century, Nan Madol was called "Metalanim". It consisted of over ninety walled

128

artificial islands covering about eleven square miles. One of the problems raised by such an immense complex is how the present island population (or their ancestors) could assemble such a complex. The natural crystalline "logs" of basalt which compose Nan Madol are usually five-and eight-sided; but some are six-sided. These stones are unworked and have been brought in from the districts of Ponapé, some by water. Evidence of swamped craft and basalt "logs" exists on the reefs. Similar but smaller structures exist on Santa Maria in the Banks Islands north of the New Hebrides. At Nan Madol, the outer walls of a large,

walled structure called Nan Dowas are fifteen feet thick. Nan Dowas is rectangular with its long dimensions within a few degrees of north (according to Hambruch's survey). Its sides are about 180 by 115 feet, and it is surrounded by thirty-foot-high walls. The largest stone is estimated at five tons.

Construction Material
Natural basalt prisms (polyhedral "cylinders")
Geographical Coordinates
6° 50′ North Latitude
158° 22′ East Longitude

Ponapé: Myth and Archaeology

According to local traditions, Nan Madol was built by two spiritmen, the brothers Olsihpa and Olsohpa. The latter became the first of sixteen rulers of the Sandeleur dynasty with absolute power over the island. This is believed to have occurred in about the thirteenth

128 Main entrance to the temple Nan Dowas, seen from a boat in the canal. At upper right, K. Masao Hadley, who takes care of the site and who bears the title "Namadaun Idehd."

century. The Sandeleurs were succeeded by the Nahmwarkis, the twenty-first of which presently rules on Temwen Island, having moved from Nan Madol. The Nahmwarkis are still the traditional owners of Nan Madol. No significant artifacts have been found which would give clues to the ancient religion. In astronomy, only two constellations seem to be important: The Pleiades ("Makeriker") and the Southern Cross ("Mel"). No significant astronomical orientations have been reported.

In the nineteenth century Johannes Kubary did extensive photography of the island. During 1908-1910 Dr. Paul Hambruch did the first comprehensive measurements, adding to F.W. Christian's earlier survey. The Smithsonian Institution then sent an archaeological survey to Ponapé in 1963. This expedition excavated three feet of the garden soil on one of the walled islands, Pahn Kadina ("Men's House"), about twenty acres in extent. Radiocarbon dates between 1180 and 1430 A.D. were found there and 1285 ± 50 A.D. for an oven on Idehd. The artifacts so far include pearl shell, round and rectangular beads made of shell, adzes of polished tridacna, shell needles, pounding stones for breadfruit, basalt knives, and fishhooks.

Astronomy in the Carolines

The level of astronomical knowledge in the Carolines, particularly when put against other elements of Micronesia's culture, is surprisingly sophisticated. Until very recently the astronomical observations of the archipelago were for the practical purpose of inter-island navigation. Several centuries of trade went on in thirty-foot outrigger canoes sailing 400 miles of open sea between the Carolines and Guam. According to one investigator, the astronomical lore of the Carolines is local in origin and was conserved by hereditary transmission of the navigator's skills. Furthermore the persons of the navigators were protected by taboos, and the occupation had the highest prestige on the islands.

These nagivators used the stars as compass, almanac, and calendar. The basic navigational problem in the archipelago could be solved by latitude sailing, just as western navigators did until the eighteenth century invention of the chronometer by which longitude could be determined. However the navigators of the Carolines could also sail thirty other points on the horizon besides east and west (the rising and setting of Altair). Polaris gave them north; the Southern Cross (at the meridian) gave them south. Twenty-eight other stellar risings and settings (including the Pleiades) gave them the other directions. Their calendar was a sidereal year of twelve star-months of varying length beginning with the heliacal rising of the Pleiades or Antares. They also had a thirty-day lunar month and, on one island, a solar calendar. As the emphasis was upon practical navigation, these calendars were only loosely equated during the navigation season.

A Psychic Impression of Prehistoric Ponapé

Ruins there originated in late Pleistoscene, very ancient time of early man. Dinosaurs at large at that time. Suffocating heat. Beings here had landed according to preconceived plan. Charting heavens, they fell too close to earth's orbit.

Their migration northward occurred as Osiris (Atlantean ruler?) was declining in illumination. (Or Sirius?) These beings wisely choose an obscure region for developing their space-oriented work. To seed a few animals with other strains to achieve an acceleration of form and function. The great ovum of the sperm whale was chosen in one experiment. Used to enhance and seed other generative processes.

They manufactured bronze here. Segments of stone-encased metal about. Their preoccupation was with altering physical matter. In the remains of charcoal are extracts from the intestines of the saber-toothed tiger. Function of enzymes studied. In a while scientists will realize that the range of animal forms was spurred by manipulators.

Tongatabu
Tonga Islands

Tongatabu Island is about 550 miles southwest of the Samoan group. Southernmost of the three Tonga groups, it is the seat of government and has an airport. The Tonga Islands are also known as the Friendly Islands. The Tongas, long rulers of Samoa, were known as daring sailors.

On Tongatabu there is an extraordinary megalithic trilithon whose construction difficulties were not much less than those posed by the building of Stonehenge, the site of the most famous trilithons. Like Stonehenge, the lintel is stablized by mortising. However, at Tongatabu the lintel is mortised sideways into the uprights instead of resting atop the uprights as at Stonehenge. The largest of the Tongatabu uprights stands about seventeen feet above ground, is fourteen feet wide at the base, twelve feet wide at the top and four feet thick. The uprights stand about twelve-and-a-half feet apart, and are oriented on an east-west axis. The estimated weight of the visible portions of this worked coral trilithon is between thirty and forty tons.

This trilithon was constructed in the thirteenth century by Tuitatui, the eleventh Tui Tonga (High Chief). His dynasty, which began about 950 A.D., was not to end until thirty-five generations later in 1865.

129 *Megalithic trilithon, Tongatabu.*

Nuku Hiva

Marquesas Islands

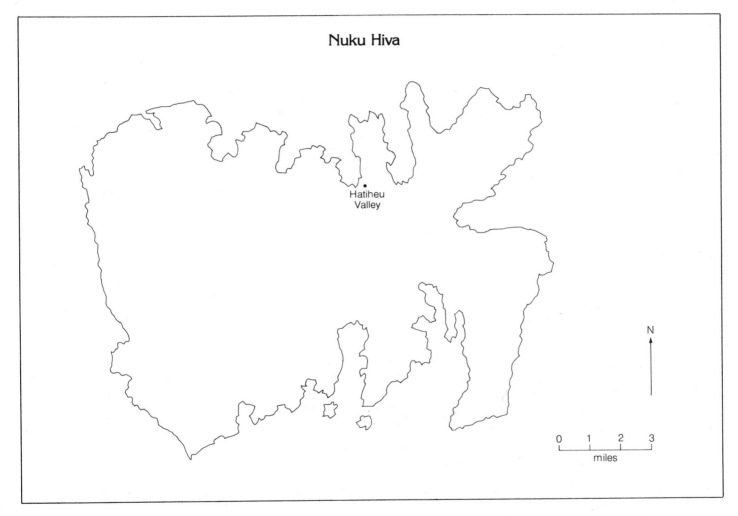

Nuku Hiva

Hatiheu
Valley

N

0 1 2 3
miles

Nearly 800 miles northeast of Tahiti lie the Marquesas Islands. While first sighted in 1596 by the Spanish navigator Mendaña, these islands really came to the attention of the western world with the publication of Herman Melville's famous novel, *Typee*. Having shipped out of New England on a whaler, the romantic youth jumped ship while it was anchored off the inviting tropical island of Nuku Hiva. Except for the evidence of cannibalism practised upon the enemies of his host tribe, Melville's stay was an idyllic one. His understated romantic interlude with the maiden Fayaway was straight out of Jean Jacques Rousseau's popular idea of the noble savage. Between Melville's visit and the expedition of Robert C. Suggs in 1956 *(The Hidden Worlds of Polynesia)*, various negative influences introduced by western seamen had reduced the once-vital Marquesan culture to a shambles. As Suggs puts it, "Marquesan society died a horrible death. By the early 1920's only 1500 confused, hostile, and apathetic

survivors remained of the possible 100,000 to 120,000 that had inhabited the islands in 1768." Their fate was typical of many cultures in Oceania (see "Easter Island"). 1768 was the date when Captain Cook's *Endeavour* called briefly at the islands. Between that time and the twentieth century, the culture was reduced by what Suggs aptly calls a "marathon debauch" marked by "violence and cruelty."

Archaeological Highlights

Suggs believes that the Marquesas were occupied as early as 120 B.C. The conventional date is about 300 A.D. Suggs further contends that the islands were settled by a well-outfitted expedition, probably from Tonga or Samoa.

The first significant archaeological survey of the Marquesas was done in 1920 and 1921 by Ralph Linton. He found no single megalithic structure equal to the Tongan sites. He found the best work on Nuku Hiva but no cut stone before the European influence. The masonry was also inferior to the Hawaiian. One Marquesan structure, a platform, was constructed with boulders weighing from three to ten tons. He found no pyramids (like those step pyramids faced with great coral

slabs) or trilithons such as those found in the Tongas and Samoa group. He did locate massive stone figures over eight feet in height on Hiva Oa in the Marquesas. Before his survey a great stone head weighing three tons was removed by the German ethnologist Karl von den Steinem.

The typical goggle-eyed stone tiki of the Marquesas has been compared with Chinese Bronze-Age statues. For Suggs this is merely a local elaboration. Suggs is also opposed to Heyerdahl's diffusion theory, saying that no Peruvian pottery or tools have been found in Polynesia.

Suggs' most interesting discovery on Nuku Hiva was made in 1956. This was Hikoku'a, a great *tohua* (ceremonial plaza) in Hatiheu Valley on the northern coast. A large platform and two large stone figures were found. They were constructed of coarse, dull red volcanic tuff. The site, sacred to Marquesans, had long been concealed from western visitors. This and other megalithic structures are believed by Suggs to date after about 1400 A.D., the beginning of what he calls the classical period. Before this time the principal artifacts are made of shell. Simple thatched huts, associated with a simple agricultural and fishing community, represent the architectural level of the culture.

130 Marquesan stone tiki.

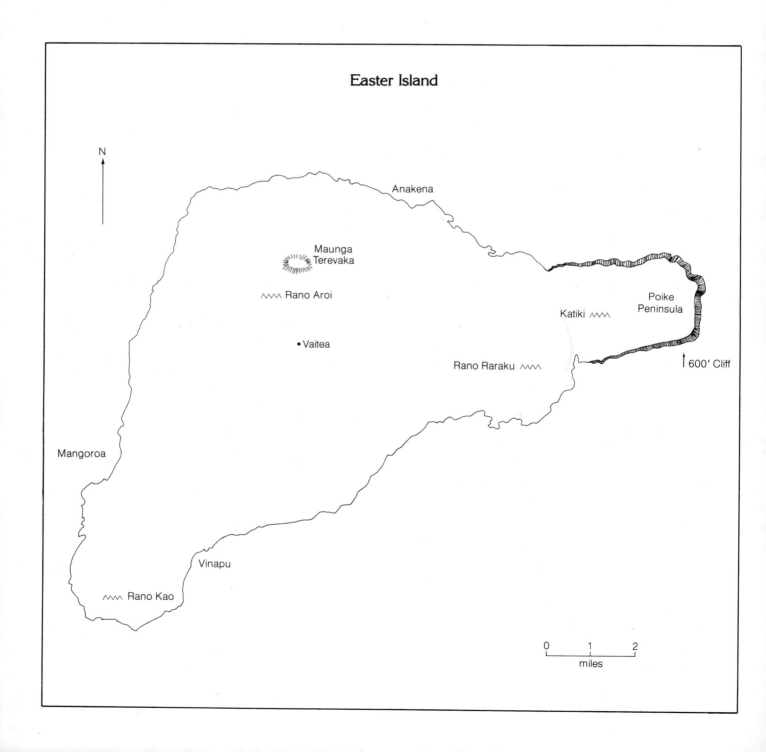

Easter Island

N

Anakena

Maunga
Terevaka

ʌʌʌ Rano Aroi

• Vaitea

Katiki ʌʌʌ

Poike
Peninsula

Rano Raraku ʌʌʌ

↑ 600' Cliff

Mangoroa

Vinapu

ʌʌʌ Rano Kao

0   1   2

miles

Easter Island

"... a dark, solemn world whose last faint heartbeats we detected — a world which may nonetheless possess a strange and unexpected relevance to our own."
Francis Mazière, French Ethnologist, 1963

Easter Island (or, in Polynesian, Rapa Nui) is a brooding island whose bleak terrain more nearly resembles the austerity of the Cornish coast of western England than the usual South-Sea island. The small volcanic island is battered constantly by wind and seas, and, until the weekly jet flights from Chile began, its isolation was apparently quite oppressive to its inhabitants. Easternmost of the inhabited islands of Polynesia, it is about 2000 miles southwest of the Galapagos Islands, 2700 miles east of Tahiti, and 2600 miles west of Valparaiso.

The island's southern hemisphere location gives it a dry season from December to the end of May and a cold, rainy season from June through November. The tiny island is a rough triangle with sides of ten, eleven, and fifteen miles and has extinct volcanoes at the corners. At one time most of its 600 giant stone statues, or *moai*, were standing around the island as silent sentinels on about 245 temple platforms, or *ahu*. Many of these twenty-five-to-forty-ton *moai* were crowned with topknots, or *pukao* weighing up to

131 Giant moai, partially excavated on slopes of Rano Raraku.

ten tons. The megalithic *moai* were sculptured from a grayish-yellow black-grained volcanic tuff, the *pukao* from a red stone. The source of these *moai* is the volcanic quarry of Rano Raraku; here are *moai* in various stages of completion, one about seventy-five feet long and weighing an estimated ninety tons.

During Thor Heyerdahl's 1955-1956 expedition to Easter Island, he was shown the actual procedures by which these statues could be erected and moved using local materials and manpower. Their significance however remains a mystery. In 1774 the great navigator, Captain Cook, was told that the *moai* were monuments to earlier *ariki's*, or royal personages — *alii* in Hawaii. This funerary role suggests a parallel with Egyptian culture, but *moai* are described by local informants as having once possessed *mana* or a beneficent power. This is reminiscent of the claims of sensitives about standing stones in Great Britain and their traditions of fertility and healing. An expedition following Heyerdahl's found very pronounced magnetic anomalies on the island. Once again, the circumstances suggest a possible connection between geophysical and paranormal phenomena.

There are more difficult questions about the island's past than the meaning of the giant *moai*. Where did they come from? Were they originally from South America as Heyerdahl claims? Or did they come from western Polynesia? Where did the sophisticated megalithic masonry of the first of the three island cultures originate? Unsettling hints come both from the archaeology and from ethnologist's interviews with those local people who still recall some of the old traditions.

In addition to the name *Rapa Nui* ("Island big") Easter Island has had two others: *Matakiterani* ("eyes gazing at the sky") and *Te Pito No Te Henua* ("the navel of the world"). Legends about the founder, Hotu Matua, claim that he came from a now-sunken archipelago to the west, Hiva. Today, this is usually taken to be an allusion to Hiva Oa, an existing island in the Marquesas. In these legends there are three possible allusions to cataclysmic earth-changes forcing the ancient migration.

Largest Moai
(still in quarry)
Length: c. 75 feet
Weight: c. 90 tons
Geographical coordinates
27° 8' 24" South Latitude
109° 20' West Longitude

132 Easter Island girl, behind her several of the giant moai.

Easter Island Chronology

1140 B.C. Current opinion as to time of the earliest settlement of Polynesia whose origins have been traced to a center in Fiji and whose influence quickly spread to Tonga or Samoa.

380 A.D. Heyerdahl's uncorrected carbon-14 date for the earliest organized labor on Easter Island (Rapa Nui). In Heyerdahl's theory Rapa Nui was settled from Peru. His evidence includes:

1 The presence on Easter Island of the *totora* reed, an American freshwater plant also present at Lake Titicaca in the Andes,
2 The presence of the sweet potato also found in the Andes,
3 Drawings on Easter Island of megalithic statues of reed boats similar to those in the Andes, one of which has three masts with sails,
4 Megalithic statues in the earliest cultural horizon which resemble the work at Tiahuanaco,
5 Evidence of fair-skinned red-haired people on Easter Island and in Andes,
6 Evidence of sun worship in both locations,
7 Blood types of present Easter Island population closer to aboriginal peoples of North and South America than Southeast Asia, supposed origin of Polynesians.
8 Small stone sculptures found by Heyerdahl in secret caves. Sculptures do not relate to South America or Polynesia.
The more conventional opinion is that Easter Island was settled from the west (Polynesia), that seeds of the *totora* reed were dropped by migratory birds (fourteen of the twenty three species which visit the island come from Peru).

690 ± 130 An uncorrected C-14 date from Easter Island which William Mulloy considers the earliest dependable one.

907-957 (± 200) Earliest *ahu* with solar orientation according to William Mulloy.

1100 Heyerdahl's estimate of date the carving of the megalithic statues *(moai)* began.
c. 1200 Hotu-Matua's migration from the west (Marquesas) to Easter Island).

1470 Quarry-work on *moai* at the extinct volcano, Rano Raku, ceases.

1680 The battle of Poike peninsula ends the Golden Age during which the megalithic *moai* and temple platforms were constructed. This battle between the Long Ears, *Hanau Eepe* ("the strong men") and the Short Ears, *Hanau Momoko* ("the weak men") resulted in the extermination, except for one man, of the Long Ears.

1722   On Easter Sunday (April 5) the western world found Rapa Nui, called it Easter Island. A Dutch admiral, Jacob Roggeveen found 261 *moai* standing on platforms. One of his crew wrote that "everything here (was) ... planted, sown, and tilled, the strips of land separated with great precision."

c. 1760   The strange cult of the birdmen began, an annual ceremony keyed to the month of July to coincide with the time of the rise of the Pleiades.

1770   Two Spanish ships called. Their commander, Don Felipe Gonzales, claimed the island for Spain, observed tall, fair men (two were about six-and-a-half feet tall) and people with black, chestnut-brown, and red hair.

1774   On the arrival of Captain Cook, the giant *moai* were observed to have been knocked down, and only a few hundred people in miserable condition were seen on the island.

1786   A French visitor, La Pérouse, found many inhabitants, confirming Cook's hunch that many were in hiding at his visit. Since then a vast system of secret caves developed from volcanic gas-pockets has been discovered. These were used as refuges and for sacred purposes.

1862   Peruvian slavers took 1,000 men (most of the male population) to work the Guano Islands off Lima. When the Bishop of Tahiti interceded, 100 survivors went back to the island by sea. Of these, fifteen reached their homes carrying smallpox which nearly finished the remaining population. The great anthropologist, Peter Buck, wrote, "no native population has been subjected to such a succession of atrocities and disintegrating influences as the people of Easter Island."

1864   Population 111 (estimated in the Golden Age at about 5,000. Today there are about 1,500).

1866   Last annual birdman cult ceremony.

1888   Easter Island annexed by Chile.

1914   Katherine Routledge, an English lady, led an expedition which found over 400 *moai*.

1934   Franco-Belgian expedition included the French ethnologist, Dr. Alfred Métraux.

1955-56   Thor Heyerdahl's expedition which included today's authority on Easter Island, Dr. William Mulloy.

1956   Thomas Bartel, German scholar, claimed to have translated the hieroglyphics of the *rongo rongo* (or talking) boards. In 1975 Hyerdahl wrote, "In spite of false claims to the contrary, the Easter Island script still remains undeciphered."

1963   The expedition led by Francis Mazière, French ethnologist.

1975   The expedition led by Antonio Ribera, Spanish underwater explorer.

Easter Island Legends

For many reasons, oral traditions are suspect for modern investigators. If you assume that our ancestors were mostly gullible, credulous story tellers, you will look at the traditions recorded by ethnologists one way; on the other hand, if you realize the actual continuity possible in societies where reliance is put upon memory instead of written records, you will have a different view. Some hint of what is known to be possible can be seen in an anthropologist's work with living Polynesian tribes. In *Vikings of the Pacific,* Peter H. Buck, himself of Maori descent, tells of Polynesians chanting 180 generations of the tribal geneology to critical audiences. It is known, too, that many prehistoric peoples, such as the Druids, transmitted their esoteric knowledge orally, training their successors in rigid oral exams. On Easter Island, one of Hyerdahl's native informants described undergoing just such training in his youth. Moderns naturally tend to underrate the possibility of accurate transmission of knowledge by this means; they are committed to a model of civilization which places more importance on a written language and written records.

A French ethnologist, Francis Mazière, sailing out of Antibes in the Mediterranean, arrived at Easter Island several years after Heyerdahl. Mazière was fortunate in that his wife was Tahitian and, as a result, at home in several Polynesian dialects. By Heyerdahl's account, he himself was on excellent terms with the Easter Islanders; Mazière, however, because of his wife's background, seems to have penetrated to an inner core of tradition missed by Heyerdahl. Of course, Heyerdahl emphasized excavation and Mazière, an ethnologist, while also involved in digging, seemed to stress the recovery of extinct traditions, hoping to find clues to the island's mysterious prehistory. Both their accounts of Rapa Nui thus represent essential complementary versions of the site of a truly exotic culture.

As Mazière's wife interviewed the islanders about their tradition, she encountered many strange statements, not the least of which was the fact that they called their predecessors, "The Others".

According to Mazière, the legend of Easter Island's settlement by Polynesians contains an allusion to a cataclysm: "King Hotu-Matua's country was called Maori, and it was on the continent of Hiva ... The king saw that the land was slowly sinking in the sea." As a result, he put all of his people into two great canoes and sailed east to Easter Island.

Easter Island itself, according to another legend, "was a much larger country" broken up by Uoke "because of the sins of its people."

Another tradition says that a tiny island about 500 miles east, Sala y Gomez, was once a part of Easter Island. Its Polynesian name, Motu Motiro Hiva, means "small island near Hiva."

In Mazière's opinion, these hints of ancient cataclysms have some support in recent discoveries which include a large underwater peak near Easter Island, a large fracture-zone nearby, and a large bank of sediment underwater in the vicinity.

These hints of now-sunken former land masses in the Pacific are suggestive of another legendary lost continent, Lemuria. The existence of either Lemuria or Atlantis is considered quite unlikely by those marine geologists and other scientists who are committed to the idea of the permanency of the ocean basins. Increasingly, however, this theory is being challenged by new evidence. For example the recent discovery of coal on the Pacific island of Rapa (Rapaiti, southwest of Mangareva Island) gives evidence of an ancient continental land mass in that part of the Pacific.

A possible clue to the first inhabitants of Easter Ialsnd is found in this native statement transcribed by Mazière: "The first men to live on the island were the survivors of the world's first race. They were yellow, very big, with long arms, great stout chests, huge ears although their lobes were not stretched: They had pure yellow hair, and their bodies were hairless and shining ... This race once existed on two other Polynesian islands. They came by boat from a land that lies behind America." Is this an allusion to Atlantis?

Easter Island Archaeology

The first actual stratigraphy on Easter Island was the result of work by archaeologists of Heyerdahl's 1955-1956 expedition, Dr. William Mulloy, Dr. Carlyle Smith, Dr. Edwin Ferdon, and Arne Skjolsvold. At that time, the earliest date for human habitation in Polynesia was thought to be about 800 A.D. and Easter Island was supposed to have been settled about 1300 A.D. Heyerdahl's samples gave him an uncorrected C-14 date of about 380 A.D. for organic remains of the earliest human activity on the island. Since then, the date for the first settlements in central Polynesia has been pushed back to about 1140 B.C. As noted earlier, compared with Old World archaeology, the work in the Pacific is yet in its infancy.

The Heyerdahl expedition found evidence for three cultural horizons, the earliest of which included the

133 Two reconstructed ahu (temple platforms); the moai in foreground has had its topknot (pukao) restored.

classical structures such as the *Vinapu ahu* (or temple platform). These *ahu* were built with large blocks of basalt. Their well-fitted masonry is similar to the best masonry of South America, the Inca work at Cuzco, Peru. This earliest architecture seems to have had no prior development either locally or elsewhere in Polynesia; in other words, it began as a fully-evolved cultural trait. This first horizon also included two megalithic stone statues which have little resemblance to the famous *moai* but *do* exhibit similarities to the pre-Inca culture at Tiahuanaco. As these megalithic statues were a part of the earliest horizon which revealed a fully developed technology, the idea of local origin for the stonework was challenged by Heyerdahl's expedition.

In the second cultural layer, the classical structures were partly dismantled, and paved slopes were built against the inland faces of the *ahu.* It was at this time that the large *moai* were sculptured and moved from Rano Rararaku. Burial chambers were also added to the *ahu.* This second horizon, the Golden Age, was suddenly terminated in 1680. The third layer, one of decadence, began at this time.

Likely the second cultural layer found by Heyerdahl was the consequence of a Polynesian migration from the west. Linguistic clues such as the word *ahu*, which derives from

central Polynesia led Dr. Alfred Métraux to claim a Polynesian origin for the islanders. Heyerdahl himself found nothing to contradict the idea of a late Polynesian migration to the island. It may have been that of the legendary King Hotu-Matua, who sent out seven scouts to the east when he found his archipelago, Hiva, sinking into the sea.

The origin of the eraliest culture is the most problematic. Father Sebastian Englert, for years a serious student of the culture and a longtime Easter Island resident, believes that there were two separate races with separate cultures. The earliest western visitors found both the Polynesian racial characteristics and also people with white skin, red hair and blue eyes. According to local traditions, these latter racial traits went back to many of their ancestors. Such ancestors may have been remnants of the first people, in place by the time of the Polynesian Hotu-Matua's arrival; as Heyerdahl pointed out in his reasoning for a possible diffusion from Peru to Easter Island, the desert sands of Paracas have yielded mummies some of which have red hair. Pedro Pizarro, who chronicled the discovery of the Inca Empire, said that the rulers were fair and taller than their subjects. Others were both white-skinned and red-headed. Pizarro was told that these people were the last of a divine race, the *viracochas*, who, with their king Con-Ticci, had sailed away before

134 *Moai on ruined platform (ahu).*

174

the reign of the first Inca. It was this legend that caused a well armed Peruvian army of tens of thousands to capitulate to a few hundred Spanish conquistadors under the command of Francisco Pizarro. White-skinned, bearded men were credited also in the legends of the Andes with having built the most impressive ruins of South America at Tiahuanaco on the shores of Lake Titicaca. This lake, of course, is also the habitat of the freshwater reed, the *totora* which Heyerdahl found on Easter Island.

In recent years, yet another discovery may have added to the relevant evidence. An aboriginal tribe was discovered in the Amazon basin with white skin and red hair.

In *Operación Rapa Nui*, Antonio Ribera claims that a charted magnetic disturbance strong enough to affect both gyrocompasses and ordinary magnetic ones exists at Maunga Terevaka on the northern coast of Easter Island. Ribera is unable to account for this anomaly because he assumes that a volcanic island like Easter would have no large iron deposits to generate the usual magnetic problems. On the other hand, the tectonic history of the sea floor in the vicinity of Easter Island, including hints of major faults, may offer an explanation of this problem. Ribera also claims that similar magnetic problems also exist at the plains of Nazca in Peru and that, for some reason, the

Peruvian government has forbidden over-flights. When I visited Peru in 1977, however, small aircraft were flying over the plains of Nazca. A third location of similar magnetic disturbances, according to Ribera, is found at Tindouf, Algiers.

Ribera also speculates that the birdman cult of Easter Island is a recollection of extra-terrestrial visits in the same way the New Guinea cargo cults started after sighting military aircraft during World War II.

In 1978, while excavating a platform *(ahu)* near Anakena beach, where Hyerdahl once had his headquarters, Sergio Rapu, director of the Easter Island archaeological museum, found fragments of white coral and red lava. Fitted together, these fragments formed a fourteen-inch curved white disk with a hole in the center; into this hole, a five-inch red lava disk then fit. The eye thus formed matched one eye-socket of a nearby *moai*. Considering the stark power of the *moais*, even today, without such eyes in place, the effect must have been awesome.

Archaeoastronomy on Easter Island

A hint of the existence of a solar cult on Easter Island was found by Heyerdahl in the local name of a cave in which selected maidens were once isolated to bleach their skin for certain sacred festivals. This cave, the cave of the white virgin, was also known as "an o keke," or "cave of the Sun's Inclination." Later, a system of holes bored in a rock at the Orongo ruins was found to indicate the summer solstice sunrise (December 21 in the southern hemisphere). Dr. Edwin Ferdon, a New Mexico archaeologist with Heyerdahl found this "first ceremonial solar observatory known in Polynesia." Still later, Dr. William Mulloy found that the Vinapu platform was also oriented at right angles to the summer solstice sunrise. Dr. Mulloy recently published a corrected C-14 date of 907-957 (± 200 years) A.D. for the earliest *ahu* (or temple platform) with a solar orientation.

It will be recalled that the first observers of the Peruvian culture, the Inca, noted sun worship. This cultural parallel is one piece of Heyerdahl's evidence for a cultural diffusion from Peru to Easter Island.

Psychic Reading on Easter Island

Geographical information—origin of first culture

Noah's ancestors—the first men on earth here at time of Lemuria's sinking. The culture was transmitted to the west from *Beings* who could see far—looking in direction southeast. Stoicism represented and the need to always be watching for the deliverance. Past memories in these people incredibly strong. Their ancestors have the story of a sinking of a far land and of stars which signalled great earth changes.

Geological history of Easter Island

The land-mass here was thrust upwards many million years ago. Deposits of rich ore from volcanic explosions. Subsequently, the land-mass drifted northward and present location is half-way between polar influences. Equatorial lines somewhat south. Belt of zodiacal energy running horizontal through island. Currents felt around the world and buildings of great monuments on line. Lime deposits in caves mostly underwater.

Function of giant statues—the moai

Always watching, as has been said, the time for the return to the skies. Earth was then understood to be a station where one was waylaid. Transmigration point in space. All souls hoped for return. Lemurian disaster threatened the concept of earth as a suitable dwelling place. It may again become so. Love and blessings.

Additional geographical information on Easter Island from a later reading

In the Western Hemisphere below the Hawaiian Island chain, visible as mountain peaks. This a subterranean ridge, rode out great cataclysmic events—a melting furnace underneath—barrages from space—a torn chunk of earth. The land-mass moved gradually southeastward—lost its edges—moved in conjunction with nearby plates extending length of west coast of South America. It moved southeast. Easter Island outpost came to rest in time of deluge and before that had submerged considerably. Ring of Brodgar likewise moved in orientation more counter-clockwise—that side (moving) north and west, Pacific side moving south.

Thunderous upheavals of mid-Atlantic Ridge and following quakes damaged much in Western Pacific—after mountain chain severed below Hawaii—now plates move in different directions.

More about the moai on Easter Island

Once facing the outward islands of the Pacific from whence were expected voyageurs from outer space—the number representing the age of their time on earth. In waiting for their saviors these peoples gradually lost the ability to out-picture their good—their remembrances faded from the time when gods and giants had walked the earth. Waiting for the giant, god-like ones to come again and lift them away.

Early peoples on earth constantly sought a return to the stars. When their spirits became earth-bound, they grew very anxious indeed and allowed no chance of their being overlooked to occur. Shown in these statues are the period of waiting. Hole in back of wooden figures put on peg and spun around. Symbolic of "taking off". Noah's ancestors were among the ones who taught these peoples. They were instructed in unlimited use of mind power. They knew how to create with thoughts. These outer islands sank during the deluge. Many survivors congregated here and re-wove their lives—(It was the sinking of Lemuria which is referred to here.)

Lanyon Quoit, Cornwall

5

Some Implications of Megalithic Culture

Instead of limiting certain elements of megalithic culture to the more or less homogeneous complex of western Europe, the present work is based on the assumption that the megalithic structures of the world represent a similar response by many different cultures to universal experiences with their planetary environment. In more isolated parts of the globe these responses continued for a much longer time.

Culture for the anthropologist is the complex of skills and behavioral patterns of a particular human group which is socially (rather than genetically) transmitted. Culture includes knowledge, language, beliefs, customs, rituals, arts, tools, utensils and food production. Much of man's prehistoric culture is based only upon inferences from the hardware (tools or utensils) — the software (most of the balance of the culture complex), having died with the culture. In other words the methodology of archaeology has forced it to define prehistoric cultures in ways that omit much of importance. (See Appendix: "A Third Archaeological Revolution?")

Certain cultural elements held in common by the various megalithic sites seem to suggest a worldwide megalithic culture. Yet, the facts make it clear that we are looking at the work of many different cultures widely separated in time. Stepping aside for the moment from the usual concept of culture we can look at the megalithic sites of the world as a dynamic system composed of various local architectural, engineering, and scientific expressions of the same basic worldwide need to understand and cope with life on a planet whose geological evolution sometimes took violent forms.

I suspect that, if this approach is taken, and that, if megalithic sites of the world are studied more comprehensively (and with more precision), the worldwide legends of destructive earth changes will be seen in quite a different light. Incidentally, the sheer number of such sites (now hidden in the sub-divisions of archaeology) will be surprising. In my research and travels for the present work, I soon came to realize that I was dealing with but the tip of the iceberg. Mystery Hill in New Hampshire, for example, represents only one of over two hundred megalithic sites in New England. The few stone circles of the United Kingdom herein treated stand for over 900 found there. The inventory of the megalithic sites of the Pacific is in its early stages.

Furthermore, the subtlety, complexity, and, so far, missing elements of the present topic render impossible anything approaching a definitive treatment. The present work was done in the hope that the emerging patterns may open the door to many new workers who can then share in a complex and demanding task. Because of its implications for man, the crucial importance of the work cannot be stated too strongly. In an age when we are beginning to see the consequences of our own discordant relationship with the earth-spirit, the pursuit of exact knowledge about ancient man's apparently harmonious relationship with his environment may have implications for our own survival.

I am quite aware that the hypothesis which I am about to put forward collides directly with two deeply-held (by now unconscious) assumptions in western culture: (1) that our own culture represents the highest state of civilization; therefore, by isolating and identifying *our* essential qualities, we can define civilization; (2) that history, and before that, prehistory represent nothing more than an evolution (and progress) toward our type of civilization. These two assumptions are among the premises of Jacob Bronowski's *The Ascent of Man*. By now, these beliefs are so deeply engrained that supposedly objective scholars can become quite emotional in defense of them, even their corollaries. For example, the idea that dynastic Egypt might have had more accurate astronomical knowledge than ancient Greece can evoke a surprisingly non-objective defense of Hellenism.

A more specialized chauvinism with which my hypothesis conflicts is the present fashion in anthropol-

ogy: independent invention. The suggestion that some elements of prehistoric culture might have been transmitted (diffused) over even a few hundred miles of open sea seems to cause something like an allergenic reaction from many scholars. Specialists who work on a particular culture seem to develop a vested interest which impels them to see all local cultural evolution as totally autonomous.

These attitudes remind me of Mark Twain's comment on the idea that man was the noblest work of God: "Well who said that?" Such chauvinism leads to cognitive filters (blinders) which protect the investigator from any evidence which does not fit his own beliefs, in this case about the evolution of man and his culture.

My hypothesis for the planet's prehistory goes as follows: what we call prehistory is but the latest chapter in a period of, perhaps, 100 to 200,000 years of organized human activity on the planet. Within this long span of time, several relatively evolved civilizations have risen and fallen. Afterwards, the evidence for their existence was all but eliminated through earth-changes produced by the planet's geological evolution. Even were evidence to be found, perhaps our criteria for civilization might obscure its meaning. The geological processes required by such a scenario were, until recently,

thought to have run their courses long before man's arrival.

To put it another way, I see the prehistory of the planet somewhere between Jacob Bronowski's linear ascent of man commencing a mere 10,000 years ago in the Fertile Crescent and Erich von Däniken's bizarre script with ancient astronauts and star wars.

During this long period of organized human activity, a series of cataclysmic events were experienced due to small changes in the orbital geometry of this planet. Such events have recently been seen both as the timing mechanism and the cause of the ice ages. Perhaps, changes witnessed in the heavens and associated with these catastrophes led ancient man to precise observations of the skies. If so, the beginning of astronomy was motivated by survival, not superstition.

Incidentally, another possible cause of instability in the earth's crust, as well as a more subtle hazard to the planet's living forms may be the periodic decline in field intensity and reversal of polarity by the earth's magnetic fields. This sequence has apparently occurred at least 177 times and coincides with the termination of geological periods — signalled by the demise of certain life forms. These fields shield the planet's biological forms from cosmic radiation until the time of a reversal. At this point the field would weaken, perhaps pass

through a null point; these changes may take as much as a hundred years. One current prediction for the next reversal is about 2030 A.D.

However offensive the theories of Immanuel Velikovsky may be to many scientists, the evidence from which he theorized is, nonetheless, our heritage from our ancestors on the planet. Add the evidence for careful astronomical observations and the engineering of important structures to withstand earth changes to the worldwide legends and myths of destructive changes affecting mankind from which Velikovsky worked, and the total thrust is sobering.

Paralleling this case is the new awareness in geology and astrophysics of violent change. As Dr. Elizabeth Baity says, "Astrophysics indicates that the concept of the universe as orderly and peaceful is startlingly incorrect; if the interest of ancient man in the heavens and their preoccupation with astra [celestial]-determined predictions seems excessive, we need not deduce thereby that they were less intelligent than ourselves — oral tradition may have given them cause for alarm."

Yet reluctance to view our planetary home as anything but a safe haven in space is certainly understandable. Furthermore it is easy to understand the problems facing the scholars. Every scientific revolution comes hard. The necessary, but radical alterations in conventional views of megalithic man's intellectual capacity required by the findings of archaeoastronomy inevitably lead to fundamental revisions in the history of science. Dr. Thom's discovery of Pythagorean triangles in megalithic structures certainly confuses the history of geometry. Mensuration, observational astronomy, and the calendar, usually attributed to the "literate" civilizations of the Middle East, might have had other origins.

We have seen a variety of megalithic engineering procedures evidently designed to provide architectural stability in the presence of seismic instability. Compared to forty-story steel and glass structures now located in the vicinity of the San Andreas fault in California, the ancients devised nearly imperishable structures. The Maltese temples, located on an island with a history of earthquakes, have survived for thousands of years. In the Andes, until the Spanish invaders stole the interlocking copper and silver keys securing the megalithic structures of Tiahuanaco, they had survived, at the very least estimate, for over eight hundred years. Spanish Colonial architecture in a similar Andean seismic risk area, Cuzco, Peru, lasted only a bit over a century until its first destruction. In 1950, only three centuries later, all but the Inca's masonry fell in another devasting earthquake.

The various techniques devised by the megalithic builders included the use of massive stones (monolithic elements), stones keyed into bedrock, elements carved from the living rock, irregular polygonal masonry, stones keyed together with metal clamps, and mortised and tenoned joints. Compare the results: Tiahuanaco was still standing until wrecked by the Spanish; Sacsahuaman is yet intact, and the essential structure of the Great Pyramid survives after forty-five hundred years. By contrast, our culture builds along interstate highway systems, motels which have been planned with a useful life of ten years for the first owner.

A more subtle matter is the possibility that the ancients were sensitive to the earth's energies and were able to locate their temples so as to derive benefits from these energies and to construct them so as to enhance these energies. Research here has only begun. We know that the ancient Chinese geomancers found certain preferred locations for building. We also know that modern dowsers have found that the earth's magnetic fields vary locally due to ground water and that the standing stones of megalithic culture were sited where the fields generated by such streams intersected. We also have seen that the earth's magnetic field intensity is subtly but measurably affected by this arrangement. In the larger context, we have also seen that major megalithic sites have a significant relationship to the intersections of the planetary grid system. What is the precise nature of the energy which is thus enhanced?

Professor Roger W. Wescott, in a review of Francis Hitching's *Earth Magic,* suggests that while standing stones *do* exhibit magnetic anomalies, their energy may have electromagnetic effects without being wholly or even primarily electromagnetic in nature. He proposed that their energy might be what East European parapsychologists call "psychotronic energy." In three years of my own university research in Kirlian photography I had begun to wonder if the electromagnetic spectrum might not be incomplete. Professor Wescott also sees a possible parallel between the energy of such sites and Wilhelm Reich's "orgone" energy, a biophysical energy with positive effects like those reported from stone and ley line arrangements. Reich's theory also includes an explanation for grassless hills and "fainting spots" — DOR, or deadly orgone energy, which is orgone poisoned by interaction with lethal cosmic rays or underground radioactivity.

In *The Mysteries of Chartres,* Louis Charpentier speculates that the horizontal stone of the megalithic dolmen may function as an accumulator of telluric and cosmic energy. In *The Stones of Atlantis,* I suggested that the dolmen may function as a resonant cavity to amplify such energies. The electronic model which I drew upon here was the magnetron which generates microwave energy. As the evidence accumulated in the present work, I began to realize that many of the dolmens included quartz in their mineral composition. Quartz is a hard, crystalline, vitreous mineral composed of silicon dioxide. It is found worldwide in sandstone, granite, flint, opal, chert, and rock crystal. In electronics circuits, quartz is a commonly used frequency-control, due to the fact that its dimensions determine the frequency to which it responds. All this led me to wonder if the capstones of dolmens were not, in some sense not now understood, a resonant element for these energies. Put another way, does the presence of quartz crystals in many dolmens serve to amplify the energies of such structures?

Finding myself again at a frontier, I asked a sensitive for her impressions of the energy patterns around megalithic structures. The result was the reading included in the first chapter. She had the impression that a radical alteration of consciousness was brought about by the total energies of stone circles. As she saw it clairvoyantly, such an environment was also conducive to the materialization of other beings, a change of state. Such a phenomenon is at least theortetically possible from Einstein's $E=mc^2$. It is also one possible explanation of certain otherwise puzzling reports associated with the UFO problem. The bizarre idea of beings materializing had earlier turned up in the course of psychic readings I supervised at Bimini Island in the Bahamas. These readings ultimately led to the extraterrestrial hypothesis about the influence of the Pleiades on our evolution thirty thousand years ago.

The theme of ancient visitors to earth was one of two major themes of the psychic readings at megalithic sites; the other being prehistoric planetary upheavals. In *The Stones of Atlantis*, I advanced the Pleiades hypothesis. It initially derived from a consensus of three psychics; later, much circumstantial evidence was found in myths, legends, star lore, ancient calendars, and archaeoastronomy. Nothing is thereby proven, but the hypothesis is not inconsistent with the evidence. Since then, evidence has grown to support an ancient global interest in the Pleiades; some of it is included in this book.

Just prior to *The Stones of Atlantis,* two other extraterrestrial theories appeared in works which are both scholarly and scientific: Robert Temple's *The Sirius Mystery* (1976) and Maurice Chatelaine's *Our Ancestors Came From Outer Space* (1978).

Many will prefer more conservative explanations for ancient interest in certain stars or in solar and lunar phenomena. Michanowsky's evidence for the visual impact of the explosion of a super nova, Vela X, some 6,000 years ago and its effect on Sumerian and Egyptian myths is a case in point. In this book we have also observed cases of ancient sites oriented to favor a winter solstice sunrise, sometimes with dramatic effects, as at New Grange. For these probably, the most tenable explanation is a solar cult: the shortest day representing the death of the old year, the subsequent lengthening representing the birth and growth of the new. The Sun's importance to ancient man's survival would have made such a belief potent.

In the Pleiades, however, we have a rather insignificant star cluster which has had a strong impact on the prehistoric mind. Pervasive in Oceanic and Mesoamerican cultures, there is also evidence for its influence in Africa, the British Isles and India. A pioneer archaeoastronomist even claims that the Parthenon was oriented to an earlier Pleiades' rising. A more conservative explanation for all this would be easier if the Pleiades were at least a spectacular asterism.

Appendix A

The Next Archaeological Revolution?

1859, the year Darwin's *On the Origin of Species* was published, also saw the beginning of a new discipline: archaeology. The English geologist, Joseph Prestwich, and the antiquarian, John Evans, visited France in that year and returned to confirm that Boucher de Perthes had indeed found hand-axes located in the same geological layer with the bones of extinct animals at Abbeville. Man's prehistoric past was thereby opened to a vast, unsuspected foreground.

For the next century, the new science of archaeology made incredible inroads into man's prehistory. Understandably, with the maturity of the new science in the twentieth century, came the feeling that the major events of human prehistory (at least in the Old World) were understood, that the outlines of the past had been conquered. In the history of science, the onset of such a static state of satisfaction usually precedes an upset. Such was the climate in physics in the 1880's — just before atomic physics. In 1950, the seemingly solid outlines of prehistory were shattered by a new discovery in radio-chemistry. This was the year that a new dating method developed by the chemist Dr. Willard F. Libby began to be accepted. The new procedure depends on the measurement of radioactive carbon 14, absorbed by once-living organisms and thereafter diminishing at a known rate.

During the decade from 1950 to 1960, the initial radiocarbon revolution was integrated into archaeological dating. Carbon-14 dates immediately upset complicated and painstakingly-established cultural sequences, especially in the Old World. Then, just when the new dating was still being assimilated, a second radiocarbon revolution was forced upon archaeology by important adjustments to the existing carbon-14 dates; they were found to be too young when compared with dates derived from the tree rings of the Bristlecone pine. In 1967 Professor Hans E. Suess at the University of California at San Diego had produced the first tree-ring calibration chart which converted carbon-14 dates to calendar years. This second revolution upset the long-cherished belief that civilization had originated in the Near East (in the Fertile Crescent) and then diffused to Western Europe. In fact, megalithic structures from Malta, to France, and to the United Kingdom are now dated as much as 800 years earlier than megalithic structures in the Near East. This includes the Great Pyramid at Giza — if we take its conventional date of about 2600 B.C.

From its Victorian beginnings, one of the major beliefs of archaeology was taken from Darwin's new evolutionary biology; the idea of cultural evolution which translates as "later equals better" or more highly evolved. For this reason, Victorians pictured our ancestors as exceedingly simple creatures, incapable of abstractions, much less any emotional or spiritual sophistication.

This view was reinforced by the procedures of archaeology. Objects can be related, one to another, in a time sequence, stratigraphically (one above another, therefore later) and an evolutionary sequence established for a particular locale: simple to complex. But what is the *meaning* of these artifacts to those who made them? In the absence of written records, an archaeologist who analyzes any object whose use is beyond the obvious, basic functions, may be nearly helpless. This fact explains the frequency of vague museum labels such as "Cult object" or "used for religious purposes."

Because of the limitations of present archaeological methods, particularly where information is sought about consciousness, I believe that the next revolution in archaeology will involve the use of psychic data both in the field and in theorizing about field results. In *The Stones of Atlantis* I explain my own use of psychics. This new approach may help solve a major question in prehistory.

In effect, based on current archaeology, prehistory tells us that suddenly, without any significant preparation, 30,000 to 40,000 years ago Cro-Magnon Man created art.

Then, later, writing suddenly appeared with the cuneiform of Mesopotamia and Egyptian hieroglyphics. Also about this time something near science in mathematics and astronomy suddenly developed among the Mesopotamians, the Egyptians, the early Chinese, and, much later, in the New World. With Alexander Marshack and others, I feel that this "suddenness" is a bit far-fetched, that there must have been a long period of preparation. Probably, also, due to natural catastrophies and wars, now unknown but evolved cultures must have risen, only to fall. Marshack is also likely on the right track when he says that the brain potential of Ice-Age man was really not less than that of man today. This recognition helps us to reconsider the current low estimate of early man's consciousness. Marshack has shown that Cro-Magnon man, in addition to his capacity for artistic expression, had the ability to observe the phases of the moon and to preserve his observations with a system of notation. Most recently, Marshack analyzed artwork on a piece of bone found in France and dating back to 135,000 B.C.!

Reconstruction of the consciousness of prehistoric man is crucial to our full understanding of the meaning of human existence on this planet. Yet, when it comes to this objective, conventional archaeology is severely limited. It might help to redefine one of the discipline's major assumptions: cultural evolution. Although the general development of culture over the past 10,000 years has been upward, it might be less limiting to view cultural evolution as *change through time,* without con-

notations of change for the better (or worse). After all, that individual cultures have regressed is a matter of historical record.

In addition to revising this assumption of archaeology, the limits of its methods must also be spotlighted. It cannot be said too often that the procedures of the discipline force it (and therefore prehistorians) to define culture in terms of hardware, or material goods, instead of software, or the consciousness of the culture. Here, of course, the archaeologist, in comparison with the anthropologist interviewing living tribes, faces enormous difficulties. Thus, it is likely that a culture with a very simple material existence yet a complex inner life (mental or spiritual) would yield very little of its true nature (its software) to the present mode of inquiry. This difficulty would be compounded if the culture's beliefs fell into the camp of philosophic idealism as distinguished from materialism. Assuming that methodological problems were overcome and that the culture's software were to be fully known, even then the evidence might be filtered out (even unconsciously) or inferences drawn from it labeled as "superstition."

In other words, the software (or the consciousness) of culture cannot always be learned from its hardware. This fact is beginning to motivate a third revolution in archaeology, one which has already seen a healthy beginning. By 1974 professional papers were being presented on the use of psychics in the field. Recently a new journal receptive to psychic archaeology has been initiated. It is called *Phoenix: New Directions in*

the Study of Man (880 Lathrop Drive, Stanford, Ca. 94305).

Accompanying this revolution is an ongoing revision of our assumptions about cultural evolution. Several basic elements were recently challenged by Marvin Harris, Columbia University anthropologist and author of *Cannibals and Kings: The Origin of Cultures.* These elements include the ascent of man, the inevitability of progress, and the triumph of technology. In particular, Professor Harris attacks the idea of progress. In the past 30,000 years new technologies have evolved, he says, to repair the damage of earlier technologies. For example, Harris does not see agriculture as a clever invention on the road to civilization. Instead, it was man's only option 13,000 years ago when he had squandered his big-game resources by hunting many species into extinction. In this, Harris expands an idea suggested by the paleontologist, Loren Eiseley, in 1970. Harris also views the life of Stone-Age man as healthier than that of many following cultures. This kind of thinking represents a direct challenge to the assumptions of widely-accepted works like Jacob Bronowski's *The Ascent of Man.*

Within the next decade these new developments in contemporary theorizing about prehistory could well lead to a new conception of man's evolution on this planet. In the process, man could emerge as a being who is not simply a slave of his biological and social development; he may also come to be seen as a creature who is working out a spiritual evolution.

Appendix B

Survey Accuracy in Archaeoastronomy

Geographical coordinates in the present work have been taken from nautical charts, Ordnance Survey maps (in the United Kingdom), United States Defense Mapping Agency charts, large scale local maps, and, in some cases, celestial observations reported from the sites themselves. My intention was to provide coordinates sufficiently accurate for preliminary calculations from astronomical tables. I assume that any serious worker would eventually take his own astronomical observations with a theodolite on the site.

As for the accuracy of many present archaeological site survey maps for archaeoastrotomy purposes, those done for other purposes (before the precision of megalithic astronomy was recognized), are often misleading. Dr. Alexander Thom, in the course of surveying over 600 megalithic sites in England and France, set a new standard. He found sites with an accuracy in their original layout of 1 in 1,000. As Professor Thom says, "Only an experienced surveyor with good equipment is likely to attain this sort of accuracy." Thus, valid conclusions about the astronomical implications of a particular site depend on accurate modern surveys.

Appendix C

Two Archaeological Controversies: The Monsters of Acambaro and The Stones of Ica

There are two collections of artifacts which the archaeological world has not accepted as authentic. If these collections were to become a part of the evidence for the planet's prehistory, some radical revisions of New World prehistory will be necessary. Some of the reasons for this rejection which Professor Charles H. Hapgood gave in connection with the Acambaro collection also apply to the strange stones of Ica:

1 The artifacts relate to no known culture.

2 The Acambaro collection represents the largest group of pieces ever found in such a small area (Over 32,000 pieces in a few acres); to a lesser extent the Ica collection presents the same problem (Over 11,000 pieces found in a relatively small area).

3 The Acambaro collection is without precedent in the survival of delicate work buried underground; the Ica stones are relatively rugged, being carved of water-worn boulders.

4 At Acambaro, the patina from earth salts usually acquired by buried objects is missing. This may be the result of the farmer who found them having washed all before delivery.

In addition to their sheer numbers, both collections share two other parallels: neither gives any indication of agriculture; both display giant reptiles (of species usually thought to be extinct by the time of man's appearance) *and* human beings together. The idea that, in two widely-separated locations of the New World, *two* fraudulent collections with so many common, yet distinct, features, collections adding up to over 40,000 pieces, are both the result of fraud is truly overwhelming!

The pottery and figures of Acambaro are fully detailed in a monograph by Charles H. Hapgood, *Mystery at Acambaro* (1973). About 1945 a German national, Waldemar Julsrud, then a hardware dealer residing in Acambaro, Mexico, was given a strange pottery figure by a farmer named Odilon Tinajero. Before the affair was over, Julsrud came into possession of over 32,000 objects of stone, pottery, jade, and obsidian. Some of these are as small as a few inches in length; others, stone statues, are as much as four to five feet in height. No effort was apparently made by Julsrud to commercialize upon this bizarre collection. In 1955 Professor Hapgood spent the entire summer analyzing the collection. He found dinosaurs and men in close association, women being attacked by reptiles, and men and women in relations with reptiles that suggested an early worship of them. He also found pottery scenes indicating a climate very different from the present. Woodland and lakeland fauna were represented; the present location is quite arid. The reptiles seemed to be of the Mesozoic Era. Elsewhere, in *The Path of the Poles* (1970), Professor Hapgood has shown a possible basis for the anomalous survival of species in some geographical locations, despite the extinction of the same species elsewhere.

There was enough vegetable matter in some of the pottery to attempt radiocarbon dating. The results ranged between 4530 and 1110 B.C. A bit later, Professor Hapgood was able to arrange for a new test, thermoluminescence, a system which gave two dates clustering around 2500 B.C.

Three years after the publication of Professor Hapgood's monograph, an article by Gary W. Carriveau and Mark C. Han in *American Antiquity* challenged the validity of these dates. In fact the writers went so far as to suggest that the pottery had been fired shortly before its discovery.

At the present writing, Professor Hapgood has a book in progress which will question these conclusions.

Thousands of miles to the south, near the mysterious markings on the plains of Nazca, about 300 km south of Lima, there is situated on oasis town, Ica. Facing the public square, is the private museum of Dr. José Cabrera, a surgeon who practises in the local government hospital. In

Dr. Cabrera's museum are to be found some very bizarre stones. Carved upon them are cultural, geological, and technological themes which call into question all of our conceptions of the prehistory of South America. Indians are seen attacking long-extinct dinosaurs; one carving accurately represents the extinct Brontosaurus. Other Indians are carrying out heart transplants and Caesarian sections while the patient is helped by acupuncture anesthesia. In a map of the world, we see the original continent, Pangaea, which existed before the continents drifted away to their present configuration. Another stone shows an Indian studying the heavens with a telescope. During our visit, Dr. Cabrera told us that, among other celestial objects, the Pleiades were included.

In his own country, Dr. Cabrera is under attack by those who claim that his 11,000 stones are fraudulent, that they were carved for him. Cabrera himself showed me a recent feature from the Sunday magazine of Lima's *La Prensa* which alleged that he had paid an Italian to create the spurious artifacts. Photos of the Indian manufacturing them were published by *La Prensa*. Since Cabrera has apparently not sold any of these stones and charges a modest admission to his museum, such accusations seem to be pointless in terms of motive.

At this writing, separate micros-

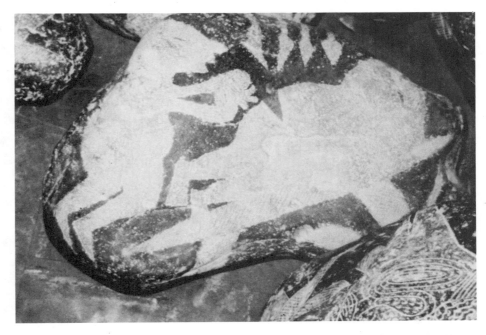

copic analyses have produced contradictory results. One investigator says the carvings are very old; another claims they are sharp and modern. One student of prehistory, J.R. Jochmans, claims that a Jesuit missionary, Father Simon who accompanied Pizarro along the Peruvian coast in 1525, saw these stones.

Both of these extraordinary collections deserve further objective analysis. Their potential importance should call out the most disinterested consideration among specialists.

135 Some of Cabrera's 11,000 engraved stones. Here, according to Cabrera, a heart transplant.

136 Two other surgical procedures.

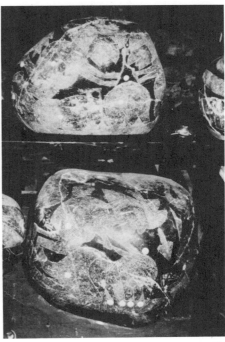

137 *According to Cabrera, a map of*
Pangaea, the original continent, as it
separated.

Glossary

American Stonehenge A stone circle in Wyoming. The Big Horn Medicine Wheel, dated about 1760 A.D. which has been demonstrated to have important astronomical alignments including the summer solstice and the heliacal risings of three stars: Aldebaran, Sirius, and Rigel.

Arawaks At the time Columbus first visited the New World, the Caribbean was inhabited by two simple Indian cultures, the warlike and cannibilistic Caribs and the peaceful Arawaks. The Caribs were in the lesser Antilles and the Arawaks in the Greater Antilles (Cuba, Hispaniola, Jamaica and Puerto Rico). Remnants of a more primitive tribe, the Ciboneys, were found in Cuba. The Arawaks had thatched huts, baskets, pottery and dugout canoes; their religion was concerned with healing.

Archaic Period North American archaeological term for the period from c. 7000 B.C. to c. 1000 B.C. characterized by plant-collecting and small-game hunting. Followed by local cultures such as Hohokam, Mound Builders, etc.

astrophysics The physics of stellar and solar system phenomena.

Azilian-Tardenoisian An Old World Mesolithic culture which followed the Magdalenian culture and existed from about 8000 B.C. to 6000 B.C. It was located on the Iberian Peninsula.

ancient measures	
Egyptian royal cubit	= .524 meter (20.63 inches)
Greek or geographic cubit	= .462 meter (18.19 inches)
Egyptian foot	= .300 meter (11.81 inches)
Greek or geographic foot	= .308 meter (12.13 inches)
Megalithic yard	= .84 meter (33.07 inches)
600 geographic feet	= 1 stadium

Aztec A Mexican culture decimated by Cortes in 1521 when the Spanish conquistador destroyed their capital city, Tenochtitlan.

Basques A Spanish people whose language seems to represent a linguistic "fossil" unrelated to the other European languages. For this reason, the language has been claimed as a remnant of Atlantis.

beach rock A limestone composed of a shell-hash cemented together by the calcium carbonate of supersaturated sea water. Formed in the tidal zone, beach rock is alternately covered and uncovered by the sea. It forms on a slope and develops a parallel system of furrows at right angles to the beach line. In the Caribbean these furrows in beach rock are typically spaced about 60

cm (c. 24 inches) and would therefore divide the blocks every two feet. The blocks of the Paradise Point megalithic site are 3 - 4 m (about 10 - 13 feet).

Bronze Age An Old World cultural period based on the use of tools made of bronze (an alloy of copper and tin) which began in the Near East at about 3000 B.C. and then spread east and west. The period, followed by the Iron Age, lasted until about 1000 B.C.

carbon-14 dating method Carbon 14 is the radioactive isotope of the inert carbon 12; both are present in the same proportion in living organisms. When an organism dies C-14 begins to diminish at a fixed rate. Back to about 50,000 years, the proportion of the C-14 to C-12 will give the approximate date of the death of the organism. Through the comparison of C-14 dates with those derived from dendrochronology (an exact dating from counting tree rings) it was learned that, because of a higher proportion of C-14 before 2000 years ago, carbon-14 dates are too young; for example, at 3000 B.C., 500 - 1000 years must be added.

Cayce, Edgar (1877 - 1945) America's foremost psychic, the success of whose thousands of medical and spiritual readings for people sometimes thousands of miles away lends considerable plausibility to his clairvoyant accounts of prehistory.

His account of Atlantis adds an exotic technology to Plato's legend. Recent archaeological and geological findings have continued to add to Cayce's credibility in prehistory.

cist A megalithic rectangular container formed of stone slabs for burial.

continental drift An idea first suggested by Francis Bacon in 1620 who thought that the Americas, Africa and Europe had once been united. As a scientific hypothesis, continental drift was fully developed by Alfred Wegener in 1912. Wegener thought that all continents were joined in one original mass, Pangaea ("all earth"), gradually separating as they floated apart on the viscous magma underneath them. Supported by paleobotanists but denied by geologists and geophysicists until the 1960's, the theory has finally begun to be widely accepted because of the work in paleomagnetism. When the plates spread out from their sea floor boundaries (as in the mid-Atlantic ridge) the molten material from the asthenosphere cools down, locking in a magnetic "recording" of the geomagnetic fields in existence at the time. As they move out, these "recordings" show the same polarity on each side of the rift and also tell of ancient field-reversals. Thus the movement of the plates can be shown (and dated). (See "Paleomagnetic record" and "Plate Tectonics")

core samples (In geology and oceanography) cylindrical sections of ocean-bottom sediments taken by coring tubes (or rock taken by hollow core drills) for analysis of their constituents.

cosmology In philosophy, the study of the origins, processes and structure of the universe; in astrophysics the study of the structure and dynamic processes of the universe.

Cro-Magnon Man An early form of modern man (Homo Sapiens) first found in southern France about 34,000 B.C. Cro-Magnon man "suddenly" appeared with skills in art and music. These sub-cultures were at once obvious: Chatelperronian, Aurignacian and Perigordian. The last was the Magdalenian which ended about 10,000 B.C.

Diffusion Theory In anthropology a theory dramatically opposed to the idea of the independent invention of similar cultural traits such as pyramids in different parts of the world. The diffusionist would explain similar cultural traits in different locations by migrations of people, often by sea. In practice, these extreme theoretical positions are seldom found. Today the tide seems to run with the independent inventionists.

dolmen like the cist, believed to have been constructed for burial purposes but a more open structure with three or four (sometimes more) vertical stones supporting a capstone.

equinox (vernal and autumnal) Times in the spring and fall when the sun crosses the equator (March and September) and days and nights are of equal duration.

fathometer A marine electronics device for recording water depths beneath a vessel.

Fertile Crescent Theory The idea that civilization first began in the Near East about 10,000 years ago. As explained by Jacob Bronowski in *The Ascent of Man,* it was facilitated by a hybrid wheat.

Gaunches A people found by the Spaniards who visit visited the Canary Islands in the fifteenth century. The Gaunches had a legend about a universal catastrophe and were surprised when the Spanish arrived that they were not the only survivors. Curiously, though an island people, they were not a seafaring group. Like Plato's Atlanteans, they once had ten kings.

geomagnetic event A relatively short-term reversal of polarity in the earth's magnetic field.

geophysics The study of the physics of earth phenomena, including the subject of meteorology, seismology, oceanography and paleomagnetism.

"Glomar Challenger" A research ship with the capability of drilling core samples in the ocean floor anywhere in the world.

Gothenburg magnetic flip A rapid geomagnetic reversal which occurred at about 10,350 B.C.

heliacal rising of a star Observation of a star as it clears the horizon just before the sunrise obscures the observed body.

joint (geology) A natural crack or fracture in rock without lateral displacement along its line, as distinguished from a fault where vertical or lateral displacement has occurred. (masonry) The space between bricks or cut stone which may be filled with mortar or left dry and closely fitted. In geology, the joint is the result of natural processes; in masonry human agency is involved. Distinguishing between the two is simple, provided the structure is intact or unaffected by environment. Such is not the case at Bimini.

Lucayan The simple Indian culture found in the Bahamas at the arrival of Columbus. Generally thought to be a part of a circum-Caribbean culture, the Arawaks (which see).

Magdalenian Culture The last of the Cro-Magnon cultures: began about 16,000 B.C. and ended about 10,000 B.C. (See Cro-Magnon man)

magnetic anomaly Due to the fact that the north magnetic pole is not at the geographic North Pole, the needle of a compass does not point true north. Instead, it points to magnetic north, either east or west of true north. This is called "variation" and is charted for all positions on the earth's surface. When the compass needle indicates more than the charted variation at a particular location, a magnetic anomaly exists, due to ferrous metal ores or other magnetic influences. Plate boundaries also exhibit magnetic anomalies. The causes of certain magnetic anomalies are still to be determined such as those which recently attracted a joint U.S.-U.S.S.R. expedition to the Bermuda Triangle area.

Maya A Mexican and Central American civilization which flourished in the Yucatan Peninsula of Mexico and the adjacent highlands of the Pacific slope from about A.D. 250 to 900, then mysteriously disappeared. Recently in Belize the origins of Maya culture have been pushed back to 4000 B.C. The Maya left evidence of a surprising level of astronomy and mathematics and produced a calendar which, due to constant astronomical corrections, was more accurate than our own.

Megalithic culture The term "megalithic" came into British archaeological usage in the nineteenth century. It derives from two Greek words, *megas* (great) and *lithos*

(stone). Megalithic culture is usually located in Western Europe and the United Kingdom, beginning about 4000 B.C. and continuing to about 2000 B.C. Gallery graves, passage graves, and dolmens are characteristic of the early part of the period; stone circles like Stonehenge and single standing stones the latter part. These later constructions are made of large, roughly dressed or natural stones. In the present work the term is expanded to include a variety of other sites elsewhere in the world. The expansion is both in time and geography. Included are New World sites such as Mystery Hill in New Hampshire, Machu Picchu in Peru and Tiahuanaco in Bolivia; Old World sites such as Malta and the Pyramid of Cheops; and Pacific sites like Easter Island and Ponapé in the Carolines. In expanding the term, it has obviously been denuded of certain cultural assumptions. Other than the above noted elements, the remaining element which many of them share is the presence of important astronomical alignments on the site. Aside from the stated elements, no other common cultural traits are assumed in the present usage with the exception of a possible shared sensitivity to the earth's energy system.

mid-Atlantic Ridge A submarine feature running roughly north and south in the Atlantic Ocean which is the active boundary of two plates spreading to the east and the west accompanied by volcanic and earthquake activity. This feature coincides with a portion of the planetary grid system.

monolithic shaped from one piece of stone, such as a sculpture.

Nazca A village of the coastal plains south of Lima, Peru nearby which are found a mysterious set of lines outlining geometric and biological shapes. Some important astronomical orientations including the Pleiades have been found. The Nazca culture is usually dated between 200 B.C. and 700 A.D.

Oceania islands of the central, western, and southern Pacific, usually including Australia and New Zealand.

orthostat upright block or slab of stone used in various megalithic constructions including tombs.

Paleo-Indian (Or Early Hunter) North American archaeological term for big-game hunters from the arrival of man until about 7000 B.C.

paleomagnetic record When igneous or volcanic rock cools below a certain temperature and solidifies, it records the magnetic lines of force

the old Imperial Palace of Constantinople (now Istanbul) in 1929, the map was apparently based on earlier maps dating back at least to Alexandrian Greek sources which were doubtless destroyed with the famous library at Alexandria.

plate tectonics The geological study of the earth's crustal movements: it is a theoretical refinement upon continental drifts. Instead of continental plates, the new concept visualizes the movements of plates, huge floating crusts, some of which carry along continents over the plastic layer below (the upper mantle or asthenosphere). The plates make up the crust (or lithosphere). In plate tectonics, the plates are deforming, shearing, separating or sliding under one another with accompanying seismic (or earthquake) activity.

precession of the equinoxes The phenomenon of precession, the conical motion of the earth's axis, leads to an apparent backward motion of the constellations of the zodiac. Each year at the spring equinox (which see), the constellation in the sky where the sun rises (due east) appears to have fallen back about fifty seconds of arc. One complete cycle takes about 26,000 years.

prehistoric In the present work, this term is expanded beyond conventional archaeological usage to include all human activities

Mesoamerican (Middle-American) Archaeological Periods	
Post-Classic (Began with Toltecs, ends with Aztecs)	c. 900 to Conquest (1519-42)
Classic (Includes Maya)	*From* 100 A.D. in Central Mexico, later elsewhere *To* 900 A.D. with collapse of Maya.
Preclassic (Formative) Farming villages and pottery appear. Olmecs about 1200 B.C.	c. 2000 B.C. to 300 A.D.
Incipient Agriculture	c. 6000 B.C. to 2000 B.C.
Palaeo-Indian Begins with a campsite at Tlapacoya, Basin of Mexico	c. 20,000 B.C. to c. 6000 B.C.

necropolis a city of the dead; applied to large cemeteries.

obelisk A tapered pillar, sometimes four-sided, used by ancient astronomers to measure the sun's shadow-length and to determine the solstices and equinoxes.

(and their polarity) of the earth's field at the time of cooling.

Piri Re'is map A map drawn in 1513 which shows both sides of South America before European explorations had discovered such geographical information. Found in

before the now-known recorded history.

sacred engineering The technology for the inclusion of a sacred geometry (which see) in a megalithic structure.

sacred geometry John Michell's term for ancient sacred architecture which has encoded within it various sacred numbers and geometric shapes, is situated at terrestrial power points on the earth's surface, and is aligned to favor certain astronomical phenomena.

Shining Ones Superior beings who, according to esoteric traditions of prehistory, once functioned as teachers or leaders. They were said to be luminous in appearance (less material in form because closer to energy than matter?)

solar cult Said of a culture whose religion centers on the worship of the sun as the creative principle of the universe which may be taken as masculine or feminine depending upon the culture. The former is more usual in which case the moon would be seen as feminine (might be the focus of a lunar cult).

solstice The two times of the year, summer and winter (June and December), when the sun rises at its greatest declination (south or north) of the equator.

Sons of Belial In Cayce's version of Atlantis, the Sons of Belial were dedicated to materialistic pursuits

such as greed, selfishness and the sexual manipulation of others. As Atlantis declined, the Sons of Belial opposed the Sons of the Law of One (which see).

Sons of the Law of One In Cayce's version of Atlantis, the Sons of the Law of One sought to preserve the original spiritual and moral understanding of the early Atlantis which was monotheistic. In the latter days of Atlantis they were opposed by the Sons of Belial whose divisive, destructive tendencies finally prevailed.

tektites Tiny fused glass shapes found in ocean-bottom sediments. They entered the earth's atmosphere as a fiery shower striking an area from the South China Sea to Australia and the tip of South Africa about 700,000 years ago. This was also the time of a reversal of the earth's magnetic field and, perhaps, the beginning of the most recent succession of Ice Ages. This horrendous event could have been seen by Java man. Theories about the origins of the tektites include the demise of a comet in the earth's atmosphere or debris from the moon's surface resulting from a meteorite's impact.

Teotihuacán The largest urban site in Middle American culture. Located in the Valley of Mexico northeast of Mexico City, it dominated the region between A.D. 300 and 750 when it was destroyed.

Some few investigators date its original construction as early as 4000 B.C.; the conventional date is 150 B.C. Astronomical and mathematical analysis of the site have revealed a very sophisticated knowledge of physics, mathematics, the solar system, and the universe.

thermoluminescence A dating method for ceramics or other objects which have been fired in an oven or kiln. Various types of cosmic radiation are absorbed into mineral crystals, especially in the clay of pottery. The radiation causes structural changes in the ring of electrons composing the clay. In the laboratory, when the structure is disturbed again (or excited), light is emitted in proportion to the original radiation. From this process an approximate age can be determined. In the present state of the art, the method is less precise than C-14. Thermoluminescence-dating measures time elapsed since pottery last heated over 500°C.

trilithon an element of megalithic constructions composed of two upright stones, capped or crossed by a lintel.

Bibliography

Books

Andrews, George F. *Maya Cities: Placemaking and Urbanization.* Norman, Oklahoma: University of Oklahoma Press, 1975.

Atkinson, R.J.C. *Stonehenge.* London: Hamish Hamilton, 1956.

Aveni, Anthony F. *Native American Astronomy.* Austin, Texas: University of Texas Press, 1977.

Aveni, Anthony F. *et al. Archaeoastronomy in Pre-Columbian America.* Austin, University of Texas Press, 1975.

Barocas, C. *Monuments of Civilization: Egypt.* New York: Grosset and Dunlap, 1972.

Bennett, W.C. *Excavations at Tiahuanaco.* Anthropological Papers, American Museum of Natural History, Vol. 34, Part 3. New York: 1934.

Bingham, Hiram. *Across South America.* Boston and New York: Houghton Mifflin, 1911.

——————————— . *Lost City of the Incas: The Story of Machu Picchu and Its Builders.* New York: Antheneum, 1963.

Breasted, James H. *A History of Egypt From the Earliest Times to the Persian Conquest.* New York: Charles Scribners Sons, 1909.

——————————— . *Development of Religion and Thought in Ancient Egypt.* New York: Gloucester, Mass: P. Smith, 1970.

——————————— . *Ancient Records of Egypt.* 5 Vols. New York: Russell and Russell, 1962.

Brown, Peter Lancaster. *Megaliths, Myths and Men.* New York: Taplinger, 1976.

Budge, E.A. Wallis. *History of Egypt.* London: Keagan Paul, Trench, Trubner, 1928.

——————————— . *The Gods of the Egyptians.* 2 Vols. New York: Dover Publishers, 1969.

——————————— . *Egyptian Religion.* New Hyde Park, New York: University Books, 1959.

——————————— . *Egyptian Magic.* Evanston, Ill.: University Books, 1958.

——————————— . *Osiris: The Egyptian Religion of Resurrection.* New Hyde

Park, New York: University Books, 1961. (Original - 1911 - *Osiris and the Egyptian Resurrection.*)

Cabrera Darquea, Javier. *El Mensaje de las Piedras Grabadas de Ica,* Lima, Peru: Inti-Sol Editores, 1976.

Charpentier, Louis. *The Mysteries of Chartres Cathedral.* Tr. by Ronald Fraser, New York: Avon Books, 1975.

Chatelain, Maurice. *Nos Acêtres Venus du Cosmos.* Paris: Robert Laffont, 1975.

Cieza de Léon, Pedro de. *The Incas.* trans. Norman, Okla.: University of Oklahoma Press, 1959.

Clark, Grahame. *World Prehistory: A New Outline.* Cambridge: At the University Press, 1971.

Cook, Warren L. (ed.) *Ancient Vermont: Proceedings of the Castleton Conference, Castleton State College, October 14-15, 1977.* Rutland, Vermont: Castleton State College, 1978.

Corliss, William R. *Ancient Man: A Handbook of Puzzling Artifacts.* Glen Arm, Maryland: The Sourcebook Project, 1978.

Daniel, Glyn. *The Idea of Prehistory.* Cleveland: World Pub. Company, 1963.

David, Rosalie. *The Egyptian Kingdoms.* Oxford: Elsevier — Phaidon, 1975.

Deacon, A. Bernard. *Malekula: A Vanishing People in the New Hebrides.* Edited by Camilla H. Wedgwood. Oosterhout N.B. The Netherlands: Anthropological Publications, 1970.

deCamp, L. Sprague and Catherine C. deCamp. *Ancient Ruins and Archaeology.* Garden City, New York: Doubleday and Company, 1964.

Edwards, I.E.S. *The Pyramids of Egypt.* Harmondsworth, Middlesex, England: Penguin Books, 1961. Rev. Edition.

Engel, Frederic André. *An Ancient World Preserved: Relics and Records of Prehistory in the Andes.* Trans. Rachel Kendall Gordon, New York: Crown, 1976.

Evans, J.D. *The Prehistoric Antiquities of the Maltese Islands.* London: Athlone Press, 1972.

Fawcett, Col. P.H. *Lost Trails, Lost Cities.* Ed. by Brian Fawcett. New York: Funk and Wagnalls, 1953.

Fell, Barry. *America B.C.: Ancient Settlers in the New World.* New York: New York Times Book Company, 1977.

Fergusson, James. *Rude Stone Monuments in All Countries.* London: John Murray, 1872.

Fix, W.R. *Pyramid Odyssey.* New York: Mayflower Books, 1978.

Formosa, Gerald. *The Megalithic Monuments of Malta.* Vancouver: Skorba, 1975.

Fox, Hugh. *Gods of the Catacylsm.* New York: Harper's Magazine Press, 1976.

Garcia Valadés, Adrian, *Teotihuacán: The City of the Gods.* Mexico City: Edicones Orto, 1978. Seventh Edition.

Goodman, Jeffrey D. *Psychic Archaeology.* New York: G.P. Putnam's Sons, 1977.

Gordon, Cyrus H. *Before Columbus: Links Between the Old World and Ancient America.* New York: Crown Publishers, 1971.

——————. *Riddles in History.* New York: Crown Publishers, 1974.

Hadingham, Evan. *Circles and Standing Stones: An Illustrated Exploration of Megalithic Mysteries of Early Britain.* New York: Walker and Company, 1975.

Hapgood, Charles H. *Mystery in Acambaro: An Account of the Ceramic Collection of the Late Waldemar Julsrud in Acambaro, Guanajuato, Mexico.* A privately published monograph. Winchester, N.H.: 1973.

——————. *The Path of the Pole.* Rev. ed. of *Earth's Shifting Crust.* Philadelphia: Chilton Books, 1970.

Harbison, Peter. *The Archaeology of Ireland.* London, Sydney, Toronto: The Bodley Head, 1976.

Hardoy, Jorge E. *Pre-Columbian Cities.* New York: Walker and Company, 1973.

Hawkes, Jacquetta. *Atlas of Ancient Archaeology.* New York: McGraw-Hill, 1974.

——————. *The Atlas of Early Man.* New York: St. Martin's Press, 1976.

Hawkins, Gerald S. *Stonehenge Decoded.* New York: Doubleday and Company, 1965.

——————. *Beyond Stonehenge.* New York: Harper and Row, 1973.

Herm, Gerhard, *The Celts,* New York: St. Martin's Press, 1976, German ed. 1975.

Heyerdahl, Thor. *Aku-Aku: The Secret of Easter Island.* London: George Allen and Unwin, 1958.

——————. *The Art of Easter Island.* Garden City, New York: Doubleday and Company, 1975. Foreword by Henri Lavachery.

Hitching, Francis. *Earth Magic.* New York: William Morrow, 1977.

Hodson, Geoffrey. *The Kingdom of the Gods.* Madras, India: The Theosophical Publishing House, 1953.

Hoyle, Fred. *On Stonehenge*. San Francisco, California: W.H. Freeman, 1977.

Irwin, Constance. *Fair Gods and Stone Faces*. New York: St. Martin's Press, 1963.

James, T.G.H. *Myths and Legends of Ancient Egypt,* London: Hamlin, 1969.

Jobes, Gertrude and James. *Outer Space: Myths, Name Meanings, Calendars; From the Emergence of History to the Present Day*. New York: Scarecrow Press, 1964.

Kininmonth, Christopher. *The Traveller's Guide to Malta and Gozo*.

Kosok, Paul. *Life, Land and Water in Ancient Peru*. New York: Long Island University Press, 1965.

Krieger, Herbert W. *Island Peoples of the Western Pacific: Micronesia and Melanesia*. Washington, D.C. Smithsonian Institution, 1943.

Krupp, E.C. (ed.). *In Search of Ancient Astronomies*. Garden City, New York: Doubleday and Company, 1977.

Layard, John. *Stone Men of Malekula*. London: Chatto and Windus, 1942.

Lewis, Harrison. *Ancient Malta: A Study of Its Antiquities*. Lovely drawings by Hilda Bruhm Lewis. Gerrards, Cross, Bucks, England: Colin Smythe, 1977.

Linton, Ralph. *Archaeology of the Marquesas Islands*. Honolulu, Hawaii: B.P. Bishop Museum, 1925.

MacKie, Euan W. *Science and Society in Prehistoric Britain*. London: Paul Elek, 1977.

Marshack, Alexander. *The Roots of Civilization*. New York: McGraw-Hill, 1972.

Mazière, Francis. *Mysteries of Easter Island*. New York: Tower Publications, c. 1968.

Meggers, Betty. *Ecuador*. New York: Praeger, 1966.

Mendelssohn, Kurt. *The Riddle of the Pyramids*. New York: Praegar, 1974.

Métraux, Alfred. *Easter Island: A Stone Age Civilization of the Pacific*. London: 1957.

Michanowsky, George. *The Once and Future Star*. New York: Hawthorn Books, 1977.

Michell, John. *The Earth Spirit*. London: Thames and Hudson, 1975.

_____ . *The View Over Atlantis*. New York: Ballantine, 1973.

_____ . *A Little History of Astro-archaeology*. London: Thames and Hudson, 1977.

Morrill, Sibley S. *Ponape*. San Francisco: Cadleon Press, 1970.

Newall, R.S. *Stonehenge: Wiltshire*. London: Her Majesty's Stationery Office, 1971. Reprint of 1959 ed.

Niel, Fernand. *The Mysteries of Stonehenge,* tr. Lowell Bain. New York: Avon, 1975.

O'Kelly, Claire. *Passage Grave Art in the Boyne Valley*. Wexford: John English and Company, 1975.

——————— . *Concise Guide to Newgrange*. Wexford: John English and Company, 1976 (abridged from 1971 edition).

Pepper, Elizabeth and John Wilcox. *Magical & Mystical Sites: Europe and the British Isles*. New York: Harper and Row, 1977.

Ponting, Gerald and Margaret. *The Standing Stones of Callanish*. Stornoway, Isle of Lewis: Essprint Ltd., 1977.

Posener, Georges (ed.) *Dictionary of Egyptian Civilization*. New York: Tudor Publishing Company, n.d. Trans. from French by Alix Macfarlane. French ed. 1959.

Reichel-Dolmatoff, Gerardo. *San Agustin; A Culture of Colombia*. London: Thames & Hudson, 1972.

Renfrew, Colin. *Before Civilization: The Radiocarbon Revolution and Prehistoric Europe*. New York: Alfred A. Knopf, 1973.

Ribera, Antonio. *Operacion Rapa-Nui*. Barcelona, Spain: Editorial Pomaire, 1975.

Riley, Carroll L. *et al.* (eds.) *Man Across the Sea: Problems of Pre-Columbian Contacts*. Austin University of Texas Press, 1971.

Rowe, John Howland. *Inca Culture at the Time of the Spanish Conquest*. Vol. II of *Handbook of South American Indians*. Washington, D.C.: Smithsonian Institution, 1946.

——————— . *An Introduction to the Archaeology of Cuzco*. Papers of the Peabody Museum of American Archaeology and Ethnology, Vol. 27, No. 2. Cambridge: Harvard University Press, 1944.

Sanginés, Carlos Ponce. *Descripcion Sumaria Del Templete Semisubterraneo de Tiwanaku*. Cuarta edicion, revisada Cochabamba, La Paz, Bolivia: Libreria Los Amigos del Libro'. 1969.

Sanginés, Carlos Ponce *et al. Procedencia de la Areniscas Utilizadas en el Templo Precolumbino de Pumapunku*. La Paz, Bolivia: Academia Nacional de Ciencias de Bolivia, 1971.

Schwartz, Stephen. *Psychic Archaeology*. New York: Grossett and Dunlap, 1977.

Shutler, Ralph, Jr., and Mary Elizabeth Shutler. *Oceanic Prehistory*. Menlo Park, California: Cummings Publishing Company, 1975.

Suggs, Robert Carl. *The Hidden Worlds of Polynesia: The Chronicle of an Archaeological Expedition to Nuku Hiva in the Marquesas Islands*. New York: Harcourt, Brace, 1962.

Temple, Robert K.G. *The Sirius Mystery*. London: Sidgwick and Jackson, 1976.

Thom, Alexander. *Megalithic Sites in Britain*. New York: Oxford University Press, 1967.

——————— . *Megalithic Lunar Observatories*. New York: Oxford University Press, 1971.

Tomas, Andrew. *We Are Not the First: Riddles of Ancient Science.* New York: Putnams, 1971.

Tompkins, Peter. *Secrets of the Great Pyramid.* New York: Harper and Row, 1971.

—————— . *Mysteries of the Mexican Pyramids.* New York: Harper and Row, 1976.

Trump, David H. *Malta: An Archaeological Guide.* London: Faber, 1972.

Underwood, Guy. *The Pattern of the Past.* London: Sphere Books, 1972. (Reprinted 1977).

Van der Veer, M.H.J. & P. Moerman. *Hidden Worlds.* New York: Bantam, 1973.

von Hagen, Victor W. *Realm of the Incas.* New York: Mentor Books, 1957.

de la Vega, Garcilaso. *The Incas.* ed. by Alain Gheerbrant. New York: Avon, 1961.

de Velasco, Juan. *Historia Antiqua.* Tomo II de *Historia del Reino de Quito en la America Meridional.* Quito, Ecuador: Edit. Casa de la Cultura Ecuatoriana, 1978.

Watkins, Alfred. *The Old Straight Track.* London: Garnstone Press, 1970.

Wauchope, Robert. *Handbook of Middle American Indians.* 12 Volumes. Austin: University of Texas Press, 1964.

Whitehouse, David and Ruth. *Archaeological Atlas of the World.* San Francisco: W.H. Freeman, n.d.

Wilkins, Harold T. *Mysteries of Ancient South America.* New Jersey: Citadel Press, 1956.

Zammit, Themistocles. *Prehistoric Malta: The Tarxien Temples.* Oxford: Oxford University Press, 1930.

Zhirov, N.F. *Atlantis.* tr. David Skvirsky. Moscow: Progress Publishers, 1970.

Zink, David D. *The Stones of Atlantis.* Englewood Cliffs, New Jersey: Prentice-Hall, 1978.

Articles

Anthes, Rudolph. "Egyptian Theology in the Third Millenium B.C." *Journal of Near Eastern Studies,* Vol. 18: (1959), pp. 169-212.

Atkinson, R.J.C. "Megalithic Astronomy — A Prehistorian's Comments", *Journal for the History of Astronomy,* Vol. 6 (February, 1975): pp. 42-52.

Aveni, Anthony F., Sharon L. Gibbs, and Horst Hartung. "The Caracol of Chichen Itza — An Astronomical Observatory?" *Science.* Vol. 188. (June 6, 1975). pp. 977-85.

Baekeland, G. Brooke and Peter R. Gimbel. "Para-Explorers Challenge Peru's Unknown Vilcabamba," *National Geographic,* Vol. 126 (August, 1964): pp. 268-296.

Baity, Elizabeth C. "Archaeoastronomy and Ethnoastronomy So Far." *Current Anthropology.* Vol. 14 (October 1973): pp. 389-449. Includes comprehensive bibliography of megalithic astronomy of over 600 items.

Brandt, John H. "Nan Matol: Ancient Venice of Micronesia" *Archaeology.* Vol. 15 (Summer, 1962): pp. 99-107.

Carriveau, Gary W. and Mark C. Han. "Thermoluminescent Dating and the Monsters of Acambaro." *American Antiquity,* Vol. 41 (October, 1976): pp. 497-499. Previous thermoluminescent dates are invalid. These pottery monsters now seem to have been fired just before being found.

Colton, R. and R.L. Martin. "Eclipse Cycles and Eclipses at Stonehenge." *Nature,* Vol. 213 (February 4, 1967): pp. 476-478. Authors claim true eclipse cycle is not 56 but instead 65 years. Therefore the 56 Aubrey holes are not solar eclipse predictors, but could be used as a device to predict lunar eclipses.

Cole, J.H. "The Determination of the Exact Size and Orientation of the Great Pyramid of Giza," Paper 39 in *Survey of Egypt,* Cairo, 1925.

Cooke, J.A., R.W. Few, J.G. Morgan, and C.L.N. Ruggles. "Indicated Declinations at The Callanish Megalithic Sites," *Journal of the History of Astronomy,* Vol. 8 (1977), pp. 113-133.

Dow, J.W. "Astronomical Orientation at Teotihuacán, a Case Study in Astroarchaeology." *American Antiquity.* Vol. 32 (1967): pp. 326-334.

Eddy, John A. "Astronomical Alignment of the Big Horn Medicine Wheel." *Science.* Vol. 184 (June 7, 1974), pp. 1035-1043.

Goodenough, Ward H. "Native Astronomy in Micronesia: A Rudimentary Science." *Scientific Monthly* Vol. 73 (August, 1951): pp. 105-110.

Hawkins, Gerald S. "Clues to Egyptian Riddles", *Natural History,* Vol. 83 (April, 1974): pp. 54-63.

Heyden, Doris. "An Interpretation of the Cave Underneath the Pyramid of the Sun in Teotihuacan, Mexico." *American Antiquity,* Vol. 40 (April, 1975): pp. 131-147.

Lynch, B.M. and L.H. Robbins. "Namoratunga: The First Archaeoastronomical Evidence in Sub-Saharan Africa." *Science,* Vol. 200 (May 19, 1978): pp. 766-768.

McClintock, Robert M. "Easter Island", *Explorers Journal,* Vol. 55 (June, 1977): pp. 62-64.

MacKie, Euan W. "Megalithic Astronomy and Catastrophies", *Pensée.* Vol. 4 (1974): pp. 5-20.

Meggars, Betty J. "The Transpacific Origin of Mesoamerican Civilization: A Preliminary Review of the Evidence and Its Theoretical Implications." *American Anthropologist,* Vol. 77 (March, 1975): pp. 1-27. See also March and September issues of following year in *American Anthropologist* for critiques.

Millon, René. "The Teotihuacán Mapping Project," *American Antiquity,* Vol. 29 (January, 1964): pp. 345-352.

Ollier, C.D., D.K. Holdsworth, and G. Heers. "Megaliths at Wagoru, Vakuta, Trobriand Islands." *Archaeology and Physical Anthropology in Oceania.* Vol. 5 (1970): pp. 24-26.

Padden, R.C. "On Diffusionism and Historicity," *American Historical Review.* Vol. 78 (October, 1973): pp. 987-1004.

Rowe, John Howland. "Diffusionism and Archaeology." *American Antiquity.* Vol. 31 (January, 1966): pp. 334-337.

Savoy, Gene. "The Discovery of Vilcabamba," *Explorers Journal,* Vol. 56 (March, 1978): pp. 32-37.

Sears, William H. and Shaun O. Sullivan. "Bahamas Prehistory." *American Antiquity,* Vol. 43 (January, 1978): pp. 3-25. No archaeological sites have been found in the vicinity of Bimini!

Severin, Timothy. "The Voyage of 'Brendan'", *National Geographic,* (December, 1977): pp. 770-797.

Thom, Alexander, *et al.* "Stonehenge," *Journal for the History of Astronomy,* Vol. 5 (June, 1974): pp. 71-90.

—————————. "Stonehenge as a Possible Lunar Observatory," *Journal for the History of Astronomy.* Vol. 6 (February, 1975): pp. 19-30.

Vokes, Emily H. "A Possible Hindu Influence at Teotihuacán." *American Antiquity.* Vol. 29 (July, 1963): pp. 94-95.

Wescott, Roger W., review of *Earth Magic* by Francis Hitching. *Kronos.* Vol. 3 (Summer, 1978): pp. 74-76.

Index

Illustration Credits

The author gratefully acknowledges the following for permission to include illustrations in this book: Aerial Survey International, Inc.; Christopher Bird; Bishop Museum, Honolulu, Hawaii; Braniff International, Exchange Park, Dallas, Texas 75235; Crown Copyright - reproduced with permission of the Controller of Her Britannic Majesty's Stationery Office; William R. Fix; French Government Tourist Office, 610 Fifth Avenue, New York, NY 10020; International Explorers Society, 3132 Ponce de Leon Blvd., Coral Gables, Florida 33134; *Journal for the History of Astronomy* and Professor A.S. Thom, Churchill College, Cambridge CB3 ODS England; LAN-Chile Airlines; *Paris Match,* 63 Avenue des Champs-Elysées, Paris, France; John Parks; Dr. Arthur Saxe; Sandra Sennett; Robert E. Stone; Jim Woodman. If we have failed to credit any illustrations reproduced in this book, we offer our apologies. Any sources omitted will be appropriately acknowledged in all future editions of this book.